AND ALL BECAUSE

They were not at all alike. She was young, terribly wealthy, and accustomed to having everything her own way. He was serious, determined, a man who worked for every penny he made, and who had no time for play. They were wrong for each other. Yet something held them together. Something that made them want to lie and hide their love from family and friends ... for there seemed no other way.

AND ALL BECAUSE

And All Because

by

Denise Robins

Dales Large Print Books
Long Preston, North Yorkshire,
BD23 4ND, England.

British Library Cataloguing in Publication Data.

Robins, Denise
    And all because.

    A catalogue record of this book is
    available from the British Library

    ISBN   978-1-84262-646-7 pbk

First published in Great Britain in 1930 by Mills & Boon Ltd.

Published in Large Print 2008 by arrangement with
Patricia Clark for Executors of Denise Robins' Estate

Dales Large Print is an imprint of Library Magna Books Ltd.

Printed and bound in Great Britain by
T.J. (International) Ltd., Cornwall, PL28 8RW

The characters in this book are entirely imaginary and bear no relation to any living person.

CHAPTER 1

There is something definitely depressing about a ballroom in the early hours of the morning after the guests have gone, the music ceased, and silence has descended upon the house.

Geraldine Wayde – she was Gerry to her relations and friends – stood by the doorway leading from the lounge into the room which so recently had been filled with a laughing, dancing crowd, and surveyed the scene of desolation with a disapproving eye.

She disliked desolation. She disliked being depressed. A few minutes ago she had been the gayest of the gay – bubbling over with spirits. Now a strange gloom fell upon her.

She could hear the faint hoot-hoot of a car break the stillness of the June night. The last car was leaving Ponders; turning out of the famous chestnut drive into the main London Road.

She looked around her, frowning a little. The electric candles in old gilt brackets – two between each amber satin panel – still burned brightly. It was a long, beautiful room with six tall windows facing south, and a priceless floor of old oak which had the polish of ages on it. Many dances and parties had been held here over a period of centuries. This room was in the old wing of Ponders, a Queen Anne house which had been restored by the Waydes when they bought it, before Gerry was born. But she hated the satin-panelling and gilt candles and the gilded Louis XVth chairs. They were of Mrs Wayde's choosing, and Mrs Wayde's choice lay in bright, flamboyant things, whereas Gerry preferred the simplicity, the severity of things old. The floor was the only part of the reception-room which she liked.

It had been a good show, she thought. Her twenty-first birthday party; and father had done her well. He always did. He never stinted cash where she was concerned and her mother was lavish – more eager, perhaps, that her daughter should be perfectly dressed and a great social success than that she should enjoy herself.

Gerry lifted a small clenched fist to her lips and yawned. Her head began to ache, and her feet too. She had danced every dance. She was tired. Somewhere in the big house a grandfather clock struck the hour of three. It was certainly time for bed.

A high-pitched voice called from upstairs.

'Gerry! Darling. Where are you, *chérie?*'

Gerry yawned again, and walked from the ballroom into the darker lounge and up the staircase, which had wonderful carved oaken rails, black with age, and walls with linenfold panelling which was supposed to be worth thousands of pounds.

On the upper landing, Gerry's mother appeared – a voluminous figure with swelling bosom and hips curving under a pale yellow nylon and lace negligée. Her hair – auburn in tint – was confined under a yellow hair-net which made her face, with its double chin and sagging cheeks, look absurd. She held a pot of face-cream in one hand and with the other tenderly stroked the lines under her eyes.

'I'm worn out, my sweet,' she said. 'But I must do my massage. Such a nuisance when Taylor's in bed.'

Gerry laughed.

'Well, I shan't do my massage. I'm for my bed – here and now.'

'So am I, darling. It was a lovely party. And you looked exquisite, my pet – *ravisante*. Your father's friend, Sir George Bracken – you know, the Member for Hartlebury – admired you immensely. That is a lovely dress, my sweet. So *soignée* – so chic. One of Roche's loveliest. A *succès fou!*'

Mrs Wayde, who bore the Christian name of 'Désirée,' had been born in France and lived there until she was fifteen. She was of English parentage and entirely English, but it was one of her pet poses to intersperse little French phrases and words with her

11

English, and to shrug her shoulders and gesticulate freely with her hands. She was never so happy as when strangers, meeting her for the first time, said: 'Surely you are French!'

She was a stupid but amiable woman. Gerry had no particular use for her, but she was very fond of her. She thought of her as 'poor old dear,' and treated her with gross disrespect. When she particularly wanted something out of her, Gerry addressed her as 'Désirée, duck.' She had managed her mother when she was a self-willed little thing of four, and had controlled her ever since.

Mrs Wayde wanted her daughter to be a success in society. No trouble or expense was spared to achieve that end. Gerry had had a very expensive education – a succession of governesses, English, Swiss, and French, none of them able to cope with Gerry, who had a stubborn will and great personal charm, as well as beauty; combined with the dangerous knowledge that she could twist most people round her little finger.

'Good night, darling,' said Gerry, stifling her third yawn.

'Good night, *chérie*,' said Mrs Wayde. 'I won't kiss you – covered in cream. *Dormez bien*, my darling.'

She withdrew into her room, waving the pot of cream. Her fat, good-natured face was greasy and shining framed by the yellow hairnet.

Gerry walked slowly along the passage, unclasping a diamond choker from her throat. It was a beautiful choker. Her father's birthday present to her. It had thrilled her for five minutes and it had cost five hundred pounds.

Suddenly she paused. She had been about to pass a room, the door of which was ajar. She glanced in and saw a young man in evening clothes seated at a small table, writing furiously on a sheet of foolscap. A look of interest and curiosity chased the *ennui* from Gerry's face. She pushed the door more widely open. So engrossed was the young man in his occupation that he did not even turn his head. Gerry regarded him in thoughtful silence for a moment.

It was a slightly stooping back that she contemplated, and belonged to a slimly built tallish man. The head was dark – so dark that it might have been called black – short, crisp hair ruffled as though the owner had been running his fingers through it.

The young man was Nicholas Hulme – private secretary to Gerry's father – and the person responsible for all the hard work in the M.P.'s household.

Gerry – in the excitement of the evening, surrounded by friends and admirers – had scarcely noticed the fact that Mr Hulme had only appeared in the ballroom for the first ten minutes after dinner, then had vanished. But now she recalled that fact. And she also remembered that he had not even asked her for a dance. That piqued her. She was a spoiled darling of the gods and used to men pleading for favours. She was annoyed that Nicholas Hulme had not begged her to dance with him.

He was always annoying her. He was such an irritating young man with his serious manner; his aloofness. He had taken the post as her father's secretary early in the spring and lived as one of the family. But neither Gerry nor her mother saw much of him save at mealtime. He was generally closeted with Mr Wayde in his study and, after dinner at night, retired to his own room. He was hard-working and conscientious. Too conscientious to please Gerry. Too grave and reticent. He was so very good-looking. He ought to be more amusing. Gerry liked being amused. He ought to admire her. She liked being admired. But he never did more than look at her occasionally with his serious eyes and say: 'Good morning, Miss Wayde' – or 'Good night.'

She had heard that he had no money. After a public-school and Varsity education he had found himself without means, through the financial failure and death of his father. He had been secretary to another Conservative member last year, and had come to Mr Wayde with excellent credentials. Mr Wayde told the family that he found Nicholas Hulme a very able and intelligent young man.

Gerry wondered what he did in his spare time. He spent so much time shut up in his bedroom. Now she fancied that she knew. He was writing a book or something. There were sheets of foolscap, closely written upon, all over the table and on the floor.

She was quite intrigued. She wondered what he wrote. She forgot that she was tired out and that it was three in the morning. She walked into the room.

'What *are* you doing, Mr Hulme?' she said.

The young man dropped his pen and swung round in his chair. Such a thin, pale face he had, she thought. And wonderful eyes – grey, brilliant, with thick brows and dark lashes. His mouth was well shaped but had a peculiarly bitter downward curve. It gave his face a cynical, even a sombre, touch. Gerry felt that he might be difficult if one knew him better. Certainly, he had most handsome and intelligent eyes. A pity he spoiled himself by being so bearish.

He was looking at her now as though he saw a ghost, she thought amusedly. He sprang to his feet. His face grew scarlet.

'Miss Wayde!' he stammered.

'Don't look so scared,' she said. 'It isn't the dead of night. It's nearly dawn. I thought you had come up to bed and gone to sleep hours ago.'

The colour left his cheeks; made him look whiter than before and very tired. There were shadows under his eyes and hollows in his cheeks which robbed his face of youth. His tail-coat had been made by a good tailor, but it was old and worn. His shirt-front was crumpled and his white tie awry. He did not look very spruce. Gerry noticed all these things and felt curiously inclined to stay and talk to him. Out of curiosity more than anything else.

'I wondered what you were writing,' she added.

Nicholas Hulme, who seemed to be dazed by her unexpected entry into his bedroom, turned and picked up a sheet of foolscap. He fingered it almost jealously.

'Oh – I was – just – doing some writing.'

'I know that,' she laughed. 'But what?'

'A – a play,' he stammered.

'A play!' she echoed. 'How intriguing. *Do* tell me about it.'

'I don't know that I can.'

'Why not?'

'I don't– I haven't told anybody,' he stammered.

'I see,' she shrugged her shoulders. 'It's a secret.'

'Yes.'

She was disappointed. Surely he might tell *her* about his play.

'Does my father know?'

'No, no, of course not.'

'You just work in secret – at nights – on Sundays – that sort of thing.'

'Yes.'

He spoke stiffly. She felt that he resented her prying into his affairs. She had always been what her father called 'a cussed little devil.' She went on questioning Nicholas Hulme out of sheer 'cussedness.'

'Have you always written plays?'

'Yes. At least – I've often tried to write.'

'Without any success?'

'I've never written one that I considered good enough to send to a producer.'

'I see. But what fun! To find dear father's secretary is a potential dramatist.'

'Please, Miss Wayde,' he said angrily. 'Don't spread it about. I – I amuse myself by writing. It's my form of recreation. But I'd prefer it not to be discussed.'

'Oh, all right,' she said, and laughed. She thought: 'Prig!'

She looked curiously round the room. She knew it, of course. It was called the 'oak room,' because it was full of old beams and some panelling, and had a four-poster bed which Mrs Wayde had bought at the sale of Herstmonceux Castle. It was a big room and

17

one of the most attractive, historically, in Ponders. But it had a north aspect and was darker and colder than most, so it was not a popular guestroom. Hence it had been allotted to Mr Wayde's young secretary when he came. Gerry remembered her mother saying that he had been quite overwhelmed because he thought it so delightful. Gerry supposed he found it inspiring. Personally she thought it looked gloomy and depressing.

It was eerie, full of shadows at this early morning hour, with only one electric lamp burning on the table at which he worked. Her quick eyes observed the lack of photographs or personal ornaments. There was nothing of a private nature to be seen except a pair of ebony-backed hair-brushes, a bottle of hair oil and a clothes-brush on his dressing-chest. And books – a dozen or more leather-bound volumes which she did not recognise as belonging to the house – in the book-case beside his bed. A studious young man, obviously. And gloomy – austere – like the atmosphere of his room.

She wondered what lay behind him; what family history; what experiences. Was there a woman in his life? Had he ever been in love? She couldn't imagine Nicholas Hulme in love.

It would take a siren to charm him from his reticence, his austerity.

She looked up at him. He was very tall and slim, but so fine-drawn he did not look ungraceful. Her head would about reach his chin, if she were close to him.

She said, suddenly, in a piqued voice:

'You didn't come and ask me to dance.'

He flushed again and gave a frigid little bow.

'I must apologise, Miss Wayde. I don't dance.'

'Nonsense. You could if you tried.'

'I haven't time to attend dancing classes.'

His sarcastic voice irritated her.

'You really are a bore!' she exclaimed.

'I must apologise,' he said again. He looked round the room as though seeking some means of escape. She could see that he was thoroughly ill at ease. She was annoyed but at the same time interested. The men, young and old, whom she knew, found it so easy to get on with her; to chat and laugh and frivol. Why should this young man treat her as though she were the most difficult creature? At one moment he was being sarcastic – she almost thought he was sneering at her. At the next he looked scared to death of her.

'Don't be silly,' she said with a little laugh. 'I didn't ask for an apology. I don't suppose you can help being a bore. But you might have come and danced with the rest of us and cheered up. Don't you like being cheery?'

19

'Yes,' he said. 'But I'm very busy. I'm here to work – not to dance.'

'I'm sure my father doesn't want you to work so furiously and exclude all pleasure.'

'But you don't understand, Miss Wayde. My pleasure lies in my work – not in dancing.'

'Oh, good life!' she exclaimed. 'That sounds altogether too good for me.'

He looked at her as though she exasperated him. Of course, this girl wouldn't understand that one's work can mean much more than idle waste of time. She had been brought up to waste her time. She wouldn't realise – how could she? – that to a man like himself, without means, and with ambition – work was everything – came first and foremost in his life.

CHAPTER 2

Once upon a time Nicholas Hulme had idled; on the playing fields at school; on the river; in the precincts of his college up at Oxford. But that was before his father, a stockbroker, had come a crash, died soon after it, and left Nicholas without means – left him to support himself, and to help financially a sister who was a young widow with two children, also without means.

He had learned not to idle. Once he had danced. Now dancing bored him. He liked his job with Austin Wayde; Wayde was a man with brains – a good fellow when he got away from that difficult affected wife of his. And Nicholas was interested in politics. But most of all he liked the work he did in his spare time. He had an incurable love of the drama, the theatre. It was the passion, the ambition of his life, to write a successful play.

He wanted to make his name and to have the money that comes with fame. For his sister's sake, for the two small nephews whom he wished to educate decently, as well as for himself.

But what did Geraldine Wayde know of these things? What could she guess of the miseries and difficulties that a woman like his sister, Macil, faced with those two kids? To Geraldine life was a song – a bubble – a dance. She probably never bothered to sit down and contemplate the other side of it – the grim and bitter struggle that life could be.

He looked at her with grudging admiration. He did not want to admire her. But he was only human and he loved beauty, and here it was in Gerry Wayde, unspoiled even by the lavish use of make-up and generous use of scarlet lipstick which he hated. But all the women – even the youngest of them that he met in this household – used make-up. It was considered smart, and Mrs Wayde, of course, perpetually remembering to be the Frenchwoman she was not, imported ideas of *haute couture* from Paris. Ridiculous in a house like this, in the heart of the country, glorious, wooded country, lying five miles south of Winchester.

There were stables here, with good hunters. Kennels full of dogs. Two hard tennis courts. A covered-in, real tennis court. Ample opportunity for sport. Gerry Wayde was, herself, quite sporting. She rode well to hounds. She played a good game of tennis. But the lipstick, the almond-shaped nails, brilliantly varnished, just that touch of artifice which Nicholas Hulme considered desecration of nature, was never missing whatever she did, inside Ponders or out of it.

Yet how pretty she was, and how very unnecessary all that powder and paint. He looked down at her, and thought that she was like an old picture in the dim lamp-light, framed in the doorway there.

She wore a white dress of crisp silk taffeta that bunched out from the slim waist; concealed the fine narrow line of her hips; fell in a wide hem of stiff tulle to the heels of her shoes. Very small white brocaded shoes with paste diamond buckles. The waist of the dress tight, showing a seductive curve of small breasts, and sewn with diamanté. She was white and shining in the lamp-light, and her arms and throat, with their faint, delicious tan from the summer sun, looked golden like her hair.

Gerry had pale, thick hair. She wore it short, parted on the side and brushed back from her forehead in crisp waves. There was a crisp quality in her hair and a natural wave which set perfectly. Her face was oval in shape, with a pointed, stubborn little chin. She had a short, broad nose, inclined to be *retroussé*, which lent her a look of delicious impudence. Her eyes were strikingly dark, in contrast to the fairness of her hair, and gave her an unusual beauty. She had rather a wide mouth with a short, enchanting upper lip and an even row of teeth.

Beautiful – and spoiled.

During the six months that he had lived at Ponders as Austin Wayde's secretary, Nicholas Hulme had watched Gerry. From the background, in the shadows, he had watched and seen many things. Enough to satisfy him that as a family the Waydes excelled in selfishness and extravagance. They were lucky enough to have money to waste. Austin Wayde had inherited a small fortune from an uncle who had made machinery up in the north. Now he was Conservative member down here. Nicholas liked working with and for him. But Austin Wayde was engrossed in politics, to the exclusion of all else. He was content to write cheques for his wife and daughter so long as they left him alone. He tolerated the brainless woman he had married in his youth. He was fond of Gerry – proud of her beauty and her charm. But he was much too concerned with politics to worry about her character. He left her moral upbringing to her mother.

Nicholas Hulme – the onlooker – had seen how totally incapable Désirée Wayde was of bringing up any child. She was a stupid, vain creature with a passion for clothes and Bridge. She adored entertaining. Ponders was nearly always full of guests, who were mainly her husband's political associates, the Bridge-playing scandal-mongers in her own social circle, and Gerry's young friends. Her great ambition was to push Gerry into a brilliant marriage. The subject of this marriage was a passion, an obsession with Mrs Wayde. She saw to it that Gerry went to a finishing school in Paris, and was perfectly turned out. It was more important in the eyes of Désirée Wayde that Gerry should have graceful deportment and pretty clothes than that she should be truthful or have a sense of honour. Such things were left to develop themselves, and Mrs Wayde hoped for the best.

What chance, therefore, Nicholas had asked himself several times during the last few months, had Geraldine Wayde to become a fine character? She had been given everything – too much – of the things that did not matter, and her moral training had been hopelessly neglected.

He had watched her – interested because he was a born writer enthralled by the study of psychology, of human nature. He had found so much in her to like. Kindness; generosity; a sense of humour. He had said little to her, but often listened. She had none of her mother's stupidity. She had her father's keen go-ahead brain; his powers of reasoning, which were useful. But she neglected her own mind. It was rarely that Nicholas saw this girl with a decent book or making her friends among the thinkers, the creators whom she came across. She danced and lazed. She had been encouraged to. She indulged in a feverish search for pleasure. She was twenty-one today and bored unless she was pursing some fresh excitement or snatching a new thrill from life.

Nicholas had heard her remark, at luncheon, that she had had so many birthday presents that she did not know who half of them were from. She had told her maid to find out and make a list. That was typical of her.

Nicholas Hulme had no use for the Geraldine Wayde that was. But he thought, sometimes, with faint regret, of the Geraldine who might have been. She could be dangerously attractive.

He felt that attraction strongly tonight, as he looked at the charming picture of her in his doorway. He was angry because he felt it. It disturbed him. He wanted to be left alone – to work in peace. He had no time, no place in his life for women. Particularly not for women like this spoilt darling of fortune.

With the loveliness of her playing like an enchantment on his tired mind and senses, the young man scowled at her.

'If you will pardon me, Miss Wayde,' he said. 'I just want to finish this scene I am on. It's very late and–'

'And you want me to push off,' she finished, putting her tongue in her cheek. She was piqued again. She was always coming up against a blank wall with her father's secretary. She was being politely snubbed. 'You aren't very gallant,' she added. 'I'm quite offended – being turned away like this!'

'I beg your pardon–'

'Oh, don't. That's the third time you've apologised. My dear Mr Hulme – you *are* an absurd person! Can't I talk to you nicely about your work? Must you always treat me in this frigid, formal sort of fashion?'

He fingered his tie, still frowning. How black his brows were, drawn together in that horrid scowl, she thought. But really he was frightfully good-looking. She would like to see him smile. He'd be terribly attractive if he smiled. But she did not remember ever having seen him smile – at her, anyway.

Nicholas Hulme was thinking:

'What does she want with me? Why does she want to pry into my affairs? She's got hundreds of friends – rich youngsters who take her about and dance with her. She has no use for me. It's only sheer curiosity. I won't satisfy it.'

Aloud he said:

'I'm sorry if you find me frigid and formal. But I'm only your father's secretary. I take a salary for my work and I haven't time–'

He stopped, reddening a little. It had been on the tip of his tongue to say: 'I haven't time to amuse you.' Gerry came to his rescue by laughing.

'You *are* funny. Quite old-fashioned. Oh, well. I suppose I owe you an apology, as I disturbed your work, so let's cry quits.'

She gave him one of her sunniest smiles. It was more than any man – even Nicholas Hulme – could resist.

She wasn't a bad sort at heart, he thought, and quite ravishingly pretty. He wished she'd hurry up and go away. He was embarrassed by the thought that she was here, practically in his bedroom, laughing and talking to him at 3 a.m., and the rest of the household in bed.

'That's quite all right. I – please – I'm sorry if you find me disagreeable,' he stammered.

'When are you not disagreeable?' She smiled again. 'Outside Ponders? I mean, if one met you away from father and politics and this place, would you be quite different?'

'I really don't know.'

'It's a shame to tease you. I'll go away. Good night!'

He bowed gravely.

'Good night, Miss Wayde.'

She moved away, yawning, pushing the thick, fair hair back from her forehead. Nicholas Hulme closed his door.

For a moment he stood reflectively staring at his carpet. He drew a pipe from his coat pocket and stuck it between his teeth. He was still scowling. Gerry's invasion of his room had interrupted his work and spoiled it. The continuity of thought had gone. The inspiration which had kept him slaving at that scene in the last act was gone. He felt sleepy. And he found himself thinking about Gerry Wayde instead of the play. He could not altogether banish the memory of her charming figure in the white dress, framed in his doorway; and that friendly, dazzling smile she had given him. After all, he *was* a bore. He knew it. Curt and even rude. But he didn't want Gerry Wayde to push her way into his private life; to invade his mind, his senses.

He felt suddenly dead tired and angry. He took the pipe from his mouth, flung himself into the chair at his table, and took up his pen. But no thoughts came. And he kept thinking about Gerry: *'Can't I talk to you nicely about your work?'* Damn it, he didn't want to talk to her about his work.

He threw down the pen with a gesture of exasperation, and began to undress.

From a distant farmyard came the faint crowing of a cock. The twitter and chirp of awakening birds. The first pallid beams of morning light filtered through a chink in the curtains. When Nicholas switched off his lamp his room was quite light. Another day had come. Once in bed he was soon asleep, and both his play and the disturbing thought of Gerry Wayde were forgotten.

CHAPTER 3

Gerry usually rode before breakfast. She loved horses and understood them. She was up at half-past eight even after the late night of her birthday party, and took Deirdre, her chestnut mare, for half an hour's exercise. She went through the beautiful park at the back of Ponders and on the by-roads leading from Graylingstone to Winchester.

Graylingstone is, perhaps, one of the prettiest villages in Hampshire. On this summer's morning it was perfect. There had been a heavy dew overnight and the hot sunlight seemed to shimmer in a pale amber mist over the winding, narrow main street with its charming thatched cottages, its Tudor inn, its cobbled pavements. It was a place yet unspoiled by modern ugliness, with the exception of one red, blatant petrol pump outside a garage which had once done duty as stables, and which looked solitary and ashamed of itself amidst so much rustic loveliness.

Everybody who saw the slim girl on the chestnut mare, greeted her. The men with a touch of their caps, the women with a friendly smile. Everybody knew and liked

Miss Wayde, daughter of the local M.P. Graylingstone was in Austin Wayde's constituency, and they gave him their staunch support here at the last general election.

Gerry had warm pink cheeks which needed no rouge when she rode Deirdre into the stables and handed her over to the groom. And she felt fresh and glowing. She had buoyant youth which could stand up to late nights, and there was no trace of fatigue on her face as she sauntered through the gardens towards the house.

Nicholas Hulme, standing outside the French windows of the dining-room, smoking and silently drinking in the beauty of the June morning, saw Gerry approaching. She had taken off her soft felt riding-hat and was bare-headed in the sun. She looked amazingly young and attractive in the well-fitting habit and white shirt. He dropped his cigarette on the gravel path and trod on it. He turned to go. He had a curious desire to escape before the girl saw him. But Gerry's quick eye had already noted the young secretary. She waved to him.

'Morning, Mr Hulme. Isn't it perfect?'

He was caught. He stood still. She came up to him, running a slim hand over the crispness of her cropped hair. It seemed to sparkle like champagne in the sun, he thought.

'Good morning,' he said in his serious way.

'I've had a lovely ride.'

'It must have been perfect.'

'Do you ride?'

'I used to.'

'Why don't you take one of father's mounts and join me one morning?'

Nicholas Hulme bit his lip. He could see that she was trying to invade his privacy again. And why – why take this sudden interest in him? For months she had ignored his presence in the house; treated him as a salaried employee and not as a friend. Quite right. He preferred it to this new intimacy which he found so disturbing.

Gerry looked up at him and then down at one neat polished boot which she tapped with her crop. She was thinking that Nicholas Hulme would look well on a horse. There was grace in his figure, and he had nice hands; thin, strong-looking fingers.

When she had woken up this morning she had found herself thinking about him. She was still piqued by his stubborn refusal to thaw to her. Piqued and intrigued.

'Do ride with me one morning,' she said.

'It's awfully nice of you, but I – I couldn't dream of it. I start work at this time – in a few minutes now.'

Gerry smiled tolerantly.

'Good excuse,' she said.

He thought:

'Why can't she leave me alone?'

He looked at her wide attractive mouth and hated the vivid red of it. It was a pity she used so much lipstick. He found himself wondering how many men had kissed those red lips. Men must want to kiss them – and she knew it – knew the strength of her own allure. He himself would like to kiss her. And not very tenderly. He despised himself for that thought. He would like to hurt her; shake her; ask her why she wanted to throw her sweetness at him like this. It must only be to satisfy an idle whim. She didn't particularly like him. He was a difficult, awkward person – engrossed in his work. She had plenty of men to amuse her ... dance with her ... flatter her.

Gerry said:

'Come and chat to me while I have my breakfast.'

'You must really pardon me,' he said. 'Mr Wayde will be down by now. I must go to the study.'

He bowed and moved away. She looked angrily after the tall figure in the grey flannel suit. Rather a shabby suit. But he looked nice in it. And his hair was not ruffled as it had been when she saw him in the early hours of this morning. It was smooth and neatly brushed; looked like black satin. Intriguing hair, contrasted with that acute pallor. She wondered if there were Southern blood in Nicholas Hulme?

He certainly did not intend to be what Gerry called 'matey.' She was baffled by her apparent inability to charm him. She was conscious of a slight feeling of shame that she should wish to do so. She ought to leave father's nice, good, hard-working secretary alone. But Gerry – thoughtless and spoiled rather than bent on evil – wanted her own way with everybody. She wanted it with Mr Hulme. She refused to be snubbed. His coldness and that maddening touch of superiority when he spoke to her, looked at her, were irritating to her vanity.

She just wanted to see what Nicholas Hulme was like when he let himself go. And he wouldn't do it.

She sat alone in the green and yellow morning-room which was full of sunlight and the last word in modern decoration – unpolished oak – crude colours – queer, futuristic oil-paintings – and decided that she was bored.

She was lunching in Winchester with the Withamburys. Ivor Withambury was an amusing young man of her own age, just down from Oxford, and a marvellous exponent of the saxophone. He was very much in love with Gerry, and they danced in town together sometimes. At one time Gerry had thought she was 'intrigued.' That was her pet word. But although she liked dancing with Ivor, she hated being kissed by him. So now she was bored. He always wanted to kiss her. She didn't care about being made love to. She had never in her life been really in love. Sometimes excited and 'intrigued.' But she had no desire to marry and settle down. She was constantly battling with her mother's passion to make a brilliant match for her.

She was bored with her present existence. There was something better to be got out of life than she got now. She knew it, without realising exactly what she wanted to get. But sometimes, definitely there came upon her the consciousness of an appalling waste of time and effort; of concentration upon nothing at all. She was by nature energetic and constructive. If she had not been born into this environment of wealth, of luxury, she might have achieved something good. She could certainly have been industrious and more contented.

Supreme discontent made the sunlit world gloomy for Gerry this morning. The feeling remained with her all day. At half-past twelve, just before she drove to Winchester in her little sports two-seater which her father had given her, she strolled into the dining-room to mix herself a cocktail. She found her father taking a glass of sherry. Nicholas Hulme stood with him, his pipe in his mouth.

The entrance of Gerry – looking charming

in a brown and yellow flowered dress of thinnest French silk, and with a burnt straw hat on her amber head – interrupted a very serious discussion on the Budget.

Austin Wayde smiled at his daughter. He was a tall, grey-haired man built on massive lines, and had a fussy, important manner.

'Morning, my dear.'

'Morning, father. Finished sweating your poor secretary?' said Gerry, with a wicked look at Nicholas, who blushed scarlet.

'Sweating is scarcely the word, my dear, surely,' murmured Mr Wayde, finishing his sherry and wiping his moustache.

'I'm sure you overwork poor Mr Hulme.'

'No – really – of course not,' said Nicholas.

Gerry's gaze met his. His eyes under their thick brows scowled at her. She was amused and went on.

'Her certainly never has time for a bit of play.'

'My dear Gerry!' Austin Wayde coughed and glanced at his secretary. 'Play!...'

'I am not here to play, and I enjoy my work,' said Nicholas curtly. He turned to his employer. 'I'll just finish that letter we were on, sir.'

He walked quickly out of the room.

Gerry shrugged her shoulders. Her expression was one of bafflement.

'What a bore he is,' she muttered.

'My dear child – he's a very nice and able

young man,' said Mr Wayde. 'But it's indiscreet of you, if I might say so, darling, to suggest that he – er – wants to play.'

'It's quite obvious he doesn't,' said Gerry with meaning.

She drove into Winchester and – not in the best of humours – destroyed any hope that Ivor Withambury entertained of getting her to go up to town and 'do a show and dance.'

During dinner that night at Ponders Gerry made another vain attempt to make Nicholas Hulme pay her some attention. He sat opposite to her. It seemed to her that he tried not to look in her direction. He addressed himself to the elder Waydes or kept his gaze on his plate. When Gerry spoke to him, perforce he glanced at her, but only for a second, and answered as briefly as courtesy permitted. She was made to feel that he was angry with her because she had 'ragged' him in front of his employer before lunch today.

Dinner over, as was his habit, he retired to his own room. To write, of course, thought Gerry. She knew now what he did all those hours in his room. He was writing a play. She felt childishly annoyed because he vanished where she could not follow. She would like to have gone up to him; made him tell her about that play; made him talk to her.

Mrs Wayde, suddenly aware that her

daughter was silent and depressed, suggested that she should telephone to the Withamburys and ask them to motor over and spend the evening.

'Get dear Ivor to come and dance with you, *chérie.*'

'No, thanks,' said Gerry shortly. 'I'm fed up with Ivor.'

'*Qu'a tu* my darling?' asked Mrs Wayde anxiously.

'A headache,' said Gerry, and walked out of the drawing-room. She fetched herself a stole, slipped it over her bare shoulders, and strolled into the garden, which was a miracle of moonlight. A perfect summer's night. The sky was a milky haze of stars. Flowers and lawns were drenched in dew. And, somewhere from the woods that fringed the grounds of Ponders, a nightingale warbled madly, filling the night with an ecstasy of song.

Gerry strolled over the lawn, shutting her eyes and ears to beauty which should have lulled her discontent, and told herself that she was thoroughly 'fed up.'

Up in his bedroom, Nicholas Hulme worked on his play. He too was conscious of a growing discontent and restlessness which might have matched Gerry's. But they sprang from a different source. He was dissatisfied with his work. He had that curious temperament of the artist who is acutely aware of his deficiencies. He hated every line he had written. He tore up sheets of foolscap and rewrote what he had destroyed.

Tonight he was not in the mood for writing at all. And why? He was crazy to finish his play. He burned with enthusiasm to have it typed and sent to Johnson Fairwright, the actor-manager for whom he was writing the play. He had created a marvellous part for Fairwright. If only he could see it; give it a chance! What a thing for him if he could launch a successful play. Throw up this secretarial job which gave a man no chance for creative work. What a thing for Macil, poor old girl, if he could make a packet of money and set her on her feet – get young Robin into the Navy, which was her burning ambition.

Why couldn't he work tonight? Why was his body so restless and his mind so confused?

Nicholas Hulme threw down his pen and got up and walked to one of the windows. He parted the curtains and looked out at the glory of the night. The perfume of syringa from a bush just below was sweet and pungent. But he disliked it. It was too sweet.

He knew exactly what was the matter with him. That girl … that maddening girl, Geraldine Wayde, with her provocative face and voice and the invitation of her lips. She had done her damnedest to flirt with him at dinner tonight. She was crazy. He was only an employee in this house. He'd be chucked out tomorrow if that awful woman, Désirée Wayde, thought her daughter was becoming romantic about him, a penniless secretary. The Waydes, both of 'em, had their eye on a title for their only child and heiress. Besides it wasn't a question of Gerry becoming romantic. She wasn't capable of romance, he told himself grimly. She was just trying to make him fool around with her; become one of those damn silly poodle-fakers – there were dozens in her set – to flatter and amuse her for an hour.

He wasn't going to be drawn into any poodle-faking with Miss Geraldine.

But she had succeeded in disturbing him and putting him off his work. Nicholas was furious with himself. He had been positively haunted by the picture of her standing in the doorway of this room after her birthday ball. The sheer beauty and charm of her in her white, billowing dress.

Tonight at dinner, when she had made him look at her, answer one of her questions, the expression in those big, dark eyes of hers had covered him with confusion. It had said plaintively: 'Won't you be nice?' He didn't mean to be nice. She was outside his circle, his scheme of things, and she knew it.

For the last hour while he tried to concentrate on his play, the thought of her pushed its way, wriggled insidiously into his mind, destroying his clarity of vision. Yes, this girl and her idle efforts to make him pander to her vanity were entirely destructive. Instead of working out a curtain to that last act, he found himself remembering the beauty of that fair wavy hair springing back from her forehead … and the velvety darkness of her eyes. Such a rare combination – blonde hair and brown eyes.

To the devil with Geraldine Wayde.

Nicholas put a pipe in his mouth and marched out of his room. He would go for a long walk and forget the girl.

CHAPTER 4

Bareheaded, hands in his pockets, Nicholas strode through the starlight, down the path beside the herbaceous border which led to the tennis courts; past a green of lawn, rippling with shadows in the moonlight and bordered by clipped yews which had the heavy, thick beauty of age, and into the orchard. Through the orchard one could reach the woods. He liked to walk through the woods on a night like this and listen to the nightingales.

And then, when he reached the bottom of the orchard past a high wall on which pears and nectarines were forming fruit, he came suddenly upon the slim figure of Geraldine. He stopped, inwardly fuming. The one person he wanted to avoid – whom he had come out to forget.

Gerry saw him and greeted him eagerly.

'Hello! Did you find the house stuffy? I did. It's wonderful out here.'

'Wonderful,' he agreed. He could not do otherwise than answer her and stand still. It would have been rude to move away – which was what he wanted to do.

'Let's stroll through the woods,' she said.

'I – I've just come back from a long walk,' he muttered, conscious of the lie.

'Take another,' she said.

He was silent. She shook her head at him.

'Anybody would think you were frightened to death of me!' she exclaimed.

He wanted to say: 'I am!' But he kept silence.

'Are you?' she inquired.

'N-no, why s-should I be?' he stammered.

'Well, then, come for a walk...'

He set his teeth. She was obstinate. She was also tactless. Couldn't she see that he didn't want to walk with her at this time of night? Couldn't she understand that her parents would object? She did what she liked. Yes, she was a spoiled little devil. But, if Mrs Wayde got any absurd notions into her head, it would jeopardise his career. But no, she didn't see that – or didn't care.

'I do want to hear about your play,' she said in a pleading voice. 'Won't you tell me?'

'I'm afraid it would bore you,' he said.

'No – honestly, I'd like to know.'

He found himself falling into step with her. They strolled together to the end of the orchard; through an archway in the old stone wall, and out on to a terrace. Here, a dry wall and rockery sloped to the wood. Gerry led the way down the rough stone steps and on to the path which had been cut between the trees. Young beeches, with deli-

43

cate tracery of leaves; exquisite; fine as lace in the moonlight.

Nicholas Hulme, thoroughly nettled, as indisposed as any man to be led against his will, followed. It was impossible to do anything but admire the charming figure in front of him. She was in green tonight; nymph-like – in keeping with the young trees – as slender and as graceful. A green silk Italian scarf wrapped around her shoulders – green shoes with absurdly high heels. Much too high for a walk in the woods and already stained with dew.

'Won't you get wet?' he muttered.

'I don't care if I do,' she said. She moved back to his side now that the path grew wider. 'I say, isn't it hot tonight?'

'Warmish, certainly.'

'Did you do much work?'

'No, practically none.'

'How far have you got?'

'To the middle of the third act...' He was being drawn, despite himself, into the discussion of his beloved play.

'Is it good?'

'I hope so. I don't know.'

'You've written others?'

'Several. But this is my–'

'Your great work – your inspiration?' she broke in, smiling up at him.

'Yes,' he admitted.

It was dark and shadowy in the woods. He

could scarcely see the girl's face. But now and then through the beech leaves came a shaft of moonlight. It turned her hair to silver. It was wonderful – that great up-springing silver wave of hair at the front of her head. She brushed it back at the sides so that one could see the tips of her ears. There were little pearl studs in them.

'She is lovely and perfectly turned out ... every detail thought out for the seduction of men,' mused Nicholas Hulme. And he thought of his sister, only nine years older than this girl, and already haggard and worn out with domestic work and the problem of rearing two children without enough money. One of those pearls in Gerry Wayde's small ears would cost as much as Macil would spend on one term at Robin's day-school.

'Tell me the title of your play,' persisted Gerry's voice.

'It's a secret...' he began frowning.

'Oh, let me in. I won't tell. Do let's be friends. Why can't we be?'

'Miss Wayde – I–'

'You don't like me,' she said swiftly and plaintively. 'I know you don't.'

'I – that's ridiculous.'

'But you don't.'

'I do.'

'Then don't despise my friendship.'

He was tongue-tied. He saw her smiling up at him. There was witchery in her eyes. How dark and soft they were under their sweeping lashes. She took his arm in a friendly way, and the contact with her made him grow hot. Did this girl really wish to be friends ... or did she know exactly what effect she had on him, he asked himself. Any man would have to be made of iron, of stone, to feel unmoved with that slim, fragrant body so close to him in the enchantment of a moonlit wood, on a summer's night. And Nicholas Hulme was not made of stone. He was a temperamental creature of moods and of strong passions. He was reticent – perhaps more controlled than most men of his age. And he had never been in love with a woman.

At Oxford there had been a girl. Not of Gerry's type ... and he had had a feverish affair with her. It had been an experience, but he had not really enjoyed it and he had hated himself when it was over. His main object in life was to work. He resented the thought of sex and the fact that a woman was a necessity in a man's life. He found that as a rule, to him, sex was of secondary consideration and work of primary importance.

But the thought of work left a man's mind – died utterly – when a damnably attractive girl – that was how he described Gerry in his thoughts – clung to his arm on a night like this, and wooed him by talking about his play.

'I must get back,' he said desperately. 'I –

you don't mind. I want to work on my third act.'

'All right,' she said, and turned round. 'If you're stuck, tell me about it... I may be able to help. What is the plot? I swear I'm as safe as a house. I'll never repeat a thing you tell me – to my people – to anyone.'

'I am sure ... but I don't want to talk about it ... please forgive me...'

'I don't know that I shall,' she said, her face crimsoning a little. She took her hand away from his arm. 'I think you might trust me.'

'I do. But I haven't told anybody – even my sister – what this play is about. It's a tremendous secret.'

'Oh, all right,' said Gerry, and shrugged her shoulders. Then she added: 'Do you live with your sister?'

'Yes. She is a widow with two kids – fine kids!'

Now he woke up. Now he was enthusiastic. She saw the light in his eyes when he said 'fine kids.' What a curious man he was.

'You're fond of children?'

'Very. Macil's boys are good fun.'

'Macil. What an unusual name.'

'Yes, it is uncommon. M-A-C-I-L – pronounced Maysill.'

'How sad for her to be a widow.'

'It's hideous bad luck. Her husband was a fine fellow. In the Navy. He died three years ago – of pneumonia. Of course she gets a

47

pension – but it isn't much and I–'

He broke off, frowning. Why was he telling Geraldine Wayde his private history? She said:

'Oh, do go on and tell me more. You help your sister, of course.'

'I try to.'

'How splendid,' said Gerry. 'Where does she live?'

'In London. Golders Green.'

'And that's your home as well?'

'Yes.'

'And how old is your sister?'

'Thirty.'

'Older than you are?'

'Yes. Three years...'

He broke off. They had reached the house. 'Forgive me if I leave you now,' he said.

How stiffly he said it. How coldly he looked at her. And she thought of the warmth in his eyes and in his voice when he had spoken of his sister's children. It was like a marble statue coming to life. She thought, luxuriously, that it would be rather marvellous to infuse such warmth into Nicholas Hulme ... to be capable of bringing such a light to his eyes. She achieved that sort of thing with other men, she knew, without effort. Too easily. There was an urge in her now to make Nicholas Hulme like other men. He had thawed just a little, down there in the woods. But not enough.

He said 'Good night,' and was gone. She frowned and walked into the drawing-room, engrossed by the thought of him. Her father sat in an arm-chair, studying a pamphlet, horn-rimmed glasses on the end of his nose and the pamphlet held well up to the table-lamp beside him. He was growing short-sighted. Mrs Wayde sat on the sofa sur-rounded by squares of canvas and patterns and a selection of coloured wools in a pink satin brocade bag. She also wore horn-rims. Her fat, over-painted face assumed a tragic expression when she looked at her daughter.

'*Mon Dieu*, darling, but you must be crazy to walk in the garden in those shoes. Look – they are soaking. Take them off. *Tout de suite, chérie.*'

Gerry hunched her shoulders.

'Good Lord, what does it matter?' she said crossly. 'I'll get pneumonia and die, and who cares?'

'What on earth's the matter with you, Gerry?' said Mrs Wayde in a thoroughly Eng-lish voice. She invariably dropped the affect-ation of French when she was cross. 'You need not speak so rudely to your mother.'

Gerry took not the slightest notice of this. She took off her scarf and trailed it on the floor.

'What are you working on?' she asked.

'A seat for that period chair in my bed-room. Come and help me choose the colours, *chérie.*'

But Gerry rejected this offer and announced that she was tired, and went to bed. This alarmed her mother. As a rule Gerry never went to bed before eleven.

Upstairs, Gerry paused outside Nicholas Hulme's door. She pictured him writing in there – running his strong, thin fingers through that jet-black mop of hair. She had a sudden sensuous vision of those fingers running through *her* hair. What was the matter with her? Why this new, crazy wish to establish some sort of intimacy between her father's secretary and herself? Nothing but pique ... because he ignored her. And yet ... there was an attraction about him ... a very strong one, of which she had only recently become conscious.

She had everything in this house that she wanted – most things outside of it – most people – for her natural charm and beauty and energy drew members of both sexes to her side. She was a girl of many friends. But the one thing she could not get was open admiration from Nicholas Hulme. He was the one person she seemed unable to win over to her side.

She walked past his door into her room, amazed at the effect his continued reticence was having upon her.

'You're a little beast, Gerry Wayde,' she reproached herself. 'Leave him alone!'

But what vain woman has ever been able to leave a man alone when he is the only one in her particular world who shuns her? Certainly not Gerry who was wilful and spoiled. But let it be said that, when she made up her mind to break through Nicholas Hulme's reticence before she was finished with him, she did not stop to consider the unfairness of it. She did not realise for a single moment that she was endangering him and his position in this house. It never struck her – because she was a careless, inconsequent child – that there would be any danger. She only wanted to satisfy her vanity and make him 'nice to her.' Beyond that she did not look.

But Nicholas Hulme looked – and saw what might happen. And that was why he fled from her and his own senses, which could easily be stirred by so much beauty and charm.

Her vanity would have been considerably fed if she could have known that he worked no more on his play that night, but paced up and down his room ... remembering the softness of her arm against his ... the fragrance of her hair ... the seduction of her, down there in the woods. How was a man to work?

'Damn women and sex,' said Nicholas Hulme to himself savagely, before he went to sleep that night.

CHAPTER 5

That next week-end – about three days after Gerry had walked with Nicholas Hulme through the woods – the Waydes entertained a house-party. During the summer months Ponders was nearly always full of guests from Friday night till Monday. And as a rule Gerry enjoyed her parties. But this particular week-end she was more bored than if she had been alone.

It was not that her especial friends were absent. They were there. Sir George and Lady Withambury and their estimable son Ivor who – despite his incurable desire to kiss Gerry – danced marvellously and amused her when she was in the mood to deal with his facetiousness. Phyllis Crozier, who had been at Roedean College with Gerry – a pretty and amusing creature, who at twenty-two was an experienced woman of the world who had twice been engaged and was now contemplating a third venture. Then there was Lieut.-Commander Edward Harrage, R.N., the third and very good-looking fiancé of Phyllis. An old crony of Mrs Wayde's; and a young politician – a friend of father's, likely, he assured the family, to distinguish himself at the next election.

A big party – an amusing and varied one. There was plenty of excellent tennis. Tea under the famous Ponders oak which spread its mighty branches over the velvety lawn in front of the house. Long drinks, short drinks, a variety of drinks, about six o'clock. Time for rest in one's bedroom; then a first-rate dinner – the Waydes had a remarkable French cook. Afterwards, dancing in the wide, oak-panelled lounge, or even on the moonlit lawn, since the weather remained so warm.

Gerry – the prettiest girl in the party – the young hostess – flattered, admired, sought after – should have enjoyed herself.

But she was preoccupied and dull – for Gerry. She frowned more often than she smiled. She refused to 'run around' with Ivor Withambury. She had little to say to father's distinguished politician. She avoided any heart-to-heart talks with her friend Phyllis. Mrs Wayde – amiable, chattering without ceasing, full of French affectations – floated around, telling everybody that darling Gerry was not well. But Gerry looked perfectly well and played tennis energetically, if nothing else. So nobody knew what was the matter, and Mrs Wayde least of all.

But Gerry knew. And she was ashamed of herself, but at the same time unable to control that maddening little feeling of pique, of thwarted vanity, that pricked at her during that week-end and 'spoiled her fun.'

Her thoughts ran continually to her father's secretary. Nicholas made himself scarce during that house-party.

He appeared at meal-time. He had to do that. But he avoided Gerry's eye. Nothing she could do made him look her way or pay her the slightest attention. She could feel that he was deliberately ignoring her. To be ignored in that way was altogether a new and hateful experience for Gerry. It reduced her to a state of nerves and irritability. She told herself that she hated Nicholas Hulme. He was a prig. A fool. What did she care for him? He was only a paid secretary in this house. Let him get on with his work and his hateful play and keep his distance. What did she care?

But she did care. Strangely. And from Friday till Sunday she brooded over Nicholas Hulme's treatment of her. Every time he disappeared from the circle, she knew that he had either gone to her father's study to work for him, or up to his bedroom to write. Every night, after dinner, he vanished upstairs. Gerry watched him go and felt an absurd desire to command him to come back; to come down and dance.

Sunday night came. Gerry danced with Ivor Withambury or with Edward Harrage.

The latter danced beautifully and was a fresh-complexioned, attractive young man who bore the clean, buoyant mark of the sea. But she found herself thinking of Nicholas Hulme. With that tall, slimly built body of his he ought to dance well. How stern he had looked at dinner tonight. Never once had he looked her way. He had sat next to Phyllis and talked – in much more friendly fashion than he had talked to *her*, Gerry decided. Phyllis had said afterwards:

'Your father's secretary is rather a lamb, Gerry. Where do you keep him? Isn't he ever on view except at meal-time?'

'No,' was Gerry's brief answer.

'He's got the most intriguing eyes and the *blackest* hair,' observed Phyllis. 'I'd be quite thrilled with him if I wasn't in love with darling Eddy.'

Gerry made no answer to this. But she decided mentally that she would never be thrilled with Nicholas Hulme. He was cold and rude and insupportable. She couldn't stop thinking about him, all the same.

During the evening, when she was walking through the hall, she ran up against him. He came out of Mr Wayde's study with a long, official-looking envelope in his hand. He bowed politely to Gerry and would have passed her, but she placed herself in front of him.

'Mr Hulme, why don't you chuck work

and come and dance,' she said.

'It's exceedingly kind of you, but I want to work,' he said in a formal voice.

She bit her lip.

'Surely for once the play can wait.'

'I'm anxious to finish it, if you don't mind.'

Gerry's fingers clenched on the diamanté bag she was carrying. So he was obstinate! Her powers of persuasion were absolutely lost on this man. She felt unreasonably angry. Her cheeks burned with colour.

'You decline every invitation I make, Mr Hulme. You are really not very polite.'

The pale face of the man coloured now. He said:

'I must apologise if I seem rude. But I don't dance, and I must work on my play. It means a great deal to me.'

It infuriated Gerry that she should mean nothing. She said nothing for the moment. She tapped one small, satin-shod foot on the floor. Nicholas Hulme gave her a swift glance and looked away. Why the devil couldn't she leave him in peace? Wasn't the lounge full of men? That young fool, Withambury, with his facetious, drawling voice and double-breasted waistcoat and narrow trousers and all the latest jokes – no doubt he wanted to dance with Gerry. There were others – men who could afford to laze and amuse themselves.

He was working; working to finish the play

that meant so much to him; that might mean everything in the future for himself and Macil and the kids. He wanted release from the kind of position he held in this household. Not that it wasn't well-paid and comfortable – what a lot of fellows would call a damn soft job. But he wanted freedom; time to write. That could only be secured if he could save money and slave at his dramas – work every second of his spare time.

It might be very pleasant to dawdle away a few hours with Gerry. She was the daughter of his employer. Charming, beautiful. She was the loveliest creature in the party. Oh, yes, he knew it. He had thought it when he came down to dinner tonight and saw her in her new black chiffon dress, so long, so graceful at the back, so short and provocative in front, showing the slimmest of legs in the thinnest of nylon stockings. There was scarcely any back to the dress. It showed a man how white and straight she was. Her skin would be like cool velvet to touch. And she wore a huge spray of diamonds pinned to one shoulder-strap. A diamond bracelet clasped her wrist. She was beautiful and desirable. A faint perfume emanated from her hair. She was made to be admired and spoiled and loved. And Nicholas Hulme knew that; felt it. He could never look at that fair shining head of hers without a curious thrill of appreciation. But it was a thrill he resented.

He wanted to cut the thought of Gerry Wayde and her beauty and desirability right out of his mind. She had disturbed his thoughts, his work, sufficiently. He wanted to be left alone.

He wanted to be rude to her, to say:

'You don't care a hang whether I live or die; whether I make my mark or not; whether I remain a slave to the rich, like yourself, for the rest of my life, or gain my freedom. They'll marry you off to a baronet or an earl before you're a year older. What the hell do you want with me except an idle flirtation? No – it's too dangerous. With me it's – all or nothing, and, by God, it's nothing so far as you or your kind are concerned!'

That's what he wanted to say. And at the same time, when she lifted those long, black lashes and looked up at him with her wide, dark eyes, he had an insensate desire to catch her in his arms and put his lips to the white, slender throat which asked for a man's kisses.

'You must pardon me if I appear rude, Miss Wayde,' he said. 'Good night.'

He bowed and left her. She turned and walked back to the crowd in the lounge. Someone had put a dance record on the big stereo-phonic radiogram which Mr Wayde had just given his family.

It was as though there was an orchestra in

the room. The others were dancing, with the exception of Mr Wayde, who stood by the open windows, holding forth on politics with one of his colleagues. Mrs Wayde – over-powdered, hennaed, in a glittering silver dress which clung to her fat figure, was dancing with Sir George Withambury and thoroughly enjoying herself. As they passed, Gerry heard her make one of her very French speeches in her succulent voice, with much gesticulation.

Gerry thought:

'Poor old mother. She's so stupid! She really thinks Sir George is interested in what she's saying.'

Phyllis Crozier passed, clasped firmly by Ivor. Phyllis was very tall and thin, with almond-shaped hazel eyes and narrow, plucked eyebrows. Her lips were vermilion. She had a husky, rather bitter voice. She was full of subtleties and cynicisms, and might have been forty. But she was beautiful, and men found her attractive. She mesmerised them. Edward Harrage was completely enslaved and dominated by her. She liked to dominate men. Gerry used to admire her enormously. She watched her tonight and wondered why. She looked rather theatrical and unhealthy. And Ivor looked awful – slinky – with his too pointed shoes. He moved like a gigolo – paid dancing partner. And he bent over his partner with parted lips as though he would snatch a kiss at any moment.

Gerry suddenly hated all these people, and herself most of all. Her thoughts would keep winging upstairs to a lamp-lit bedroom where a young man bent feverishly over a paper-littered table and wrote ... wrote ... wrote. A man who had work to do. But why couldn't he abandon it for one evening and dance with her, as she had asked him to? The persistent way in which he ignored her filled her with a desire to match her will against his; to defeat him.

The music ceased. Phyllis strolled up to Gerry.

'That was *marvellous*. Ivor danced divinely. Why are you so depressed, Gerry, sweetie?'

'I don't know,' said Gerry abruptly.

'Where's that nice secretary with the raven hair?'

'I couldn't tell you.'

'Won't he come and dance?'

'No. I don't suppose so.'

'I'm sure he would if *you* asked him, darling,' murmured Phyllis, unconsciously hitting a raw place.

Gerry snapped at her.

'I don't want to ask him.'

Phyllis stared, then laughed. She took a small gilt box from her bag and opened it. She powdered her face and added fresh colour to her lips.

'You've got 'em tonight, Gerry, my lamb.'

'Liver,' said Gerry and moved away.

She suddenly cordially disliked her best friend.

Mrs Wayde rushed up to her.

'*Chérie* – what *is* wrong. *Do* be nice to your father's friend. He's so clever and he's coming into a baronetcy, darling. I–'

'Are you trying to match-make, dear mamma?' Gerry broke in grimly, 'because I'm not in the mood for it.'

Mrs Wayde turned her eyes heavenwards.

'The chances you miss – the *brilliant* chances, Gerry!'

'I don't want to get tied up to anybody,' said Gerry. 'Leave me alone.'

In a very ill humour Gerry went to bed once the party broke up and the guests retired.

She sat on the edge of her bed, warming her bare toes before an electric fire. When the central heating was not working, during the summer, Gerry used an electric fire, at bed-time. She was a luxurious person and she detested the cold. Even on these warm June nights it grew chilly in the early hours of the morning.

It was half-past one. Taylor, her mother's maid, was in bed. Gerry's room advertised that fact. She was not, by nature, tidy. The black dress hung over a chair. Nylon stockings, pale yellow lingerie, satin shoes all in a graceless heap on the floor. The dressing-table low, semi-circular, with a triple mirror and plate-glass top, was a confusion of bottles and jars. All the luxurious pink cream-pots and lotion bottles of Elizabeth Arden. A tall, crystal spray of perfume; a gold and tortoise-shell toilet set. A tray full of odd rings; necklaces; nail files; a polisher; face-powder; lip-stick. All the dozen and one luxuries which a pretty woman likes to consider necessities.

It was a very charming bedroom. Soft, faded blue Persian carpet. The low divan bed, with a circular back of polished walnut wood, had extending arms on either side that held books and papers. Gerry liked to read for ten minutes, no matter how tired she was. Overhead, attached to the bed, was an amber shaded light with a little chain. There was a serpentine bureau of dark golden walnut. A wardrobe of the same smooth satiny wood. Three long, low windows, with curtains of Wedgwood blue silk taffeta, and palest amber net. Gerry had turned out all the lights except the one burning over the bed. She liked this dim light. It was mysterious and soothing.

She wore no dressing-gown. Only a black lace nightgown and wrapper of the same lace. She looked very young with her sleek, fair, short-cropped head.

She was in a restless frame of mind. She

had been tired when she came to bed. But now her nerves were alive, jumping. She was not in the mood for sleep. She sat staring at the rosy glow of the electric fire, her brows drawn together. She was thinking about Nicholas Hulme. She wondered if he was still writing in his room which was not far from hers, just down the corridor.

What a strong will he had! What an intangible personality! Could no woman make him unbend? Supposing she went along to his room now, in this attractive night-attire, and talked to him. Would he be beguiled? Perhaps. After all – he wasn't a stone. And he wrote plays – dramas, no doubt, about the loves, the passions of men and women. He must *feel* what he wrote. He had an artistic temperament. Temperamental people are usually most volcanic when roused.

She visualised Nicholas Hulme being volcanic, and was fascinated by the picture.

She had never deliberately played the vamp to any man in her life. Yet she felt an irresistible desire to play the vamp to Nicholas Hulme. She had been snubbed and ignored. It roused all her fighting blood.

She lit a cigarette and smoked it, brooding over the thought of Nicholas Hulme.

She heard footsteps outside her room, the creak of a board. She knew that board. It always creaked just outside her door. She jammed her cigarette down on an ash-tray on the table beside her. She walked to the door and opened it tentatively.

She saw a man's figure in a green Paisley dressing-gown. Her pulses gave a peculiar leap. It was Nicholas Hulme. There was a towel over his arm. His hair looked rough and wet. He had just come from the bathroom. There entered into Gerry a spirit of sheer mischief – perverse rather than evil. The urge to beat down Nicholas Hulme's cold superiority; to *make* him thaw to her against his will.

Without thinking, without bothering about consequences or morals, with just that obstinate desire to conquer – she called to him.

'Mr Hulme. *Mr Hulme!*'

Nicholas stopped dead. He swung round. He saw the slim, thinly-clad figure of the daughter of the house and stared at her, amazed.

She put a hand to her throat and called to him again, as though she was choking.

'Oh, Mr Hulme – *quickly!*'

Nicholas thought she must be ill. He dropped his towel and ran to her.

CHAPTER 6

'What is it? What's the matter?' he asked.

He had reached Gerry's door. She backed into her room. She panted and half-shut her eyes.

'Oh, quickly ... I'm frightened. I'm scared to death!'

'Frightened? What of?'

'There's someone ... something in my room!'

Nicholas stared round the room. It was his first glimpse of Gerry's bedroom. He had a confused glimpse of silken curtains and a luxurious bed with an amber light burning over it; lace-edged pillow-cases and sheets; thick, soft carpet and a general atmosphere of disorder which was very feminine and charming. But everything looked peaceful.

'Who is there in your room? What can be?' he exclaimed.

'Oh, I don't know,' stammered Gerry. 'But I'm frightened to death.'

He was in the room almost before he knew it. He scowled at Gerry in the way so familiar to her, his thick, dark brows drawn together. He ran a hand over his roughened hair and tried to smooth it. Gerry thought how black it looked; wet and glistening. His face was smooth and freshly shaven. He looked tired but absurdly young in his dressing-gown.

'But what frightened you?' he asked her.

She put a hand to her head and looked round.

'I – I don't know. I was just going to get into bed. I heard a creak ... then a shadow seemed to fall on the curtains.' She pointed to the windows. 'I wondered if anybody had got into my room – climbed up the casements. Oh, please look behind the curtains!'

Nicholas hesitated. He looked down at her doubtfully. Was she really scared? Certainly she was flushed. Her eyes were glittering. He marched across the room and firmly parted the blue taffeta curtains. Not a soul to be seen. No lurking cat-burglars! All the windows were clear. The moon slanted in from a sky ablaze with stars. The garden was quiet, misty, beautiful in the moonlight.

Nicholas turned back to Gerry. She was watching him, wondering how he would behave; what he would do next.

'There isn't a soul there,' he said.

She bit her lip and intimated that she was still frightened.

'I know I heard someone. I'm frightfully nervous at night. And everybody seems asleep. It was so quiet...'

'Your mother is still awake. I heard her

voice as I passed her room. Shall I call her for you?' said Nicholas.

'No, no,' said Gerry hastily. 'It doesn't matter. But *do* look under my bed.'

'Don't be absurd; there isn't room under the bed for a cat,' he said, and laughed.

It was the first time Gerry had ever known Nicholas Hulme to laugh – to smile at her. It made his thin, grave face amazingly attractive; cut two deep lines on either side of his mouth. He crossed the room toward the door.

'I don't think you need be afraid,' he said. 'There isn't a soul in the room. I expect you heard the board creak in the corridor or something.'

Gerry suddenly swayed and closed her eyes.

'I – I feel faint.'

Nicholas ran to her. He put an arm around her shoulders. He was very embarrassed and rather angry. Surely she wasn't going to faint. It was ridiculous. Modern girls didn't faint. That was a Victorian pose.

'I'd better call your mother,' he said gruffly.

'No. I – I'm all right,' she stammered. She opened her eyes and leaned against him. 'Just a moment ... don't leave me ... for a second.'

He stood still – even rigid. He was furious with himself because his heart was pounding madly. Gerry's full weight was against him. How slim she was; much too lovely and seductive in her black lace nightgown. The crisp, shining waves of her hair touched his cheek. There was a faint delicious scent about her. It hung about the whole room. Gerry's particular perfume. It was only too familiar to him.

'So stupid of me ... to be so ... nervous,' she whispered.

'But you're all right now,' he said awkwardly.

'Yes, I – I think so!'

'Then I'll say good night.'

She suddenly turned to him before he could take his arm away from her. She looked up at him with dark appealing eyes.

'Are you going to be – so horrid to me? Won't you ever be my friend – Nicholas?'

He dared not move or speak. His heart was thudding. He felt that his whole body was on fire. He wanted to push her away and could not. There was something so sweet, so alluring about this girl. He felt his forehead go damp. The way in which she said his name. Nicholas! She had never called him that before. All these months he had been 'Mr Hulme.'

'Won't you be friends, Nicholas?' she whispered.

'Yes ... of course ... naturally,' he said and his voice was strained. 'Now – good night.'

'Good night,' she said, and lifted her face with a quick, provocative movement.

The blood hammered in Nicholas's head. And then his control seemed to snap. All the desire that had lain in him for days, weeks, to yield to the fascination of this girl – culminated into a blind mad moment of passion. He was strong, but, like so many strong, reticent creatures, when he broke – he broke badly.

A mist blotted out the beautiful, uplifted face of the girl. He felt himself shivering. He was like one suddenly intoxicated. He caught her in both arms and set his lips to her mouth.

It was long, fierce kiss. It took away Gerry's breath. It also tore away all pretence and idle play. This was something real and urgent – this close, almost savage embrace; this pressure of hard, unrelenting lips on hers. The cold, difficult young man who was her father's efficient secretary; the reserved, unbending Nicholas; was all primitive man in this moment. He was a vibrant, glowing creature, and she – who had never really been kissed by any man in such a way before – went to pieces. Her silly vanities, her self-ishness, her insincerities went down like ninepins before such an onslaught. She saw, too late, what she had done; what she had roused.

She had got her way. She had made

Nicholas Hulme unbend. But she had also got a little more than she had bargained for. Yet in that moment, clasped to him, breathless, her face quite white, her lips bruised under his kisses, she did not hate him – did not fight against his passion. Neither did she respond to it. She was too startled and shocked to do anything but submit in a curiously apathetic fashion.

He, drunk with the softness and beauty of her in his arms, went on kissing her; mad; oblivious to the danger of the situation; on fire for her.

Afterwards, long afterwards, Gerry felt that it was as though she had flung herself into the vortex of a hurricane; into the crater of a volcano – and was too stunned to battle with such terrific elementary forces, to help herself.

The next thing she knew was that Nicholas had pushed her away from him, and her mother's voice was breaking the silence – a shrill, horrified voice:

'Gerry! *Mr Hulme! Mon Dieu* – what is this?'

Gerry recovered herself. Something was drumming, singing in her ears. She gasped and put a hand to her head. She saw Nicholas, very straight and stern, and white as a ghost, standing beside her. She saw the fat ridiculous figure of her mother in a mauve satin dressing-gown entering the room. The inevitable hair-net framed the fat, flabby face. Two round, horrified eyes stared at Gerry. The voice repeated:

'Gerry! *Mr Hulme!*'

Then Gerry came alive to the acuteness of the situation. She tried to laugh.

'Mother, really!'

'Don't "mother" me, Gerry,' interrupted Mrs Wayde. Her face was scarlet and her plump body shivered with rage. *'Quelle horreur!* You – my daughter – and this – this *man!*'

The last word was uttered in a tone of scathing contempt. The flabby, crimson face turned to Nicholas.

'Leave my daughter's bedroom, Mr Hulme. You shall hear from her father in the morning. You cad! You monster – to come to her room – to dare to touch her – an innocent, helpless girl–'

'Be quiet, mother, please!' broke in Gerry. She felt icy cold, and she was trembling. She could not allow her mother to continue in *that* strain. She dared not look at Nicholas; dared not imagine what he was thinking; how he would deal with this situation. Mrs Wayde continued in a low, dramatic voice, forgetting to be French:

'I had left my glasses down in the lounge. I was going to fetch them. I saw your door open and the light on. I came along to speak to you and I saw *this*. Good heavens, and what if Lady Withambury had seen, or your father's friend – Mr Denlington! It would be a scandal. All over the constituency.' – Mrs Wayde liked to think in political terms – 'a secretary – attacking his employer's daughter – in his employer's own house!'

'Oh, for God's sake – *stop!*' interrupted Gerry desperately.

Mrs Wayde, beside herself with rage, went on:

'I shall see that you leave the house in the morning, Mr Hulme. Meanwhile – kindly go.'

An instant's silence. Nicholas Hulme looked down at the elder woman's flushed, furious face. He was not surprised by her temper and virulence. He had known all the way along that there were long claws under this lady's velvet glove. He understood well enough. Fury and indignation – that a mere paid secretary should dare to kiss the daughter of the house – the heiress reserved for a brilliant marriage. The *innocent, helpless girl.* Gerry … who had asked for what she got tonight; had asked to be kissed; had pursued him and disturbed him and worried him for weeks. Well – now perhaps her vanity was satisfied.

It was abominable luck that Mrs Wayde should have come along, of course. His heart sank suddenly, like a stone, at the thought of tomorrow morning. Mr Wayde would believe the worst of him and chuck him out, of course. This was the end of his career as a politician's secretary. Tomorrow would find him amongst the unemployed; his reputation in shreds.

He turned and looked at the girl who had helped to tear it; who had, in fact, ruined him. A moment ago he had held that soft, charming figure in his arms, had kissed her madly ... yes, he had gone mad for a few seconds. She had driven him mad. She looked white and frightened. No doubt she was a little frightened now that the mischief was done. She hadn't really been scared when she had called him into her room. That had been a trick. A trick which had succeeded. But she was frightened now.

Passion no longer raged in Nicholas Hulme. He gave Gerry a cold, bitter look – a look so bitter, so accusing, that she withered under it. Then he bowed to Mrs Wayde.

'Of course, it was entirely my fault,' he said. 'Miss Wayde is not to blame. I will tell Mr Wayde that I will leave the house in the morning.'

He walked out of the room.

Gerry cried:

'No – stop – wait–'

Her mother seized her arm.

'You little fool, Gerry. Don't dare call him back. He's done harm enough.'

'But he hasn't. It's me that's done the

harm,' said Gerry hysterically. 'Me ... *me...*' she beat her breast with a clenched fist. 'I ought to be shot. Oh, my God ... I ought to be shot!'

She tried to get past Mrs Wayde and to follow Nicholas. She wanted to fall at his feet and beg his pardon. She couldn't bear the way he had looked at her ... the bitter scorn in his eyes! Mrs Wayde hung on her arm with relentless fingers.

'Don't make a bigger fool of yourself than you've already done, Gerry. If you're implicated in an – an affair with this young man, then you're a senseless little idiot. A paid secretary – a penniless nobody – and you can pick and choose. Are you out of your mind? Your father would be petrified if he thought you were in any way to blame. Understand – you're *not* to blame. That man forced his way into your room and attacked you.'

'But he didn't–' panted Gerry. She burst into tears. 'Oh, let me go to him.'

Mrs Wayde dragged her to her bed.

'Stop this. Get into bed, Gerry, and pull yourself together. Be thankful that none of the guests have heard this.'

Gerry sank on to the edge of the bed. She trembled violently. The tears rained down her cheeks. Her head buzzed so that she could not think. Her mother was, for the moment, stronger than she. She was forced to stay there – to listen to that voice which told her again and again that she was not to blame and that Nicholas Hulme had tried to seduce her and would be sent away in the morning.

Somewhere, in the corridor, a door shut and a key turned in the lock. Nicholas Hulme had gone into his room.

Gerry turned and buried her face in her pillows.

'What have I done?' she moaned under her breath. 'Oh, my God, *what have I done?*'

CHAPTER 7

There was no sleep for Gerry that night. Mrs Wayde did not leave her room for an hour after her unfortunate entrance into it. To her, of course, it was a mercy that she took it into her head to go and talk to her daughter. She believed that she had nipped in the bud what might have been a disastrous affair. Nicholas Hulme was a good-looking, personable young fellow, and there was no knowing how Gerry might be affected if he chose to flatter her by falling in love with her. The repeated questions which she hurled at Gerry, mingled with French ejaculations of indignation against the miserable young secretary, met with replies which were, on the whole, unsatisfactory to Mrs Wayde.

'No – he hasn't ever made love to me ... no, he has never kissed me before ... no, he's never come inside this room before ... no, no, *no*, I tell you, mother! He *isn't* my boyfriend. Don't be so stupid. We just lost our heads a few minutes ago – that's all.'

'You mean that *he* lost his head,' Mrs Wayde corrected her balefully. She unfastened the strap of her hair-net as though

76

it choked her. Her cheeks were a mauvish shade which toned with her satin wrapper. Her large bosom heaved. 'He is entirely to blame. Not you. He said so.'

Gerry ceased crying. She sat straight, rigid, white except for two feverish spots on her cheek-bones, staring ahead of her.

'He said so – yes. But I tell you he wasn't the only one to blame. He wouldn't have come into my room if I hadn't encouraged him.'

'That,' said her mother, 'is a mad and foolish thing to say and I forbid you to say it, Gerry.'

Gerry gripped the bed on either side of her with two hot little hands.

'I shall tell father so.'

'Your father would be disgusted and horrified and he wouldn't believe you. He will say as I do that you are trying to defend this young man out of pity – because you don't want him to be sacked. 'But he will be sacked. *Ma foi! Mais c'est tout à fait horrible!*'

Gerry set her teeth.

'Go away and leave me alone, mother. I'm worn out.'

Mrs Wayde eyed her doubtfully, then, gathering her dressing-gown securely around her ample figure, marched to the door – the picture of wrathful majesty.

'*Mon enfant,* you can thank God that I and not one of our guests discovered Mr Hulme in your room. Imagine the talk. *Quelle horreur!* And your father an M.P. ... known to everybody in the district ... you might have more consideration for a man in the public eye.'

Gerry stared in front of her. She saw suddenly the hideous unfairness of this thing – of the whole scheme of life as her mother – both her parents, in fact – chose to live it.

If Ivor Withambury had been found in her room kissing her, there would have been a row – yes, but it would have been overlooked. Ivor was a rich young man and heir to a baronetcy. Her marriage to him would be a good thing. Or to Arthur Denlington, another future baronet, and a fine politician, likely to be elected for the mid-Fairfax division, in the autumn, if the present parliament was dissolved. Had he been found here, tonight, with her in his arms, Mrs Wayde would have chided him but given a smile with the chiding.

Nicholas Hulme, the paid secretary – the young man who was nobody and nothing – was to be sent away in disgrace. It was wrong – disgracefully wrong.

Horror and compunction smote Gerry. She would have given all that she possessed to undo the harm she had done. She had never meant such calamity to evolve out of her vain longing to attract a smile, a word of admiration from Nicholas. If only she could go back … but one can never go back. She realised that. The meaning of Omar's words: 'The Moving Finger writes, and, having writ, moves on…' was brought home to her forcibly. For the first time in her lazy, useless, inconsequent life, Gerry knew what it was to feel remorse.

It was not those burning, passionate kisses that Nicholas Hulme had given her which hurt or humiliated her. But the look of contempt, of bitterness, which he had flung her as he walked out of her room. And the greatest humiliation was the thought of the shameful thing that she had done when she had led him on – tricked him into this bedroom tonight.

'What have I done…?' she asked herself again and again.

Long after her mother had left her she sat there, shivering and repenting. It was full daylight – the dawn of another perfect June day – before she got into bed, and then it was not to sleep. For the first time in her recollection she had a 'white night' and did not close her eyes. She got up and bathed very early – long before her usual habit. When Taylor came in with her tea at eight-thirty, the usual hour when Miss Geraldine was called, she was astonished to find the bed empty and Miss Geraldine up and dressed.

In the big, historic room with its Jacobean

four-poster, the room wherein so much inspiration for good work had come to him, Nicholas Hulme had passed what was probably the worst night in his career. And there had been one or two bad ones. The night, for instance, when his mother had died … when he was a boy of thirteen … and had been sent for, hurriedly, because Mrs Hulme had been thrown from her horse on the hunting-field and had broken her back. Nicholas had adored her, and she had died holding on to his hand. That had been a dreadful night, unforgettable, even for a child so young. And then there had been the other awful night of Mr Hulme's sudden demise, following his final failure in the City. Death from a stroke, brought on by the strain and worry of crashing disappointments. Nicholas had been older then, a young man up at the Varsity. But at twenty, even when faced by tragedies, one is still enthusiastic and eager about life, and there is hope abundant. He had youth and health and brains and good friends to help.

Only yesterday he had written to Macil and said:

'Things look pretty hopeful, old girl. I shall finish my play by next month if I am lucky. I'm stuck on the third act, but I am waiting a moment of inspiration. Don't worry about Robin's school. I may be able to let you have a decent cheque next week...'

And what now? Far from being able to send Macil a 'decent cheque,' he would be going home; to Macil's flat in Golders Green, where he had a shake-down when he wanted it. The only home he knew these days. He would have to face her; tell her he had lost his job. Been chucked out ... for kissing the daughter of the house in her bedroom at one in the morning.

The vulgarity of it. The loathsome idea of it all. Rage and disgust burnt fiercely in Nicholas Hulme's very soul that night. He did not attempt to sleep. He did not go to bed. He paced the big lamp-lit room, smoking one cigarette after the other ... walking up and down until he was so physically tired, aching in every limb, that he had to sit down. He turned out the lamp and sat in front of the open casement and watched the dawn break; watched the exquisite beauty of the morning light break over the misty beech woods, and lift the shadows from the garden. He knew it was the last time he would ever see the sun rise on the Wayde's home.

His eyes were sore, the lids inflamed. His lips and throat felt dry from too much smoking and no sleep. There was a sick, heavy feeling in his heart.

What luck ... what damnable luck ... for

such a thing to have happened … just when he was working so well and so hard. Austin Wayde was pleased with him. He might have kept this post for some time to come. And he would have finished his play. It would never be finished now. He wouldn't have time or opportunity. He would have to tramp round; tout round for a job. And without anyone to say a word for him. Austin Wayde wouldn't recommend him for a job – a cad, a bounder who assaulted his daughter in her room at dead of night. God, what a thought!

Nicholas leaned his aching head on his arm. There was a very bitter taste in his mouth and great bitterness in his heart. And the one person he never wished to see again in this world was Geraldine Wayde.

She had got her way … she had defeated him with her wiles and her cajolery and her unquenchable thirst for admiration. All his self-restraint, his reticence, had gone down under an avalanche of passion, of uncontrollable desire for her. The most terrible thing of all now to Nicholas Hulme was the knowledge that desire was not dead. He hated the thought of her and what she had done to him … but he still wanted her. All through the bitterness of those cold, grey hours of the morning he remembered the thrill of her lips, the seduction of her in his arms. A man might remember these things and not cease to want them until he was dead. That was the damnable part of it. He despised himself for it.

And God, how he despised her! She had ruined him. It might be weak and caddish of him to say, 'The woman tempted me,' but, in heaven's name, wasn't it true? Hadn't he fought against her, strived to keep away from her, to dispel her enchantment, to remember that she was not for him?

Tomorrow he would be turned out of Ponders in disgrace. Not a pretty thought. It was not only the immediate loss of an excellent post and of his reputation that he regretted. It was all that the loss meant in the future. Nobody knew better than Nicholas how difficult it was for a man to get a decent job these days. A man without capital, might be weeks, months before he found anything suitable. After all, he had literary talent but no definite profession. It was the professional men ... the chartered accountants, the mechanics, the engineers who could find work ... not the artists of this world.

It was a dreary outlook. And as for the hopes of finishing a play and getting it produced ... they had gone west with every-thing else tonight.

Poor old Macil! What a blow it would be to her. Poor, hard-working, patient Macil!

Overwhelming anger against Gerry – the cause of all this unhappiness – consumed

Nicholas while he sat there before the open casements staring out at the dawn. He got up suddenly and walked to the table littered with foolscap – the manuscript for his play. He looked down at the top sheet. *At Boiling Point*. That was the title of it. The title he had refused to tell Gerry. *Damn Gerry!* Damn the play and everything else.

A red mist came before Nicholas's eyes, and in a moment of terrible, uncontrolled despair he seized the sheets of foolscap and tore them in half – scattered them wildly on the floor.

'To hell with *At Boiling Point*, to hell with everything.' He shouted the words as he destroyed the sheets – shaking with frenzy.

When he had torn the last in half he flung himself on his bed and lay very still; his ravaged face on the curve of his arm.

CHAPTER 8

Gerry hung about the lounge and the hall from half-past seven until eight. She did not care what the staff thought. Up and down she walked, keeping an anxious eye on the staircase. She was waiting for Nicholas Hulme to come down. She must see him before he went away – if he was really going for good. She *must* see him – apologise – make the only amends within her power.

It was a warm, mild morning. The sunlight slanted in through the big windows on the staircase and made the polished oak look like dark bronze. A faint perfume of flowers came from the garden.

It was a beautiful, colourful summer's day. But to Gerry it might have been raining or snowing for all she cared. Her eyes were blind to beauty. She felt cold and nervous and unutterably wretched. She dreaded facing Nicholas Hulme. Yet she knew that she must see him; speak to him just once again before he went away.

She stood a moment at the front door and looked with unseeing eyes down the wide paved path which was flanked with weeping ramblers – great masses of pink roses on the slender trees. One or two birds were hopping and twittering on the old stone bird bath which stood in the centre of the pathway. A pearly mist hung over the distant beeches. That meant another hot day. But Gerry looked at the woods and shivered, ashamed of the remembrance of an evening when she had walked there with Nicholas Hulme and tried to make him flirt with her.

'What a little beast I have been,' she thought. 'Oh, if only I could wash it all out.'

She heard footsteps on the staircase and swung round, her heart beating violently. She saw Nicholas Hulme dressed in a dark grey suit; tweed coat over one arm; a suitcase in his hand. So he was ready to go – now – at once.

He came to the foot of the staircase. She went forward to meet him. When he saw her the blood rushed to his face. It receded quickly and she saw how white he was. There were dark circles under his eyes. He looked ill. He glanced at her with an expression of cold indifference which she found unbearable. He would have passed her but she spoke.

'Oh, please – Mr Hulme – listen to me – one moment.'

He stood still. He was forced to look at her, but still with that chilly indifference, as though she were a complete stranger.

Gerry was not used to asking people for

forgiveness; to humbling herself. But there was generosity in her nature, and now, when she knew herself at fault, she was generous with her apology.

'I must tell you how frightfully sorry I am – about last night. Oh, please, don't curl your lips like that. I know you must loathe me – despise me – but I *am* sorry. Honestly, I never dreamed – I never wanted–' She broke off, husky, stammering.

Nicholas looked at her unmoved. His face might have been carved out of granite. In a vague, detached sort of way he saw that she was labouring under some intense emotion. She was very pale and distraught and her eyes were suffused. But just how genuine her contrition was he neither knew nor cared. He was finished with Geraldine Wayde.

'Won't you accept my – my apology – please,' she stammered. 'I – I'm dreadfully sorry. It was my fault. I know. I didn't mean anything – dreadful to happen. I mean – if only I'd thought – that my mother – that you'd lose your job–' She couldn't get it out. She was nervous and stuttering.

Then Nicholas spoke.

'I'm afraid I can't discuss last night with you,' he said in a frozen voice. 'Good-bye.'

'No – don't – oh, really – you can't refuse to believe that I'm most dreadfully sorry!' she exclaimed. Her face grew red and puckered like that of a child in distress. 'You *must* believe that I am sorry.'

'I'm afraid that you being sorry can't undo the harm that has been done,' he said coldly. 'Please let me pass.'

'But father must be told – you can't be sent away disgraced and blamed – it isn't fair.'

'No – it isn't fair,' he agreed coldly. 'But that is what'll happen. It's inevitable. Please let me get by. I see no use in prolonging this conversation.'

Gerry moved back. Her heart-beats seemed to shake her body. Her throat felt choked and hot. She felt a frantic desire to fall at his feet and implore him to forgive her. He looked ghastly. His eyes were so awful. Oh, *what* had she done? It was too frightful...

'I'll tell father that it was my fault – I swear I will!' she stammered.

'Please don't trouble. It won't make things any better for me and might make them worse for you. Good-bye.'

He would have passed on but a loud, angry voice from the upper landing made him pause. Simultaneously he and Gerry looked up. Mr Wayde was leaning over the banisters.

'I think the less you two have to say to each other the better. Hulme, you will oblige me by going to my study. I will join you there.'

Nicholas squared his shoulders.

Now for the peroration. It was only what he had expected. Yesterday – a kind friendliness and comradeship in work with Austin Wayde,

M.P. This morning, cold anger and disgust. His cup of bitterness filled to the brim.

But Gerry said frantically:

'No, father – you're making a mistake. Come here. You must listen to me. Mr Hulme – you aren't to go.'

With frantic little fingers she caught hold of Nicholas's arm and hung on to him. He reddened and tried to get away. Damn it … if only she'd let him alone. She was making things ten thousand times worse.

Austin Wayde came down the stairs. He looked a handsome, dignified man with his grey hair and clipped moustache, his fine, massive figure. He was always smartly tailored – this morning in light grey flannels. At times he was inclined to be self-important and dictatorial, but on the whole he was a pleasant, attractive man. At this precise moment all amiability was wiped from his face. He looked flushed and angry. When he reached the hall he eyed his daughter with none of his usual tolerance. His wife had treated him to a bad half-hour on the subject of his secretary's disgraceful conduct with Gerry.

'Gerry, will you kindly let go of Mr Hulme's arm and leave us,' he said. 'I wish to speak to Mr Hulme alone.'

'But you must hear what I have to say first,' exclaimed Gerry. 'I don't know what mother has said.'

'Enough to convince me that I was greatly mistaken in Mr Hulme's character,' broke in Austin Wayde. 'As for you, Gerry, your mother assures me that you are not to blame ... but you modern girls ... well, dammit ... a little more dignity and poise, ahem' – he coughed loudly – 'might dissuade young men like Hulme' – he shot a wrathful look at his secretary – 'from daring to take such liberties.'

'Mother doesn't know what she's talking about!' said Gerry wildly. 'Look here, father. I encouraged Mr Hulme and–'

'Please, Miss Wayde, let me talk to your father alone,' interrupted Nicholas, sick at heart with the whole affair.

'Yes, Gerry. Kindly leave us, my dear,' said Mr Wayde. 'You don't realise what you are saying. You wish to make excuses for this young man – very nice of you – but there are no excuses possible for his scandalous behaviour last night. Good God!' Austin Wayde passed a finger across his moustache. 'Daring to enter your bedroom ... my secretary ... a trusted employee under my roof ... good Lord!'

Nicholas writhed and set his teeth. Gerry felt that she would go out of her mind.

'Father, I tell you I asked him to come in!' she said desperately. 'I did ... it wasn't Mr Hulme's fault ... you mustn't send him away...'

'Now, Gerry, enough of this,' said Mr Wayde. 'I am not going to listen to a lot of hysterical nonsense. Your mother assures me that there was nothing between Hulme and yourself – no serious affair – isn't that so?'

'Yes, but–'

'Very well. There is not even the excuse that you were – er – in love with him.'

'No – but–'

'Nor Mr Hulme with you.'

'No, sir, but–' began Nicholas.

'Then it's sufficient that you walked into her bedroom in the early hours of the morning and forced your attentions upon her!' broke in Mr Wayde, his voice rising with his temper. 'Now kindly go to my study at once. Gerry, I'll listen to no more explanations from you.'

'Oh, my God,' said Gerry in a low, strained voice. 'Won't you try and understand...'

But Austin Wayde had no intention of trying to understand. He was no more anxious than his wife that an affair of any kind should be tolerated between his daughter and heiress and an impecunious secretary. Hulme was a gentleman, and till now he had thought him a decent fellow – but this was scandalous and unpardonable. That he should enter Gerry's bedroom – in his dressing-gown – compromise her – endanger her good name. His, Austin Wayde's good name. Think what a scandal there might have been in Hampshire if this had become public property.

Nicholas walked into Mr Wayde's study. Gerry stood at the foot of the staircase, leaning against a post. Her face was pinched and white. She saw now, more clearly than ever, what a dreadful thing she had done. Dreadful because it was unremediable. Neither of her parents would admit that she was at fault. They did not choose to admit it. And Nicholas would shoulder the whole burden of disgrace.

In the study the two men faced each other.

'I am bitterly disappointed in you, Hulme – bitterly,' said Austin Wayde. 'You have no possible excuse to offer.'

'No – none,' said Nicholas.

'Of course, my daughter is trying to exonerate you because she is sorry for you.'

'Yes,' said Nicholas. His face was stony.

'I shall give you a cheque for a month's salary and you must leave my house this morning.'

'Yes.'

'As for future references–' Wayde cleared his throat. 'It will be difficult for me to speak highly of a young man who has behaved so dishonourably under the roof of his employer.'

Without flinching Nicholas accepted this. He felt that he was in a stunned condition of mind; that nothing could hurt him. Acute feeling had died, at dawn this morning, after he had destroyed the cherished manuscript of his play in a bitter moment of madness.

Austin Wayde made a few more speeches – accusing, condemning, censuring Nicholas heavily for his conduct. He continually re-iterated the words: 'My young daughter ... my little girl...' suggesting an added rebuke to Nicholas because Gerry was so young – and a young girl is easily taken advantage of.

'You must be thankful, Hulme, that it was my wife and not I who saw you in her room. Without doubt I would have lost my temper and thrashed you,' were Austin Wayde's last angry words.

Nicholas – white to the lips – said:

'May I go now, please, sir?'

Austin Wayde coughed and glanced at him uneasily. The boy had taken the whole thing very coolly and quietly. Not a word of excuse or appeal. It was a damnably uncomfortable affair – damned awkward for him, too. He was losing a most efficient secretary.

He permitted Nicholas to leave.

'Your things are packed? Yes, very well. I will tell Jennings to take you to the station. You will, I presume, catch the next train to town.'

'Yes,' said Nicholas.

With a cheque in his note-case and the taste of ashes in his mouth, Nicholas walked out of Mr Wayde's study into the garden to await Jennings and the car.

Gerry was there – waiting for him again. Would she never leave him alone? Yet faint pity for her entered his heart when he saw her face. It was so unlike the pretty, beguiling face of the old Gerry. It was blotched and stained with tears. She had been crying violently. Why? What was she worrying about? She had got her own way ... she had torn down his defences last night. Nobody blamed her for what had unfortunately been discovered. He was ruined. But life for her was as rosy, as full of brilliant prospects as ever. Why should she make a scene?

He tried to avoid her. But she came up to him, her handkerchief pressed to her lips.

'Are you – really going?'

'Yes.'

'Father has dismissed you?'

'Yes.'

'My God – it's rotten – it's not fair,' she said in a passionate voice.

'I should advise you,' said Nicholas, 'to go in and not be seen out here with me. It will only cause fresh trouble.'

'I don't care,' she said wildly. 'I can't bear this to have happened. Won't you say you forgive me?'

He looked down at her. He was inclined to believe that she was sorry. But pity and the desire to pardon her were far from his heart in the bitterness of this hour of disgrace and dismissal. Upstairs in his room lay the torn sheets of his play. Hope and inspiration both had gone. This calamitous finale to his career as Austin Wayde's secretary had robbed him of any desire to write again. Perhaps that was the worst thing Gerry had done to him. And there was the heartbreaking thought of his sister and the kids ... their disappointment.

'Please, please forgive me,' said Gerry hoarsely.

She was so close to him that he could catch that faint elusive scent which was her own. He had a shattering vision of her in her black nightgown, the passion she had stirred in him ... the softness of her lips crushed under his kisses. She had ruined him, and yet he wanted to drop his suitcase now, catch her in his arms and kiss her savagely ... hurt her...

The blood rushed to his head.

'It can't matter to you whether I forgive you or not,' he said violently. 'We shall never meet again. Now, for God's sake, go away and leave me in peace.'

She felt as though he had lifted his hand and struck her across the face. She fell back, dumb before his bitterness. She knew herself unforgiven. And it was, perhaps, in that moment that the scales fell from Gerry's eyes.

Suffering acutely from real remorse, real grief, she came face to face with one outstanding and poignant truth. She loved Nicholas Hulme. She loved him. She had known it in the dim recesses of her mind when he had been caught up in the tornado of her own making last night, and he had taken her in his arms and kissed her so desperately. She loved him and she had ruined him. She loved him and he was going away – when she would have given half her life to make him stay. In undeserved disgrace he was going; refusing her his forgiveness. That was the hardest part of all to bear.

When she looked at him, that sudden shock of realisation of her love for him upon her, she felt that it was only the beginning of a punishment that would last all her life.

She put a hand to her lips. She almost cried out aloud: 'Nicholas … Nicholas?'

He turned his back on her. There was something very grim and unbending in the sight of his back; the stern outline of him against the sunlight. Her eyes smarted. Her heart beat swiftly and hurt her. She whispered his name: 'Nicholas…'

He did not look at her again. In sudden agony and shame she turned and ran into the house. She tore upstairs, like one running from a nightmare. She collided with the tall figure of Phyllis Crozier, who – in a sleeveless, canary-coloured cotton frock with a yellow straw hat pulled over her sleek, dark heard – looked like a mannequin displaying costumes for the Riviera.

'Hello, darling,' said Phyllis. 'Where are you rushing to?'

Gerry did not answer. Miss Crozier, staring at her, was startled and amazed to see a white, distraught little face with tears streaming down the cheeks. She began to question her, but Gerry broke loose from her. She couldn't bear Phyllis. She rushed into her bedroom and locked the door.

For a few moments she lay across her bed and gave way to a fit of wild sobbing. Between the great, aching sobs, she kept on saying convulsively: 'Nicholas … Nicholas … Nicholas…'

If only she could go back – wipe out what had happened. She felt that the inability to undo the harm she had done would drive her out of her mind.

Spent with sobbing she lay rigid, her face buried in the curve of her arm. Then she heard the wheels of a car crunch on the drive and rushed to the window. She saw her father's Rolls moving slowly away from the house. She knew Nicholas Hulme sat in the car. He was being taken to the station. Sent away in disgrace. Sacked at a moment's notice by her father, who refused to believe he was not at fault. That was the awful thing – that both her parents refused to believe what she told them.

The dark blue bonnet of the Rolls flashed

in the sunlight as it rounded a bend in the drive. Then it disappeared. A dreadful sensation of despair gripped Gerry's heart. In all her spoiled, luxurious life she had never suffered as she suffered now. Remorse ... and the painful and bitter knowledge that she loved the man whom she had hurt and driven away.

She would probably never see him again. That was a dreadful thought. For the first time in her existence she knew what it was to love ... to be in love. Yes, she was in love with Nicholas Hulme. That had been made plain to her this morning when he had refused her his forgiveness. That was the hardest part of her punishment. She had never contemplated falling in love in this fashion, nor wished to. She had shared none of her mother's ambitions for a brilliant marriage. And now she knew that when one cared, money, a title, position, did not, could not come into it. One just cared – that was all. The fact that Nicholas Hulme was nothing and nobody did not matter. She loved him.

If he had wanted her to, she would have walked out of this house today and followed him barefoot; thrown up everything for his sake; made any sacrifice in order to prove to him her love and her remorse for the thing she had done.

Gerry's mind seethed with these feverish thoughts as she walked up and down her bedroom; her handkerchief a tight, wet ball in her clenched hand; her face streaked with tears. Her eyes felt as though there were burning weights on the lids. Her temples throbbed and buzzed. She had not had her usual cup of tea. She felt a little sick. But she could think of nothing but the awful fact that she loved Nicholas Hulme and that he despised her. She would never see him again.

How blind, how mad she had been not to realise all this before, not to foresee that her vain, inglorious attempts to attract Nicholas had been born not merely of vanity and pique, but of strong, deep feeling for him. He had attracted her; had always attracted her. But until today she had not understood that she loved him.

Perhaps last night, when he had lost his head in this very room and held her so passionately in his arms, she had known and understood. She had thrilled, unconsciously, to his fierce kisses, and had not wanted to resist him.

She faced herself and the truth grimly in this hour. She knew that only one thing in life was worth anything to her. Nicholas Hulme's love. And she would never win it. She would never see him again. Even if she did, he would not forgive her.

Gerry stood still and covered her face with her hands. A heartbroken feeling swept over her. She whispered to herself.

'Oh, why, why didn't I know … why didn't I see what was going to happen? Oh, my God … what am I going to do now?'

Somebody knocked at the door.

'*Chérie*,' said Mrs Wayde's voice, 'aren't you coming down? Aren't you dressed yet?'

'Yes – I'm coming,' said Gerry in a dead voice.

She walked to the wash-basin which was fitted in a corner cupboard in her room. She sponged her face with cold water. Then she looked at herself in the glass and was shocked by the reflection. She looked ghastly – chalk white – eyes ringed with blue shadows – eyelids inflamed. Even with make-up anybody would see that she had been crying violently.

She could not go downstairs and face a hearty crowd at the breakfast table. Mother, eyeing her with suspicion after last night. Father, fussy and irritable and put out by what he called the 'scandalous behaviour' of his secretary and his dismissal. Phyllis being inquisitive. Ivor Withambury, facetious. No, no, she could not face them.

She slipped off the tennis shorts and shirt she had been wearing, put on a nylon bed-jacket, and climbed wearily into bed. She rang the bell for Taylor. She said:

'Please bring some coffee and rolls and tell the mistress that I have a headache and will come down afterwards when I have had some aspirin and some sleep.'

'Yes, miss,' said Taylor, and departed, somewhat surprised to see Miss Geraldine, who was usually full of health and spirits, looking so 'queer.'

As soon as the maid had gone a feeling of awful restlessness seized Gerry. She could not stay in bed. She could not rest or stop thinking about Nicholas. Nicholas going back to his sister's flat in Golders Green – yes, he had told her that was his home – unjustly dismissed from his post. The idea maddened her. The spirit of justice was strong in Gerry – always had been when she was a small child. She could not bear the injustice of what had happened to Nicholas through her. All kinds of wretched memories kept coming into her head about Nicholas. The fact hat he was poor – that his sister was a widow, hard up, with two children to support. He helped her to support them. The loss of his job and reputation with his employer was a very serious thing; a terrible thing for him. Why hadn't she had the sense, the grace, to realise how she had jeopardised his career by her careless pursuit of his favours?

'Oh, damn,' said Gerry miserably, and fresh tears stung her eyelids. 'Oh, Nicholas, if only you knew how sorry I am!'

She walked out of her room. She was drawn as though by a magnet to the room

Nicholas had occupied. Nobody was about. Everybody had gone down to breakfast; up bright and early on this glorious June morning.

Gerry found Nicholas's door open. She walked in and stood staring disconsolately around her. The morning sun never came in here through these north windows. And even in summer the atmosphere of the room struck cold. But this morning it seemed to Gerry to have the gloom, the stillness, the chill of a vault. Here, indeed, something had died. Something warm and vibrant. Nicholas's hopes ... they were dead. His fervent aspirations to work hard, save money, and write a successful play.

One of the maids had already stripped the big four-poster bed of its sheets and folded the blankets. But there was an atmosphere here of untidiness, of that desolation which hangs over a bedroom which has just been vacated.

All Nicholas's things – his brushes – the personal touches of which Gerry had taken note the other night – had gone. Only the memory of him – the lingering personality – was here.

She looked at his writing-table. That was so reminiscent of him. She seemed to see the slim, tall figure stooping over it; the bent head with the thin, strong fingers ruffling and threading through the thick, black hair.

An awful pang smote her heart. If only she could call him back ... see him here ... hear him tell her that he understood how sorry she was ... knew how she suffered ... and would forgive her.

Then she noticed that there were many pieces of foolscap lying on the table, in the paper-basket, and on the floor. Dozens of white, torn sheets. She frowned and walked to the desk. She picked up one of these sheets. She found the small, irregular hand-writing ... the illegible hand typical of a writer ... difficult to decipher. But it only took her a second to see that this was a play. There were the names of the characters in the wide margins. Short speeches of two or three lines. Phrases crossed out and revised. An untidy author's manuscript.

She stared at it, shocked into the realisation that this was Nicholas's play ... the play on which, of course, he had been working. But why had he torn it up and left it behind?

The colour rushed to her cheeks. Her heart beat violently. Surely she hadn't done *this* to him, too. Made him tear up his cherished play? Surely his disgrace, his un-deserved dismissal from his job with her father, hadn't preyed on his mind so that he had lost all ambition and deliberately destroyed his play?

With trembling fingers Gerry picked up other sheets of the foolscap. She could not read what was written because there was a mist before her eyes. But she saw that the halves could be fitted together.

She went down on her hands and knees and gathered all the scattered pieces. She searched the room diligently – found every piece of foolscap which had any writing on it. Found even the title page.

AT BOILING POINT
A Play in Three Acts
by
NICHOLAS HULME

So it *was* his beloved play. And he obviously had no copy. This was the original. It was not typed. He had not finished it.

Gerry shivered from head to foot when, finally, she stood in the centre of the deserted room with the torn manuscript in her hand. This was the most bitter moment of all to her. To feel what irreparable harm she had done a fellow creature through her vanity and inconsequence. And to a creature whom she loved now better than anybody she had ever known.

It was bad enough that he had lost his job and his reputation. But this was worse – much worse. That he should have destroyed his beloved play. He must indeed have been hurt and maddened to do such a thing. His play which meant so much.

She could see him standing here before her as he had stood late that night after her birthday ball, telling her shyly, awkwardly, how much the play meant to him. And again in the moonlit woods when she had strolled with her arm through his, and he had said that the play meant everything – that his future and his sister's depended upon the success of it.

And this was what she had done to him. *This!*

'Oh, Nicholas, why did you tear it up – why did you do it?' she cried aloud.

Her scalding tears fell on the manuscript. She carried it back to her own bedroom, weeping bitterly over it. Later she would sort out all the halves – read it – make herself decipher it – put it together – keep it. If she could find out where he was she would post it to him – beg him to go on with it. That he should have destroyed it was tragic and unbearable to her because she knew herself responsible for the tragedy.

She locked the torn manuscript away in a drawer of the little walnut bureau in her room. She crept miserably back to bed and hid her face in the pillow, exhausted by her futile grief.

CHAPTER 9

Macil Robertson rose every morning at a quarter to seven. She dressed Tony, her three-year-old baby, and Robin, aged six. She cooked breakfast, and afterwards, when Mrs Smithers, the good-natured 'daily,' arrived to keep an eye on Tony, she took Robin to the kindergarten which he had just commenced. She then returned to the flat, prepared lunch, and took Tony out in his push-cart and did her shopping.

The afternoon meant Robin home from school again; the two children to take out till tea. The children to amuse till bedtime. Then supper and an evening of sewing for them, or herself, and mending for both.

That was Macil's daily routine – the usual monotonous grind of life. The life she had led ever since her husband died. She was a brave, patient woman – still a girl – only just thirty. She had adored her husband – handsome, breezy, amusing, Tom who had had no right to marry on a naval lieutenant's pay with no private income. But so long as he had been alive, Macil had laughed at hardship and been ideally happy, and learned amazing economy considering that she had been brought up in luxury with Nicholas in their father's lifetime.

She adored her two small sons – they meant everything now that Tom was dead. Poor Tom, his laughter, his humour, his sunny personality so tragically wiped out by that attack of pneumonia just after Tony's birth.

But no woman, no matter how patient or philosophical, could enjoy the life which Macil led nowadays in her cheap top flat in Golders Green. Macil, in particular, hated stagnation. She had Nicholas's ardour and enthusiasm for life; his ambitions. She was a born musician – she would have liked to have studied music. She had what all the Hulmes possessed – the creative instinct.

But with no money and two small sons to provide for and their education to save for, life could be nothing to Macil but a mere existence – an effort. The friends who knew her, who visited her, and those in town whom she visited – all very much better off than herself – wondered sometimes 'how she did it.' How she managed to smile through all the disappointment and drudgery and difficulty. Sometimes she didn't know herself how she did it. She just achieved things by sheer will-power and with her intense love for her children as a driving force.

Nicholas, her brother, and the only member of the family left to her, was particularly dear to her these days. She was in sympathy with him. They understood each other. They were tremendous pals. And she adored him for his goodness to her and her sons. What she would have done without the moral and financial support which Nicholas had given her since Tom died, she did not know.

She felt particularly pleased about Nicholas at the moment because of that letter which she had had from him yesterday.

He seemed to be in such a first-rate post in Austin Wayde's house, and he enjoyed politics, dear old boy, and had the evenings for his own work. Macil was delighted about it. There was the play … always the play to work at and hope for. He was trying hard to save money so that he could settle down and work really hard at his writing. One must have capital behind one to do that. Plays were a toss-up; only one in a hundred succeeded. Not everybody could write a *Mousetrap*.

But the tone of his last letter was very hopeful and gave Macil hope.

She was altogether astonished and startled when, at half-past eleven that morning, while she was in her tiny kitchen making an apple-pie for the children's lunch, she heard a familiar treble knock on the front door.

That was Nicholas's own particular knock. But it couldn't be Nicky – unless he had come up from Hampshire on business for Mr Wayde and had run in to see her.

Macil wiped her hands; took off her overall and smoothed her jumper. She also ran a comb speedily through the thick, dark hair which was so like Nicholas's, and which she wore bobbed. She went to the front door and opened it.

She saw her brother standing on the mat with a coat and suitcase. A taxi-driver was struggling up the stairs with a trunk.

'Nicky – so it *is* you!' she exclaimed delightedly. 'My *dear* – how lovely!'

In the excitement of the moment and the darkness of the little hall, she did not see his face very plainly. She hung on to his arm, and he bent and kissed her.

'One moment, dear, I'll just settle the taxi.'

Then, while he helped the driver in with the trunk and tipped him, Macil began to wonder what all this luggage meant. They walked together into the sitting-room – a low-ceilinged room at the very top of the building, with two windows from which one could see the whole of Golders Green and the outlying suburbs. It was rather close and stuffy up here on a hot June morning. But Macil had grown used to it.

The heat and stuffiness struck Nicholas rather forcibly after the exquisite freshness of Graylingstone air and the big, beautiful rooms at Ponders. But this was home. Macil's home was his.

He had wrestled with a veritable demon of

despair all the way up to town in the train. But the acid had bitten deeply into him. His eyes were full of glom as he looked round him at the familiar objects. The furniture was good, antique stuff saved from the wreckage of their old home. And there were some nice pieces of china and glass which had belonged to Tom; one or two decent pictures. It was a tasteful, well-furnished room. But the hideous red bricks of the fireplace; the cramped feeling up here; the whole atmosphere of economy – annoyed Nicholas intensely this morning. Macil ought to be in a better home than this. And he had hoped to make a success of things. To send her and the kids down to the country. How *they* would have appreciated a place like Ponders, or even the lodge by the gates of Ponders, he thought bitterly. And now all hope of that was gone.

Damn Geraldine Wayde. He hadn't been able to stop thinking about *her* during the hour and a half of that journey from Graylingstone…

'Now, Nicky, what's all this mean.' Macil's voice interrupted his unhappy reflections. 'You and all your luggage. My dear – I'm thrilled, but–'

'You won't be very thrilled when you know,' he broke in.

She stood before him, staring up at him. She was a tall woman, but he was two inches taller. The first flush of pleasure at his unexpected arrival had died down. She was anxious now. She saw his face in the full light. It was white, and his eyes looked as though he had had no sleep for days. He looked positively ill, Macil told herself, her heart sinking. What on earth had happened? There was some disaster here, she could see it. She could scarcely bear the bitterness in the downward curve of his lips.

'Oh, Nicky!' she said. 'What's happened, my dear?'

He lit a cigarette.

'Sorry, Macil – do you want one?'

'No. But sit down – talk to me.'

'I can't sit down. I'm as restless as the devil…'

He began to walk up and down the room. And she, infected by his restlessness, found that she could not sit down, either. So she stood leaning against the mantelpiece watching him. From the kitchen came the high treble of Tony, chattering to Mrs Smithers. But Macil had eyes and ears only for her brother, her cherished Nicky – who was, who must be – in some terrible trouble.

Nicholas smoked swiftly in silence for a second or two, then he looked at his sister.

'I'd better get it off my chest, my dear. It's a damnable thing. But you've got to know. I've left the Waydes for good.'

'Left them? You mean–'

'I've been sacked – yes,' he said grimly.

'But Nicky,' said Macil, horrified. 'You can't have been sacked. Why? What for? You were doing so well. You told me Austin Wayde liked you. You were only just beginning on this forthcoming election stunt. *Why* have you been sacked?'

He stared at his cigarette. He found it awkward – beastly – to explain to Macil – yes, even Macil to whom he told most things; with whom he was such pals. But it had to be told, and the sooner the better.

'It sounds unbelievable, Macil, but I was chucked out because I was found by Mrs Wayde in her daughter's bedroom, in the early hours of this morning – the said daughter being in my arms.'

Silence. Macil Robertson looked at her brother's grim, white face and then blushed suddenly and violently.

'I don't believe it!' she said indignantly. 'You're joking, Nicky. Don't be absurd. *You!* Why, nobody would make me believe you capable of doing such – such a damn silly thing,' she finished.

'Thank you, my dear,' he said. The hard line of his lips softened. He looked at her with gratitude. 'That's very nice of you.'

'Nicky – you're joking – ragging me.'

'I'm not, dear. I wish to God I were.'

She looked at his haggard young face and saw that there was no joke in it. The hot colour stained her face again.

'Nicky, my dear – but how on earth–'

'Oh, it's a rotten, beastly story, Macil. Of course it was my fault inasmuch as I did go into Gerry Wayde's bedroom and I did kiss her–' He broke off. His nostrils dilated slightly at the memory of the almost brutal kisses he had pressed on Gerry's lips. How soft, how curiously yielding that slim, charming figure had been in his arms. If he could only wipe out the thrilling memory of that … remember only that he hated her; loathed her for ruining him.

'It was her fault, then,' said Macil stoutly. 'I'll bet anything in the world it was her fault. She must have led you on, Nicky. You're not the sort of man to go into a girl's bedroom unless he's been encouraged. I know that.'

'You're a dear, Macil,' said Nicholas gratefully. 'As loyal a sister as a man can want.'

'It isn't only loyalty. I know you. She did encourage you – ask for it – didn't she?'

'Perhaps we won't discuss that,' he said sombrely, and turned to the window. From the mantelpiece he could see nothing but the sky – hot, glaring grey – so unlike the clear blue in the country.

Macil lit a cigarette and put it in the little cherry-wood holder which she kept in the pocket of her jumper. Her under lip quivered very slightly.

113

'Well, my dear boy, we won't discuss it, then,' she said. 'But you've shattered me completely. I simply can't take it in.'

'Facts remain. I've lost my job.'

'Did – did Mr Wayde have a row with you?'

'Both he and Mrs Wayde naturally rebuked me as the would-be seducer of their beautiful daughter.'

'Oh, don't, Nicky.'

'Sorry, darling.' He laughed – not a very happy laugh – and began to walk up and down the room again. His sister followed him with an anxious gaze.

'I could kill the beautiful daughter,' she said suddenly in an angry voice.

'I wanted to – in the early hours of this morning.'

That told plainly enough that in his heart Nicholas held Gerry Wayde to blame. Macil, up in arms on his behalf, had a swift vision of Miss Wayde seducing her brother. Of course, Nicky was so terribly good-looking and attractive. He would appeal to any woman. But why couldn't she have left him alone, under the circumstances? There he was working hard for her father ... trying to save.

'Oh, I could kill the girl!' muttered Macil again.

'Well, that's no use. I believe she's very sorry for her share in it now,' said Nicholas, with irony in his voice.

'That doesn't help you.'

'No. And anyhow, being a perfect little gentleman I must blame myself. I did go into her bedroom. I did kiss her. The Waydes had every right to chuck me out. I shall not get any backing from old Austin, M.P., if I want another secretarial job, and there we are.'

Macil's eyes filled with tears – she who had borne so much suffering in her own life and so rarely cried. But she knew her brother, and she could see that he had been through hell. It was marked on his face. Naturally – he was a particularly sensitive person. Such a dismissal, such loss of dignity and good character would hurt him damnably.

'Oh, my poor old boy,' she said.

'You're a brick, Macil. I wonder you don't tell me I've been several kinds of a fool.'

'I don't suppose you have. I don't know the facts, but I can guess exactly what happened. And now–'

She broke off. Her courage failed her momentarily. She remembered that Nicholas had been going to help pay for Robin's kindergarten, and to send them away to the sea in August. The kids needed sea-air and a change. She, herself, badly needed a rest and change. But all hope of that was dead.

Nicholas looked up and caught her gaze. He saw the tears on her lashes. He saw how white she was and much too thin. The grey eyes, so like his own, were sunk in her face.

And he noticed about this cherished sister of his little details that many men would have missed. The fact that her fingers – which in the old days, he remembered, had been a white and exquisitely manicured as Gerry Wayde's – were rough and reddened by continual washing of dishes and the children's clothes. Her hair had grown long at the back; needed cutting. Her thin knitted dress was a streaky faded green. She had had it dyed last year and was still wearing it to work about the flat. Poor old Macil, poor old girl. And there would be no redress, no rest or holiday for her this year, after what had happened. They would have to save every halfpenny till he got another job.

He sat down and scowled furiously at the ground. He felt that women were lucky to be able to cry. There were times when a man could weep – howl like a kid.

'Oh, *God,* damn and blast it!' he broke in savagely. 'It's the most filthy luck. I don't mind for myself so much. It's you and Robin and Tony – I could cut my throat for … for the whole thing…' he broke off, pitched his cigarette into the grate, and fumbled for a packet of cigarettes.

Macil swallowed hard. She could have broken down and cried from sheer disappointment very easily. But she pulled herself together. She told herself that she was used to knocks; she ought to be armour-plated. And she was older than poor Nicky – three years older – the mother of two sons. He was like a son to her, poor Nick. She must keep her end up and help him. This business wasn't very surprising after all. Nicky was one of the best; straight as a die; as conscientious a worker as any man could employ. But he was cursed with a temperament – the intense outlook of the artist. Hadn't she got it, too! She knew well enough that it made one do things; one had mad moments. She had them often since darling old Tom had died. She had been starved for love – cried out for it – conquered self for the sake of the children.

Nicky was a man … much more difficult for a man who has no children, no memories, nothing to help him achieve a victory every time his blood flared up. She understood. She went up to him and stroked his head.

'Chin up, honey. It's no use worrying now. We must find you another job.'

'Yes, the sooner the better. God knows how or where. I must answer every advertisement in the papers and go and see every bloke I know. It's going to be difficult, Macil. Poor old Sir Frank Sallsberry's dead and buried. It was he who got me my first secretarial post, you know.'

'I know,' said Macil, smoking hard. 'But why not ask Charles Petrie. He was elected for Barshire with your able help a year ago.'

'Yes, my dear, but imagine me going to Petrie and saying: "I want a job." He'd say; "Haven't you been working for Austin Wayde?" And I'd have to say: "Yes, sir, and I was chucked out because I made love, at midnight, to Miss Wayde…"'

Macil made a gesture of exasperation.

'Yes, it's beastly. But you see my position.'

Macil saw it. A very serious position. Even in this lax age, when idle love-making seemed to be the order of the day and no-body thought anything of it, the secretary to a public man must not be found in his daughter's bedroom at midnight. Poor old Nicky. He must have lost his head com-pletely. But that wretched girl … Geraldine Wayde – oh, that *wretched* girl!

'I'm afraid I'll have to chuck up the idea of pleasant secretarial posts to politicians,' said Nicholas grimly. 'I shall have to tout round in the hard world of commerce, my child.'

'But your literary work, Nicky – your play.'

'My play!' He gave a harsh laugh. 'It's gone to hell.'

'What do you mean?'

'I mean that I tore the damn thing up in the early hours of this morning.'

Macil shook her head.

'Oh, Nicky – you needn't have been so temperamental as that!' she said in a grieved voice.

He flung out his hand.

'What did it matter? It wasn't finished. I should never finish it now. I wrote it full of inspiration down there. It was a glorious old place – full of peace and atmosphere. I wanted to write. I used to work half the night. But after what happened – I couldn't work – I know it. My play!' He gave another bitter laugh. 'That's gone into the waste-paper basket – like most of my other attempts.'

'Oh, Nicky!' said Macil. It was all she could say in the face of this fresh disaster.

'Never mind, old girl,' he said. He looked up at her with an unhappy smile. 'One day I may write again. But I've got to put those ideas behind me now. It will be a question of forgetting I'm a playwright, and slogging from dawn till dusk at some really hard job. But the first difficulty is – find the job.'

'Yes,' said Macil. 'But I'm sorry about the play.'

Nicholas thought of the torn manuscript in his bedroom down at Ponders. And he thought of Gerry, a changed, white-faced Gerry, with tears in her eyes, begging for his forgiveness. Bitterness and disgust of the whole affair racked him unbearably. He walked to the door.

'I'd better unpack. Where do I sleep, old thing?'

'Your usual cupboard, Nicky. The little room Robin has. He can sleep on a camp-bed in my room.'

'It'll be an awful crush for you.'

'No. I like having Robin with me, and Tony will shriek with joy. Of *course* you must have your old room. This is your home as well as mine.'

Nicholas looked at her dumbly. He wanted to hug her and tell her that she was the bravest and nicest woman he knew. But brothers don't easily say those things to their sisters. He only said gruffly: 'Thanks awfully, my dear...' and followed her out of the room.

Later, while he unpacked in the tiny, long-shaped bedroom wherein he generally slept when he was on holiday, he heard Macil's brisk voice telling Mrs Smithers to run out and get another chop for lunch.

'Mr Hulme has come home unexpectedly. Isn't that nice for me, Mrs Smithers ... yes, one more chop ... and oh, you might get a bottle of beer. He likes beer for his lunch. Tony, isn't it lovely, darling? Uncle Nicky's home. Run along and talk to him while he unpacks...'

Nicholas bent over his suitcase. His eyes felt hot and moist. Dear old Macil – bless her! – talking brightly and happily like that as though there were no calamity or disgrace attached to his homecoming. And she couldn't afford beer. He must remember to pay her for it. What wonderful creatures women were – women like Macil.

He remembered, suddenly, walking

through the moonlit woods at Ponders, with Gerry – Gerry, exquisite and nymph-like in her green dress, her little green shoes and her blond hair shining silver. He had told her about Macil and she had said: 'How sad for her to be a widow.'

How sad ... how tragic ... but what could spoiled, sheltered Gerry Wayde know of the things Macil endured, or realise how her vanity, her thoughtless conduct, had increased the hardship here in this home.

He wished to God he had never seen Gerry; never known her. He wanted to put her completely out of his thoughts, just as he had gone completely out of her life. But he knew to his cost that he would never be able to forget her. He would go on remembering her and that moment in her bedroom ... in shame for her and for himself ... in unending bitterness.

CHAPTER 10

Gerry had a scene with her parents on the evening following Nicholas Hulme's departure from Ponders. It was not a pleasant scene for any of them – and particularly disagreeable for Gerry. For the first time in her life she felt at enmity with both her father and mother. Hitherto they had indulged her and spoiled her. Any little 'dust-up,' as Gerry called it, had been about extravagance or some difference of opinion, but it had never been a serious matter, and had always blown over and been amicably settled. As a rule Gerry came out on top – smiling and victorious.

This was quite a different sort of row. A grave one which left some bitterness on either side. And Gerry did not triumph. She was defeated. It was difficult for her to accept defeat. Especially over the subject of Nicholas Hulme's dismissal.

All day, after Nicholas had gone, she had lain in bed, refusing to allow anybody in her room and pretending that she had a severe headache – even a temperature – which prevented her from getting up and joining the house-party. She did not wish to face her friends. They sent up messages of sympathy and departed after luncheon – all with the exception of Phyllis Crozier. The gallant Commander returned to a job at Portsmouth, but Phyllis, whom Gerry in a moment of weakness had suggested should remain a few days at Ponders, stayed on.

Gerry had to get up. If she stayed in bed she knew that she would only arouse suspicion and cause a lot of talk. Phyllis would insist on coming into her room for a heart-to-heart talk. She dreaded that. So, about seven o'clock, she rose and went downstairs. Her head was aching. She certainly looked ill. No amount of make-up could remove the traces of the tears she had shed; of the real, acute grief she had suffered.

She went straight into her father's study. She felt that she must speak to him; make an appeal to him about Nicholas – clear his good name if she possibly could.

She found Mr Wayde at his desk, writing letters. Her mother at that moment happened to be there, talking to him. So the three-cornered argument around Nicholas Hulme commenced.

Mrs Wayde began it by being dramatic about her daughter's appearance.

'*Mignone,* you look *ghastly* ... my poor darling. You are ill. We must have the doctor–'

'No, mother,' interrupted Gerry. 'I'm not ill. Not physically ill – anyhow. But I'm going off my head with misery.'

Mrs Wayde caught the double row of jade beads about her fat neck and jangled them. She eyed Gerry knowingly. She could see what it was, she thought. The foolish child was being sentimental about that outrageous young man who had – thank heaven – departed from the household before further harm was done. She had a sudden startling recollection of her daughter in the lace negligée, abandoning herself – yes, the whole curve of her body had been abandoned – to the embrace of Mr Hulme. And, as she had told Austin several times since then, it was most fortunate she had discovered the affair and put an end to it. It was unthinkable that Gerry should be mixed up in a scandal with a young man like that ... no money ... no position ... nothing to commend him but his good looks. She would never have had him to live in the house, but she had been so sure Gerry was sensible and not interested in men. Mrs Wayde felt grieved about it all. Gerry evinced no interest in the clever, affluent young men her mother chose for her. She had said, repeatedly, that she had no intention of marrying until she was twenty-five.

'My darling,' said Mrs Wayde very sweetly. 'I think you are exaggerating the importance of – er – what has so unfortunately happened ... I mean, with regard to Mr Hulme.'

The colour rushed to Gerry's face.

'But I haven't exaggerated it. I keep trying to make you and father understand that you've behaved very unfairly and improperly to Mr Hulme.'

Austin Wayde, who had been writing, suddenly swivelled round in his chair, removed his horn-rimmed glasses, and glared at his daughter.

'My dear Gerry – I suggest that you have no right to accuse me of unfair or improper behaviour to any of my employees! I thoroughly understood the position, and I acted as I considered right and correct.'

Gerry began to shiver with sheer nerves. She wore a brown floral silk cocktail dress. She had put on rouge, but she had put it on badly tonight. Her face was white; a pallor accentuated by her dress. The patch of colour on both cheeks was obviously unnatural, shown up by the sunlight, which even at this hour still shone brilliantly. She said in a low, quick voice:

'Father, I'm sorry, but I must disagree with you. I told you this morning – I tell you again. Mr Hulme was not to blame for what happened.'

'Don't be ridiculous, Gerry,' said her mother.

Gerry swung round on her.

'Mother, you found Mr Hulme in my room, kissing me. I know that. But I asked

125

him in. I *made* him come in.'

Mr Wayde coughed, and put on his glasses again. He looked through them at his daughter reproachfully.

'Really, my dear, the way you make that statement – as though you were proud of it–'

'It isn't a question of what I'm proud of or ashamed of. If you want to know, I'm ashamed – terribly ashamed. But not only for making him come into my room – for ever allowing him to do so – to endanger his good name with you. Oh, you *must* believe me, father. It was dreadfully unfair for him to be blamed and sent away at a moment's notice like that.'

'My dear girl,' said Mr Wayde in his pompous voice, 'whether or not you – er – encouraged Mr Hulme, he grossly betrayed my trust in him by entering your bedroom and making love to you.'

'Besides, she didn't encourage him, Austin. She's a silly child to keep on saying that. *Mon Dieu,* it's only out of kindness. The darling girl is kind-hearted and sorry for that outrageous young man.'

Gerry doubled her hands.

'Mother, if you keep on saying that I'm defending Mr Hulme through kindness, I'll – oh, I don't know what I'll do!' she said between her teeth.

'*Chérie, chérie,* you really must not be so hysterical,' said Mrs Wayde in a soothing voice. She walked to her daughter and put an arm about her. '*Vraiment*, I am astonished. I thought you were so level-headed and–'

'Oh, leave me alone!' broke in Gerry, flinging off her mother's arm. She turned to her father again. 'Father, you must listen to me. Mother doesn't understand. I know what I'm talking about. I *did* make Mr Hulme come into my room. I said I heard a noise and was scared – I asked him to look under my bed and–'

'Come, come, Gerry,' interrupted Mr Wayde. 'All this may be quite true – regrettable though it is – but it doesn't excuse Mr Hulme for making love to you – even if you did ask him to – er – look under the bed. Such stuff and nonsense!' he added crossly. He was feeling irritable. He, personally, had felt the loss of a most efficient secretary all day.

'But good heavens – just kisses. It was harmless enough!' cried Gerry, her eyes blazing. 'Anybody'd think we were living in Queen Victoria's reign.'

'I see no point in discussing it, my dear,' said Mr Wayde, and picked up his pen.

To his astonishment, Gerry rushed at him and seized the pen from his fingers.

'You shan't go on writing – you shan't ignore me, Father. You don't seem to realise what you've done in chucking Mr Hulme out of the house like this. How is he going to find another job? He hasn't a bean. He told me so. He has a widowed sister dependent on him. It's frightful – to have sent him away like that. Don't you see?'

Mr Wayde stared at her, open-mouthed. He had seen Gerry in a temper, as a small child. But for years he had known her as a gay, cheerful, charming girl whom he could pet and spoil and show off to his friends. This white-faced passionate young woman staggered him.

'My dear,' he protested. *'Really!'*

'But can't you see?' she persisted. 'It's ruined him!'

'But he shouldn't have behaved as he did.'

'But I keep telling you – it was my fault!' she wailed. The tears sprang to her eyes. She was distraught; she had the most burning longing to exonerate Nicholas, and these people would not help her, would not understand.

'That may be, but once and for all, Gerry, I dismissed Mr Hulme for improper behaviour, and my actions were absolutely justified,' said Mr Wayde, losing his temper. 'I've had enough of Mr Hulme. I'm sick of the subject. If you were encouraging his attentions, then you were most reprehensible. And that is that.'

Gerry fell back, panting as though exhausted by her violent emotions. She stared at her father. She put her locked hands up to her lips.

'Reprehensible,' she repeated under her breath. 'Yes, I know. I *know*.'

'I shall begin to believe that you were becoming sentimental about Mr Hulme,' put in her mother. '*Mon Dieu,* it's as well he's gone. An affair between you and your father's secretary–'

'Well – what of it?' interrupted Gerry in a high voice. 'I wouldn't be the first girl to have a love affair with a secretary – or a groom – or a chauffeur, if it comes to that!'

'Good God!' exclaimed Mr Wayde.

'You're out of your mind, darling,' said Mrs Wayde, and piously thanked heaven once more that she had nipped this affair in the bud.

'There was no question of a love affair between Mr Hulme and myself, anyhow,' said Gerry, the tears suddenly pouring down her cheeks. 'You needn't worry. He *despises* me. But no more than I despise myself – for ruining him.'

'My dear child, you are being dramatic and stupid and exaggerating the importance of the whole affair,' said her father.

Gerry closed her eyes; blinked away the blinding tears. If only they could realise – how important it was – what terrific importance it had assumed. Now that she knew that she loved Nicholas – loved him with all her heart and soul. But she wasn't going to tell them or tell anybody in the world about that. What was the use? It would be her secret; her bitter, secret punishment.

'Father,' she said huskily. 'However stupid you may think me, I do so want you to be fair to Mr Hulme.'

'I have given him a month's salary and that is all he deserves,' said Mr Wayde.

'Much more,' said Mrs Wayde. 'When you think how he might have compromised our girl – why, Lady Withambury might have seen him go into her room – it fills me with horror – to think how narrowly we escaped scandal.'

'Yes, of course,' agreed Mr Wayde, frowning. 'And however foolishly Gerry behaved with the young man he had no right to take advantage of her. She is a mere child. And he, what? – twenty-six or seven – old enough to have learned control, and how to conduct himself under his employer's roof. He was a gentleman – at a public school – the Varsity – and I treated him as such. He came to me with an excellent report from Charles Petrie. Who was to know he was untrustworthy? It is most regrettable, but there it is. And now, Gerry, my dear, kindly refrain from mentioning Hulme's name in the future. This affair is much better forgotten – wiped out. I, for one, will not remember it.'

'Nor I, darling,' said Mrs Wayde, smiling. 'It was just a little foolishness on your part.'

Gerry gave her mother a look which that good lady did not altogether like. It was so unutterably reproachful and tragic. She felt very worried about the way in which Gerry was behaving about Mr Hulme.

Gerry looked at her father. He was bending over his desk, writing again. The sunlight fell on his bent, grey head. It shone like silver. He looked very handsome and imposing at his work. She had always been very fond of him – good friends with him. But in this moment he seemed a stranger; someone who refused to help her, to understand. And mother ... mother had made it her business not to understand. She was too keen on her match-making; too busy worrying about marrying her off to an earl or a duke. In this hour Gerry almost disliked her mother.

She made a last appeal.

'Father,' she said desperately. 'Won't you even – just to please me – send Mr Hulme some kind of recommendation – help him to get another post? He *is* without any private means, you know.'

'My dear girl – that is his affair,' said Austin Wayde, glancing up at her. 'I am willing to speak very well indeed of his capabilities as a private secretary, but if I am asked about his personal character, I shall find it difficult to forget what happened in my daughter's bedroom last night. Now do run away, my dear, and let me finish my letters.'

Gerry stood very still, staring in front of her.

'Oh, my God,' she said under her breath. 'Oh, my God, what *have* I done?'

She turned and walked blindly out of her father's study. She paused in the hall and pressed her fingers to her eyes. They ached and burned. Her heart was like a stone, heavy within her. She saw that she was up against a blank wall with both her parents. She wanted, more than anything in the world, to undo the harm she had so thoughtlessly done to Nicholas Hulme, and she was powerless to do so. She was up against an insurmountable barrier. She could never now retrieve the wrong. Nothing she could do or say, no amount of humbling herself, of shouldering the blame, was of any use at all.

He had gone – in disgrace. In disgrace, so far as her father and mother were concerned, he would remain. And it would, of course, affect his whole career; perhaps his life.

She thought of the tragic, torn manuscript of his play which she had pieced together while she was in bed, and locked away in her drawer. She felt sick with misery and too nervous – strange that she, Gerry, should be nervous – to go back and ask her father for Nicholas's address so that she could post the play to him.

He had only been gone from this house ten hours. It seemed to her like ten years. She imagined him thinking about her in anger; in contempt. And it hurt dreadfully. Nothing had ever hurt so much as Nicholas's contempt.

'Oh, if only I could do something ... if I could only make some sort of amends,' she thought.

Phyllis Crozier strolled down the stairs, dressed for dinner; tall, slim, sinuous, in white crêpe with jet necklace and earrings. She saw Gerry standing there despondently in the hall with her fingers to her eyes. She hastened to her side.

'Hello, darling. Are you better? I'm so glad you're down. What's up? Touch of 'flu? Ought you to be up?'

Gerry raised her face and looked at her friend.

'Yes, I'm all right now,' she said dully.

'Dearest, you look ghastly!' exclaimed Phyllis, never very tactful.

'I daresay. I've had a bad head and too much aspirin. Let's mix a cocktail.'

They walked into the lounge. Gerry thought:

'In a few minutes we'll be having dinner and there'll be just four of us. There ought to be five. Nicholas ought to be here. If only he were here ... oh, if only he were here ... and we could go back ... to yesterday ... when it was all right!'

But that wasn't strictly true. It hadn't been

133

all right yesterday. It had been all wrong for the last week or two; ever since she had commenced that shameful pursuit of him; that endeavour to make him nice to her.

'Gerry – is anything wrong – I mean, is it only that you're seedy, darling?' she heard Phyllis's inquisitive, rather drawling voice. 'Be a sport and tell me.'

'There's nothing to tell, Phyl.'

'But this morning you rushed up the stairs past me, looking like death. And that nice secretary with the lovely black hair was just going to the station. I saw his luggage. Has he gone for good? You didn't tell me he was leaving. Has anything happened to *him?*'

Gerry's nostrils quivered, but she bit fiercely into her lower lip. Nothing would induce her to tell Phyllis about Nicholas.

'Nothing's happened except that he – he had to go – suddenly – on private business,' she said.

Phyllis Crozier glanced at Gerry and put her tongue in her cheek. She didn't quite believe that. She was rather inclined to believe that naughty little Gerry had been carrying on a secret affair with the good-looking secretary. It was rather sad that he had gone. Such a *lamb* ... so intelligent ... and such wonderful brilliant eyes.

'Won't he come back, dear?' she persisted with the subject of Nicholas.

'I don't know,' said Gerry.

'Was he in love with you, darling?'

'Not in the least,' said Gerry, and wanted to laugh aloud in sheer misery.

'Well, as I told you yesterday, if it hadn't been that I'm *frightfully* in love with darling Eddy, I'd have been quite smitten with Mr Hulme. I loved his black, black hair.'

Gerry closed her eyes. If only Phyllis would stop talking about Nicholas. His black, black hair ... oh, yes, any woman might love it ... she knew now that she had loved it. She could see it, so plainly. His dark head bending over his work. Oh, the tragic, torn manuscript; the tragic murdered hopes. *She* had murdered them.

'Nicholas, forgive me,' she said inwardly, in an agony of grief.

Feverishly she drank the cocktail that Phyllis mixed for her. And she thought:

'I must forget Nicholas. I must forget him or I shall go right out of my mind!'

CHAPTER 11

A month went by. The bright golden month of June drifted into a moody July. The fine weather broke. The countryside suffered from continual thunderstorms and long spells of rain. Down in Graylingstone it continued to be hot, but it was a damp heat; enervating and tiresome. The sky was more often grey than blue. The nights were clear and starlit, but, somehow, as soon as dawn broke the clouds rolled up and another showery, sultry day set in.

Normally, Gerry would have fretted at this undesirable weather. It meant poor riding, intermittent tennis, and no chance to arrange picnic parties or week-ends on the river. Nothing could be more depressing than the river with a lack of sunshine and the constant menace of rain.

But the weather did not matter to Gerry this July. Nothing seemed to matter very much. Her whole outlook on life had changed since the calamity of Nicholas Hulme's dismissal from the household. She herself changed. Mrs Wayde grew thoroughly anxious. Mr Wayde, busy with the prospect of a general election in the autumn, paused once or twice in his busy career to worry about the alteration in his daughter's attitude, but left his wife to solve the problem.

Within a month Gerry had lost flesh. She had never been plump, and now she was positively thin. Her shoulder-blades stood out – were conspicuous when she wore low-necked dresses. The contours of her face had sharpened. She was all eyes, and they were eyes that no longer sparkled. They were full of sadness. She was pale and languid and seemed disinclined for any of her old occupations. She appeared to her mother to have lost interest in life itself. She no longer wanted to rush round in pursuit of gaiety. She no longer possessed the feverish passion for thrills; the desire to be surrounded by friends. She drove Mrs Wayde to distraction by refusing one invitation after another.

'You're mad, *chérie*,' Mrs Wayde declared on one occasion, when Gerry rejected Lady Withambury's proposal to take her out to Majorca for three weeks. 'Absolutely mad. You used to like Ivor. You *love* Majorca. You'd meet all kinds of interesting people. The Withamburys know everybody. And, if you go on turning down all these invitations, people will begin to drop you.'

'I don't mind if they do,' Gerry replied.

'But, *mon Dieu*, what has come over you, child? Do you intend to mope around home like this for the rest of your life?'

Gerry shrugged her shoulders.

'I don't know. I just don't feel like the Withamburys and Spain or any of these parties.'

'Are you ill?' demanded her mother irritably. 'If you are ill than you must see a specialist.'

'I'm not ill. I'm quite well.'

'You can't be well. You aren't yourself. *Cela va sans dire!*' Mrs Wayde rolled her eyes. 'You, who used to be the life and soul of the place.'

'Well, I'm not the life and soul of it now,' said Gerry with a short laugh.

Mrs Wayde stared at her daughter. How blue she was under the eyes. The child wasn't sleeping properly. She was smoking furiously, too, and was obviously a bundle of nerves. Ridiculous for a girl of twenty-one.

Since that day in her father's study when Gerry had opened up the subject of Nicholas Hulme, Mrs Wayde had deemed it wise not to mention his name. But now – driven by real anxiety on Gerry's behalf – she spoke of him.

'Gerry,' she said, 'I'm going to speak my mind to you, darling, and be quite frank. *C'est nécessaire, je crois.* Now listen. Ever since Mr Hulme–'

'Don't let's talk about Mr Hulme,' broke in Gerry swiftly. But across her face there came a burning flush which settled her mother's suspicions for good and all. It *was*

138

a question of this Mr Hulme – drat him. Just as well that Austin's new secretary was a sensible, middle-aged woman.

'I must talk of him, Gerry. I am your mother, darling,' she persisted. 'You ought to be able to talk to me about anything. This change in you is breaking my heart, you know.'

Gerry looked at the fat, worried face under its ridiculous crown of dyed, dark reddish hair. Breaking her heart! Poor old Désirée duck! She was, no doubt, a devoted mother. But if only she had been differently devoted. If only she had not indulged her, schemed and planned with passion to make her thoroughly desirable in the marriage market, and left her character to develop itself.

For the last four or five weeks – suffering as Gerry had not thought it possible to suffer – deliberately shutting herself away from people and idle pleasure – she had had so much time to think. To use her brain which she now realised had been dormant. Frantic with grief and remorse over Nicholas Hulme, torn in two with an intense feeling for him which grew and increased as the days went by, she learned a new philosophy of life. She saw now that she had wasted her time and her days. How indolent and useless she had been. How contemptible she must have seemed to Nicholas who was a worker, a thinker, a man with an object in life.

She had had no object – at least, not a worthy one. She had only wanted to enjoy herself and to attract attention. And these things had been her downfall. Bitterly she deplored the Gerry who had been. But what could she ever become, even now? She was hemmed in by too much money, leisure, luxury. She knew herself for the victim of the environment in which she had been brought up. But that did not console her.

She had asked her father for Nicholas's home address. Mr Wayde, aided and abetted by his wife, who wanted Nicholas Hulme to drop altogether out of Gerry's life, told her that he knew no address. Hulme, he assured her, had said that he would send an address for correspondence to be forwarded, but had not done so.

Gerry did not know whether to believe this or not, but she was forced to accept the answer such as it was. And she had no other means of tracing Nicholas. She knew no personal friends or even acquaintances of his. She had wanted to write to him; to send on his manuscript and implore him to continue with his play. She was not even allowed that much consolation. It is a very bitter thing to know that one has wronged a fellow creature and can in no way make amends. And it was the bitterness of this which was biting so deeply into Gerry these days. She was eating her heart out for the chance to make reparation to Nicholas. She asked herself day after day what he was doing … whether he had secured another job easily … whether his sister had suffered much through the loss of this job at Ponders.

Day after day she hungered for news of him; hoped against hope that he would write here – perhaps write for something he had left behind. But he had left nothing and no news came.

Night after night Gerry went to bed early and lay awake tormenting herself by the thought of him. The longing to see him again and to ask his pardon and obtain it obsessed her. And with this obsession her newly awakened love for him thrived and deepened, until the thought of him, the mention of his name, was like a knife-thrust in her heart.

At intervals she unlocked the drawer which contained the torn manuscript. She had most diligently and carefully joined the jagged ends of the halves together with the transparent cellotape with which one renovates music script. She read and re-read it. She knew every line of it, almost by heart – every character. She thought it a most brilliant piece of work. She was tortured afresh each time she reflected that she had been the cause of diverting the author of such a play from his purpose, of spoiling his inspiration.

Sometimes when she remembered him

and her mental pain became almost unbearable, she sat down and wrote to him.
Letters she knew she would never, could
never send. But the wild outpouring seemed
to ease a little of the agony.

*'Oh, Nicholas, if you knew how I am suffering
you would forgive me,' she wrote on one occasion.
'You would, I know, because you understand
human nature. Nobody could have written "At
Boiling Point" and not understand. Oh, Nicholas, I'm so sorry I was such a little beast. I'll do
anything to make up for it. Anything. Only say
you forgive me. Please, please, forgive me.'*

The letter was blotched with tears, twisted
up and burnt. Then back came the old hopeless feeling of remorse, of hunger for him.

August came.

The grey days vanished. There commenced a spell of fine weather. Ponders was
bathed in hot sunshine. The gardens drow-
sed and shimmered in golden warmth. The
fruit trees in the orchards ripened, and on
the old grey walls the pears and nectarines
grew heavy and luscious amidst their
delicate leaves. The herbaceous borders were
gay and bright with many-coloured flowers.
The roses opened eagerly and were doomed
almost at once to scatter their fragrant petals
on the baked brown beds. Lack of rain
robbed the lawns of some of their vivid green

and the hard tennis courts looked cruelly hot and scarlet in the blazing sunshine.

But there were attractive, cool places in the adjoining woods where one could lie down on soft moss under the spreading beeches and find rest and a dim, green enchantment.

During the hot spell, Gerry spent most of her leisure in those woods; lying there under the trees with her hands behind her head and her eyes fixed wistfully on the lace-work of leaves above her; or reading books sent down from the Times Club. But she could not read with any enjoyment; could not concentrate on novels. Books about love and passion which, hitherto, had left her unmoved, hurt her now. She could not bear them. The surfeit of literature about the War bored her. She was too young to remember all the agony of the War. She opened book after book and then abandoned them.

She was utterly unable to forget Nicholas Hulme. There in the woods the recollection was so vivid.

It was about the second week in August that she went up to London with her mother to do some shopping. Mrs Wayde wished to choose some new curtain material, and went off to Heal's. Gerry promised to meet her for lunch at her club in Dover Street, and, feeling disinclined to hear her mother chat vigorously with shop assistants, strolled down Piccadilly. She gasped with the heat in spite of the thinnest of cotton dresses, and a dark blue straw hat with a drooping brim which shaded her eyes from the sun.

She paused outside Dalbeattie's, the new big motor-car people near the Ritz. She liked cars and loved driving. Only last week her father had said:

'That little racer of yours is done for, Gerry. Jennings tells me you want new pistons. Why not turn her in now and buy a new car? I'd get a little coupé if I were you. I'll give you one for Christmas and you can buy it now.'

That was typical of Austin Wayde. He was a generous man, careless with his money, and the donation of Christmas presents started in his household at midsummer and continued till December.

Gerry had not taken any notice of the handsome offer. But this morning, looking through the huge plate-glass windows of Dalbeatties, she was attracted by a beautiful little green and silver car with a long, narrow bonnet. A Triumph. She had been crazy to own a Triumph two months ago. All the papers lately had been saying that it had the finest acceleration of any car of the same horse-power.

'Shall I go in and have a look at it?' thought Gerry.

She did not particularly want a new car. She was indifferent about it. Just as she was indifferent about everything. Languidly, without enthusiasm, she strolled into Dalbeattie's.

A marvellous young man with a tooth-brush moustache, an immaculate suit of clothing, and shirt and collar of palest pink, walked up to her – also languid and without enthusiasm. He looked to Gerry like a tailor's dummy.

'Good morning.'

'Good morning,' said Gerry. 'I want to have a look at that Triumph coupé.'

'Certainly,' said the tailor's dummy.

'I'm thinking of selling my racer. Your firm might do an exchange for me,' said Gerry.

The tailor's dummy woke up. The beautiful, dark-eyed vision in blue was bent on business, was she? Better call the gentleman who arranged these matters of exchange.

'One moment, madam,' he said, showing his teeth in a brilliant smile. 'I'll just ask someone to speak to you.'

Gerry nodded and walked to the Triumph. She opened the door and gazed inside, appreciating the low, comfortable-looking seats, the smart olive-green leather up-holstery. A nice little job. She wondered vaguely if she would take father at his word and buy the Triumph. It was £650. That seemed an expensive Christmas present. But what did it matter? Nothing mattered.

'Good morning,' said a voice behind her.

145

'Can I tell you anything about the Triumph?'

Gerry swung round as though she had been shot. Her heart gave the most violent jerk. She recognised that voice. Deep, rather brusque. How often in the past it had said to her those words, coldly polite: 'Good morning.'

'Oh!' she gasped *'You!'*

She found herself staring up into the face of Nicholas Hulme.

CHAPTER 12

The shock was so great that for the moment Gerry felt physically ill. The big, spacious show-room, full of shining, brand-new cars, began to revolve slowly round her. Through a kind of haze she saw Nicholas ... stared at him ... the man she had wanted to see, prayed to find. She staggered a little and leaned back against the car, clutching at it with her hands. Her bag dropped to the ground.

Nicholas Hulme stood very still. It was also a considerable shock to him to find that his prospective customer was Geraldine Wayde. Just for an instant, not expecting to see her of all women in the world, he had not recognised the slim, fashionably dressed girl in blue cotton. She had been bending over the car with her back to him.

He was embarrassed, and angry because of his own embarrassment. But his whole body tingled curiously at the sight of her, after an interval of two months. Two of the longest months in his career. Wretched, difficult, heart-breaking days spent in pursuit of a job.

He was astonished that she should turn so white. He could not fail to see how she was affected. When she leaned against the car and closed her eyes he grew alarmed. This was no sham faint – like the one with which she had tricked him into her bedroom at Ponders. He set his teeth at the remembrance of that night. He looked at her anxiously.

'I – you – are ill?' he found himself stammering. 'Can I get you a glass of water?'

Gerry opened her eyes. The show-room ceased to revolve. The faintness passed. But her face was still livid and her heart continued to pound, pound, so that it hurt her.

'No thanks. I'm all right,' she said under her breath.

'You wanted to see the de luxe Triumph?'

He spoke coldly, formally, as though they were complete strangers. But Gerry hardly heard what he said. She was looking at him with her eyes large and dilated. The wild expression in them astonished Nicholas. She looked as though she could not believe her own eyesight. Then she said huskily.

'Oh, if you *knew* how glad I am that I've found you at last.'

He stared at her.

'Found me? I don't quite understand...'

'No, you wouldn't. But I've wanted to see you – ever since you left Ponders. I tried to get your address from my father. He either couldn't or wouldn't give it to me. I've been nearly crazy – trying to find out where you lived. I knew it was with your sister. That was all I knew. And that didn't help. It's been unbearable–'

She broke off, panting. Her face changed colour. She was in such a condition of nervous excitement that she did not know what she said.

Nicholas stooped, picked up her bag and handed it to her. She did not even say 'thank you.' She continued to look at him with her big, wild eyes.

Nicholas grew more embarrassed.

'I don't quite know what you mean – why you wished to find me,' he said in his most chilling voice. 'I don't think there was any necessity for us to communicate, was there, Miss Wayde?'

'Oh, don't,' she said brokenly. 'Don't. You don't know what I have suffered. Don't speak to me like that. I know you're frightfully proud. I used to be, too. But I haven't any pride left. Not an atom. I've been through *hell* these last two months – absolute *hell*.'

He opened his lips to make another cold and crushing remark, but closed them again. He was horrified to see two large tears gather in her eyes and roll slowly down her cheeks. She was crying – *crying*. He was staggered. Yet he could not sneer at what she said or think that she was acting a part. She had changed in looks; changed unbelievably. He had never seen anybody grow so thin, so white, in such a short space of time. She was a ghost of the vivid, beautiful Miss Geraldine

149

Wayde of Graylingstone. She was still beautiful – yes. She would never be anything else with those eyes, that mouth. But what a mouth … today … a curve of tragedy. What, in heaven's name, had happened to the girl?

He was too embarrassed to make any comment on her last speech, so it was Gerry who broke the silence.

'I've got your play – all of it – quite safely!' she blurted out.

'My play?' he repeated. His brows drew together in the scowl so familiar to her.

'Yes, *At Boiling Point*. You tore it up. But I saved it – pieced it together – mended it.'

Nicholas flushed darkly. The mere sound of that title *At Boiling Point* was an echo from the past, best forgotten. It recalled hopes, ambitions, long since trailed in the dust.

'Oh – I see,' he said shortly. 'You need not have troubled. I tore it up. I meant it to be burned.'

'But you couldn't,' said Gerry. She clasped her hands together, nervously locking the slender fingers. 'You *couldn't* have meant that. Your wonderful play – you worked so hard on it. It *is* wonderful. You ought–'

'I beg your pardon,' he broke in. 'All that is over and done with. I'm no longer interested in that play. I have a new interest – here – in cars.'

She looked at him. She was trembling. How coldly he spoke to her, yet how terribly glad she was to see him again. His face, his voice, his manner awoke a hundred memories. Standing here, so close to him, she was flooded with an almost painful ecstasy of emotion. For two long months, madly in love, she had dwelt on the thought of him. She had hungered and thirsted for his forgiveness. And now, after despairing that she would ever find him, she had come across him in this amazing way. Oh, what stupendous luck, that she should have been seized with a whim to see the new two-seater Triumph. All her life she would associate that car with this terrific, this crucial moment.

Feverishly she took in every detail of his appearance. He was as she had remembered him. So tall; so finely drawn; with his 'black, black head' as Phyllis Crozier had described it; his curiously bitter mouth; his grey, piercing eyes under the heavy brows and lashes. He was unchanged. And yet … she could see that he was far from well. If she had grown thin, he, too, had lost flesh. He had always been lean. But now his clothes seemed too big for him; the line of his jaw was attenuated. His cheeks were hollow. He was a bad colour – in fact he looked to Gerry a sick man. And at once, because she was now a woman in love, she forgot herself and her own suffering and grew anxious about him.

'Oh, tell me – everything,' she said. 'Tell me what happened to you when you left

Ponders. Please tell me.'

'It can't possibly interest you–' he began.

'But it does. I want to know. Don't you – can't you understand – how much I want to know,' she broke in. 'I've been frantic with misery because of – what I did.'

So she wanted to rake up that painful ghost. Nicholas set his teeth. God, and it *was* painful, too. She said she had been through hell. So had he ... so had poor Macil. And through it all he had been haunted by the memory of this girl. Despising himself, and her, he had nevertheless been unable to forget the almost brutal ecstasy which he had known when he had held her in his arms and kissed that wide, provocative mouth of hers. It was no longer smiling and provocative. It was peculiarly dolorous. He wanted to hate her; to look at her with bitterness and contempt and say, 'You ruined me.' And he could only look at her and feel painfully embarrassed by the grief that was written on her face.

'Tell me what – happened to you,' she pleaded with him.

Because she reproached herself with being his downfall she knew no pride; only the intense longing to hear what he had been doing, how he had fared.

He answered briefly:

'I haven't much time to spare. I'm here to sell cars. That is all I can tell you. I got this job – ten days ago.'

'Only ten days ago. You've been doing nothing till then?'

'Nothing but rush after jobs – dozens of jobs – all day, every day – and not get 'em in the end.'

The bitterness in his voice tortured her.

'Oh!' she said. 'Oh, how *damnable!*'

'Please don't let it trouble you.'

'But it does. It does. Aren't you ever going to see how sorry I am – how frightfully sorry – for what I did?'

'I'm sure you are sorry,' he said coldly.

'But you don't allow that that can make amends. No,' said Gerry. Another great, hot tear rolled down her cheeks. 'I can't. I know it, too. Nothing I can do or say will ever make amends. I've been realising that – for weeks – until I've been half off my head.'

Nicholas fingered his tie. He looked away from her, through the plate-glass windows at the stream of traffic rolling in the sunlight up and down Piccadilly. The sight of those tears glistening on the girl's cheeks unnerved him. Like any other man he hated to see a woman cry. And damn it, he thought, why should this girl be as upset as all this about that wretched business? It was an old story now. He would never have believed that Gerry Wayde could be concerned deeply about anything, anybody, except herself. Perhaps when he thought of her as a heartless and contemptible coquette he had not quite given her her due. Having seen the harm she had done she was genuinely distressed. That was to her credit.

'Please,' he said stiffly, 'don't upset yourself about me. I am quite capable of taking care of myself and getting on my feet again.'

'But here – selling cars – you with your brain, your capabilities – it's awful!' she said.

Nicholas's nostrils dilated a very little. He looked down at her, his face hard and grim.

'Selling cars on occasions can be quite a profitable business. I am fortunate to be here. An old pal of mine who is a director of Dalbeattie's got me the job. Otherwise I'd still be searching for one – without a reference, you know.'

She winced. 'Oh, don't – please,' she whispered.

'I am sorry,' he bowed.

'You're frightfully hard,' she said. 'Hard as nails. Of course. You must – loathe me.'

'I don't loathe anybody.'

'But you must hate the sight of me,' she said in a frantic little voice. 'I caused all the trouble. Oh, after you'd gone, I swear I spent hours trying to make father and mother believe I was to blame. But they wouldn't–'

'They were justified. What I did – I did of my own free will.'

'You're sneering.'

'Believe me, I am not. A man may be

154

coerced, but if he gives way – it is his own funeral.'

'But it *was* utterly my fault. I know it. You know it,' she said.

'Don't let's rake it all up again.'

'But don't you see – I can't go on.' She clenched her hands very tightly. 'I simply can't go on.'

He stared at her.

'Can't go on – what do you mean?'

'I mean – that I shall go mad – if you don't say that you believe that I am terribly sorry.'

He averted his gaze.

'I am sure you are sorry. I do believe it.'

'But you won't forgive me.'

'There is no question of forgiveness. We – aren't likely to see each other again after today. Our lives lie apart.'

'I see,' she whispered.

She stood silent for an instant. She put a hand in a delicate suede glove up to her cheek and touched a tear that still glistened there. She felt profoundly miserable. Nicholas believed that she was sorry but he could not forgive her. Naturally. Why should he? As he said, they would probably never meet again after today. Those words put her right out of the circle of his existence, of his thoughts and his emotions. She felt desolate – derelict and hopeless on the sea of her unhappiness. He could not know and she could never tell him that she had grown to love him, and that nothing and nobody else mattered to her any more.

'Tell me,' she said after a pause. 'Did … did it affect you and your sister very badly … your leaving father's employ … like you did? I'm not asking out of idle curiosity, but because I've thought so much about you both.'

The fact that she remembered Macil touched him. But he did not wish to be touched by anything this girl said or did. He answered all the more abruptly.

'We got on all right.'

'You don't look well,' she said wistfully.

'I've not felt very fit. I get no fresh air or exercise.'

'And you used to love the country – love Ponders – you must detest London.'

He felt a strange desire to ask her how things were down at Ponders. He had often thought how gorgeous it must be down in the old Queen Anne house with is perfect garden, this August weather. But pride forbade him to question her.

'You must hate this job,' she spoke again. 'Hate it … selling cars … *you!*'

'I can't say I love it,' he said. 'But it's a job.'

That told her so much. Up till ten days ago he had not had a job. He must be hard up. It was unbearable to her. She turned suddenly to the Triumph.

'I – want to buy it,' she said in a low voice.

Nicholas took a notebook from his pocket.

He smiled grimly. It was a queer enough position ... that he should sell a car ... to *her.* If she bought that car it would mean a very decent commission for him. God knows he needed it. But he wouldn't let *her* know that. He hadn't sold a car this week. So much depended on these sales. It was not a well-paid job outside the commission.

There seemed no hope now of sending Macil and the kids away to the seaside. He, himself, of late, had felt rottenly ill. Depressed; no vitality; scarcely able to lift his head from the pillow in the mornings. 'Thoroughly run down' – that's what the doctor would say. He knew it. He *was* run down. He slept so badly. It was intolerably stuffy in poor old Macil's top flat. And they had been on poorish rations lately. There had been enough, of course, but not enough of the right and nourishing kind. No more beer these days! That was because little Tony had been ill. He had had to have his tonsils out. All the money that Nicholas had saved at Ponders had gone on doctors; a hospital nurse for a week; the special medicines and food he needed. And now the poor little kid was in need of a breath of sea-air. His mother was worn out with nursing, cooking, worrying... God, they hadn't much to thank Gerry Wayde for.

Yet, this morning, when Nicholas looked down at Gerry's altered face, saw the way the slim, gloved fingers wiped away the tear on her cheek, he could not hate her. He could even pity her.

He made pretence of writing notes in his book. In a formal voice he said,

'I understand you want to make an exchange, that you have a Benvex you want to sell.'

'Yes,' she said. She forced herself to attend to business and blot out the anguish of her thoughts. 'You know the one – my little yellow racer.'

Yes, he knew it.

'It was a last year's model, wasn't it? And you want to exchange it for this model of the Triumph?'

'Yes.'

'I'll discuss it with my manager and let you know how much we are prepared to allow you,' he said.

She looked up at him, cut to the heart by his polite and frigid voice. She said desolately,

'Thank you.'

'You are at Ponders, I presume? I can write there?'

'Yes.'

She told herself that he would get the commission if she bought the car through him.

'You can consider this coupé definitely sold to me,' she said recklessly, and decided that she would settle things with father tonight.

Without telling him or mother that she had bought the car through Nicholas Hulme. Whatever happened they mustn't know that.

Nicholas – tired and dispirited by his job – felt a faint spark of gratitude. Thank God he had sold something. That would be a great help to Macil.

Gerry's head was aching. Her whole nervous system had suffered through the shock of encounter with Nicholas. She suddenly took off her hat and smoothed back her hair. He found himself looking down at the familiar blonde head with fair waving hair and remembering the beauty of it in moonlight. He told himself that he was a weak-minded fool, and removed his gaze from the beautiful hair.

'Will you give me your address?' she asked him. 'I want to post back your play.'

He reddened.

'I don't want it. Please burn it. That's all over and done with.'

'But won't you ever write again?'

'I have written every night since I left Graylingstone. I have written a new play.'

'I'm so glad,' she said. 'But don't you really want–?'

'No,' he broke in violently.

He had destroyed *At Boiling Point* and wiped it from his memory. He had no desire to see it again, to attempt to finish it. It was connected with a very hard, bitter moment of his life and he wanted to forget it.

'Very well,' said Gerry.

She put on her hat again. Slowly she moved toward the door of the big show-room. Nicholas walked with her. A sudden, dreadful feeling of grief came over her that this was the final parting – that she would not see him again. She wanted to tell him so many things. Tell him how she had thought and fretted and repented of her useless, butterfly existence. Tell him about her new philosophy; her wish to do something in life worth doing. She wanted to beg him to allow her to help his sister, the children. She could say none of these things. She was inarticulate; up against the old wall of his reserve and his reticence.

She found it very difficult – even impossible – to believe that he had ever swept her into his arms and hurt her lips, her body, in that violent, intimate embrace.

'Good-bye,' he said at the door. 'I'll let you know, at once, about the price we can allow you for your Benvex 3-litre twin carburettors. That's the model. Yes, I know. Good-bye.'

'Good-bye,' she said. Her eyes, large, feverish, stared up at him. She held out her hand.

Nicholas flushed. He only just touched the small, gloved fingers with his, then turned away from her.

She walked away from Dalbeattie's; a forlorn figure, moving slowly and reluctantly up Piccadilly towards Dover Street.

CHAPTER 13

When Gerry announced, somewhat feverishly, at dinner that night, that she had
exchanged her Benvex racer for a new
Triumph, Mr Wayde was mildly astonished
but not displeased. Mrs Wayde was delighted. This meant that Gerry was waking
up – taking an interest in life again. And
certainly she thought the child had seemed
more herself up in town; more talkative – not
so despondent as she had been lately.

'Well, well … I did say I'd give you a new
car for Christmas,' said Austin Wayde.
'What did you get on the Benvex?'

'I don't know yet,' said Gerry.

'But surely, *mignonne*,' said her mother,
blinking, 'you haven't bought it without making sure of a good price for your old car?'

Gerry, very flushed, shrugged her shoulders.

'Oh, I'm certain to get a good price. I went
to Dalbeattie's. They're the best car people
in town now.'

'Yes, Dalbeattie's are all right,' said Mr
Wayde. 'But you seem to do things very suddenly and recklessly, my infant.'

Gerry had nothing to say to this. She was

seeing the thin, weary face of Nicholas Hulme, as he took down notes in his note-book in the show-room; wondering what her father would say if she told him she had bought the Triumph through his one-time secretary?

'I shall know what price I'm to get on the exchange tomorrow morning,' she said. 'Then I'll drive the Benvex up and take over the Triumph. Will you let me have a cheque, father?'

'Yes, my dear. It's an extravagance, but I promised it.'

Gerry stared across the dinner-table. When they three dined alone she never sat in her usual place without looking at the opposite place – where Nicholas used to sit. Tonight the memories of him were particularly vivid. That was because she had seen him that morning. She thought:

'I'm glad he'll get the commission. Oh, I wonder if he's frightfully hard up. He looks so ill.'

She had worried all day over Nicholas's thinness, his hollow cheeks, and the very fact that he was a salesman in Dalbeattie's. Nicholas, with his talents, his ambitions – a motor-car salesman. And all through her. But better not to let that thought haunt her. It had tormented her enough – too much.

She had said what she supposed would be a final good-bye to Nicholas this morning.

Yet as long as they were in communication about the Triumph, they would be in touch. Even though it was cold business through his firm. She found herself looking forward, absurdly, to the letter which was to come tomorrow.

For the first time in many long weeks she slept without waking until the maid called her. Then she sat up quickly, and anxiously took the letters from the tea-tray. There it was – a large, square envelope with *'Dalbeattie's Ltd.'* on the flap. She opened it. She did not know what she had really expected, but it was merely a formal typewritten letter, beginning 'DEAR MADAM' and signed 'A.G. HESLOP, *Manager.'* It made her a reasonable offer for the Benvex racer in exchange for the Triumph, providing the firm found the Benvex in decent condition.

Gerry lay back on her pillow and shut her eyes. What a fool she was. Of course, Nicholas had placed the matter in the hands of Mr Heslop, the manager. She would no longer deal through Nicholas. But he would get the commission on the sale of the coupé. So she wrote at once accepting the offer and confirming her purchase of the Triumph. She suggested that she might drive her racer up to London on the morrow.

For the next twenty-four hours she was in a nervy, excitable state. She dwelt on the possibility that she would see Nicholas again when she took her Benvex along to his firm. She did not suppose he would have anything to say to her that could comfort her. He would be cold and formal. It would only hurt her. Yet she felt she must see him.

She was doomed to disappointment. When she reached Dalbeattie's the following morning she was received graciously by Mr Heslop, the manager of the firm. The tailor's dummy with the toothbrush moustache was there. But there was no sign of Nicholas.

Gerry, with a dry sensation in her throat, made a tentative remark about the 'assistant who had sold her the new car,' and Mr Heslop said:

'Oh, ah, yes, Mr Hulme. He is not here today. I am afraid he is laid up.'

At once the world went dark to Gerry. She held her breath. Then with apparent un-concern she said:

'Oh, is he ill?'

'A bad chill, I hear. He looked very seedy yesterday and I don't fancy he is a very strong,' said Mr Heslop. 'His sister came along down from Golders Green where they live and told me he had a temperature and that she had persuaded him to stay in bed. Not easy to manage ... such a conscientious worker.'

Gerry knew. How well she knew what a conscientious worker Nicholas was. And his sister had come here this morning to say that he was ill in bed. He had a temperature. Gerry at once visualised him as seriously ill. She felt stricken. She was seized with the insane desire to rush to Golders Green and see him. But she knew that it was out of the question. How dreadful that she should love Nicholas and he was ill and she had no right – less right than anybody – to go to him.

She could not resist asking for his home address.

'I'd like to drop a line to him and thank him for the trouble he took in selling me the car,' she said casually.

Heslop found Nicholas Hulme's private address and gave it to her.

Gerry wrote it down in the little notebook in the Russian leather bag which she carried. She drove away from Dalbeattie's in the new Triumph. But the luxurious coupé, the sweetly running engine, might just as well have been the old racer with an engine knock and noisy gears for all she cared. Any pleasure that she might have felt in taking over the new car from Nicholas had died. She drove down Piccadilly heavy-hearted and anxious. Nicholas was ill. How ill? If only she knew. If only she had seen Nicholas's sister this morning. If only she could drive to Golders Green now, this very moment.

Gerry's eyes stared desolately ahead of her at the bright sunshine.

'How deathly to love somebody who

doesn't love you and hasn't any use for you,' she thought. 'It's like death to me.'

Such an aching longing to do something for him possessed her that in a reckless moment she stopped the car outside a wine merchant's. She went inside, chose a case of half a dozen champagne, and ordered it to be sent to Mr Nicholas Hulme at his address.

'Shall I put a card in it, madam?' asked the assistant.

'No, nothing,' said Gerry, and walked out again.

It was very little comfort to send him that anonymous gift, but it seemed to her better than nothing.

When that case of champagne arrived at Macil Robertson's flat, Macil took it in, surprised and pleased. Poor old Nicky wasn't ready for it yet. He was thoroughly seedy – in bed with a temperature and a bad cough and a splitting head. He just wanted to be left alone to doze. But when he was better the champagne would do him good. She wondered what kind friend had sent it.

Nicholas was not well enough to care. When his sister told him about it he only said:

'Very decent of someone, but I can't imagine who sent it. We don't know many millionaires.'

He tossed and turned in a hot bed; feverish; racked with pain; distressed for Macil's sake as much as for his own that he should have fallen ill. It only made more work for her. She had enough to do as it was. And now she had to nurse him and try to keep Robin and Tony quiet, and she wasn't very well herself. But she refused to admit it. Macil was the kind who wouldn't admit defeat until she was at the last gasp.

Nicholas said, several times:

'Thank God I sold that Triumph yesterday. That'll mean a decent commission, Macil – something.'

Macil thanked God, too. They needed it. Nicholas did not tell her that he had sold the car to Geraldine Wayde. The name of Gerry had not been mentioned between them since he had come home that day and told her the story of the disaster at Graylingstone.

Nicholas tried to get up the next day, and got as far as shaving and putting on a pair of socks, then collapsed. Macil put him back to bed. He coughed incessantly and his temperature went up to 104. In horror she sent for Dr Agnew, the man who had attended Tony when he had tonsilitis.

Agnew examined Nicholas and said at once, 'Bronchitis, and if he isn't careful it will mean pneumonia. There's a patch now that'll want watching. If I were you, Mrs Robertson, I'd put him in a home.'

Macil, her heart sinking to zero, said:

'We can't afford that doctor. I'll get a pal of mine to take the children for a day or two and I'll nurse him myself.'

'Nobody could be better,' said Peter Agnew, who, tired, harassed G.P. though he was, always found time to stop and admire Macil Robertson. He thought her the finest and most capable woman he had ever met and an extraordinarily charming one into the bargain. He was a confirmed bachelor, but he had often thought since he came into contact with Macil, during Tony's illness, that if ever he forswore his freedom it would be for the sake of a woman like Mrs Robertson. It was given to him as it is so often given to the medical profession, to see that heartbreak and privation behind the scenes. And he bowed before the fine courage which this woman – still a girl – brought to life, and the smiling way she faced the little disasters attached to her children and her brother.

'Don't overdo things,' Agnew counselled her. 'You look pretty tired as it is.'

'I'm all right,' said Macil. 'But if Nicky has bronchitis I'm going to nurse him. He loathes strange people about him when he is ill and I don't blame him. Tell me what to do and I'll do it.'

Dr Agnew told her what to do. She felt confidence in him. She had felt it when Tony was so ill with his septic throat. She liked the tired, hard-working doctor. He was small and lean and had thick, greyish hair and a queer, kindly face, rather like a monkey's, with very small, bright eyes. But there was something in him that inspired confidence, and he had a charming voice and nice hands.

'I'll be in again first thing in the morning,' he said, and departed.

Macil set to work to gather all her courage then, and to forget how her head ached and how sore her feet were from constant running about after Nick and the children this hot weather. When she set out to do a thing she did it. There was a certain Miss Belfore in Golders Green, a middle-aged woman with a house, a garden, and nothing much to do. This Miss Belfore had met Macil and her children casually, one day about a year ago – the introduction made through Robin's overtures to a Cairn terrier which was Miss Belfore's special pet. She had become a firm friend since that day and had always implored Macil to call on her for assistance with the children when she needed any.

Macil had not, so far, taken advantage of this offer, but she took it now in this hour of need. Before darkness fell that night Robin and Tony were installed in Miss Belfore's house, having promised their mother solemnly to be 'terribly good.' Macil – thankful beyond words to have a little respite, dearly though she loved her small sons – had nothing to do then but look after her brother. The flat became extraordinarily quiet. Nicholas coughed and gasped for breath and was a very sick man for several days. Macil, who had moved him to her own big bedroom, hardly left his side. Tom, her darling, had died of pneumonia, and if anything happened to Nicky, she thought she would not be able to bear it. Nicky's bronchitis *must* not be allowed to develop into pneumonia.

Between them, Macil and Peter Agnew fought off the dread illness. Nicholas was racked and tormented and really ill for the first time in his life. But he pulled through. The patch disappeared, and he came out of it, a lean, pallid spectre, all bones and eyes. But he passed the crisis.

Dr Agnew ceased to worry about his patient and turned his attention to Macil, who would become the next one if she did not have a little rest. She was brave and laughing, but she was tired out. In a few days she would have to have the children back.

'If only you and those kids and that brother of yours could get out of this flat down to the country,' said Agnew, frowning at her when he came to see Nicholas one morning about a fortnight after Nicholas fell ill.

'It can't be done, doctor,' she said. 'We're broke. And, as it is, the manager of Nicky's firm has written to say he can't hold the position open indefinitely. We may find Nicky out of work again. We've got to save every penny.'

'Oh, Lord,' thought Peter Agnew. 'Where's the justice in life. Here's this dear, wonderful creature worked and worried to death and can't take a holiday ... and in Bond Street this very morning there are females spending hundreds on a new coat. It's damned unfair.'

After he had gone, Macil went into the kitchen to make some Ovaltine for Nicky's eleven o'clock fare. The front-door bell rang sharply. She sighed, and without taking off her overall, went to the door and opened it.

A girl, fashionably dressed in a flowered dress of pale, cool green, and with a small green hat pulled low over her fair head, stood outside. She carried a huge bunch of roses. She looked to Macil expensive and extremely pretty in her delicate dress; like one of the roses she carried. Altogether out of place on the dark, shabby landing with its worn lino and the paper peeling off the walls.

She drew near Macil and lifted what Macil thought the loveliest face she had ever seen, with its large dark eyes, long lashes, and pencilled brows.

'Are you...' she began in a shy, halting voice. 'Are you ... Mrs Robertson?'

'Yes,' said Macil, 'I am Mrs Robertson.'

'I ... I've come to ask ... how ... Mr

Hulme is.'

Macil stared. She had no idea who the expensive and pretty young woman was. But she smiled at her.

'That's awfully nice of you. My brother is better; he's been very bad, but he is better today.'

'Oh ... I'm glad ... so glad.'

'You're a friend of my brother's,' murmured Macil. 'Won't you come in. Perhaps he'd like to see you.'

She was astonished and alarmed to se the girl flush burning scarlet, then turn white. She looked as though Macil had given her a mortal wound. She said under her breath:

'Oh, no ... he won't want to see me. But I wanted to know how he was. I heard through Dalbeattie's that he was dangerously ill.'

'He has been, but he's out of danger now and I trust will remain so,' said Macil. 'Do come in.'

'No,' said the girl in a panic-stricken voice. 'Oh, no, thank you. But please give him these. Good-bye.'

She pressed the roses into Macil's hands and would have fled down stairs, but Macil called to her.

'Won't you please give me your name?'

'No, really,' said the girl and vanished before Macil could speak again.

Macil, baffled, shut the door and walked

into her brother's room. Nicholas lay against his pillows, looking a sick man still, and with eyes grown large and bright.

'My dear,' said Macil, 'the most weird thing. A marvellous vision of youth and beauty called to inquire after your health and refused to give her name – refused to come in – looked scared to death and rushed away as soon as I said you were all right. She left you this glorious bunch of flowers.'

Nicholas frowned at her and the roses.

'Who on earth was it?'

'I don't know. She was the prettiest girl I've ever seen. Very fair hair and the loveliest dark brown eyes with the longest lashes imaginable. She said she'd heard from Dalbeattie's that you were ill.'

Nicholas's whole face flushed. He caught his breath. He knew immediately, from that description, who it was. Gerry. Gerry had called – had been outside the front door five minutes ago.

Those roses came from Ponders. Of course. He could see that. The lovely scarlet and golden and pale pink blooms. They were not from a London florist's.

'Who was she, do you think, Nicky?' inquired Macil, unwrapping the roses from a covering of tissue paper.

He said in a grim voice:

'Geraldine Wayde.'

Macil almost dropped the flowers.

'Geraldine Wayde! *That girl!*'

'Yes. Look out of the window. See if there's a green car at the door.'

Macil ran to the window and leaned out. She returned to her brother's bedside. Her usually kind eyes were hard.

'Yes. A brand new green and silver thing.'

'A Triumph,' said Nicholas.

'You mean that it was to *her* you sold that car?'

'Yes. I didn't tell you at the time. There was nothing to tell.'

'I see,' said Macil. She frowned at the lovely mass of roses which were already filling the room with perfume. And she thought:

'That girl – that girl who hurt Nicholas so badly – how dared she come and bring him flowers?'

Nicholas lay back in his bed, fumbled under his pillow for his cigarette-case, and thought:

'Why did she bring me the roses ... why did she trouble to find out my address? She can't really care. Damn it, why doesn't she leave me alone?'

Yet he had a sudden disconcerting vision of her standing before him in Dalbeattie's show-room, wiping away a tear on her cheek; and heard her broken little voice saying, 'I can't go on ... I've been through hell ... aren't you ever going to see how sorry I am?'

He remembered that ... and against his

will, his mind swept back ... much further back ... when he had held a slim, vibrant young body in his arms and felt the maddening sweetness of her lips.

He lit his cigarette with unsteady fingers.

'My dear,' said Macil. 'Perhaps it was Miss Wayde who sent the champagne.'

'Perhaps,' he said shortly.

'But why, Nicky–'

'I don't know,' he said.

'Conscience, perhaps!'

'Perhaps, Macil.'

Macil, tired and hot, pushed a strand of hair back from her eyes and walked to the door with the roses.

'It seems peculiar to me. She looked scared to death of me, and when I suggest that you might like to see her, she almost burst into tears. Oh, well – do you want the roses in here?'

'No,' he said curtly. 'Put 'em in the sitting-room.'

But he thought a lot about those roses and Gerry's unaccountable kindness. Certainly the champagne must have come from her, too. Later that evening when he knew his sister was out shopping, he dragged himself out of bed and walked into the sitting-room. He stood a moment feeling weak and dizzy, and stared round the room. Roses every-where – of every colour – transforming Macil's room into a bower. He could see them as they grew in the sunlit garden down at Ponders. And he could see Gerry in a green dress and little green shoes, walking with him in the moonlight through that same garden.

'You cursed fool, Nicholas Hulme,' he said to himself bitterly. 'Fool of fools – to remember anything but the fact that the girl vamped you and ruined your whole career. Bah! Go back to bed and forget her.'

He went back to bed, but he could not forget her.

CHAPTER 14

Then, suddenly, distressingly, on the very night that Miss Belfore returned Robin and Tony to their mother, Nicholas had a relapse. He got up too soon. He insisted upon getting up and dressing, hoping to recommence work without Dr Agnew's permission. It was crazy. His temperature shot up and he went back to bed with another and worse bronchial attack. This time it verged very closely on pneumonia.

Macil was distraught. As a rule level-headed, competent, and able to face things with a smile, she staggered under this new blow. Miss Belfore, her stand-by, had that very day left London for her annual holiday at Broadstairs. There was nobody but Mrs Smithers, the char, to give a hand with the little boys. And Nicholas, coughing his heart out and barely conscious of his surroundings, needed constant vigil.

Peter Agnew would have liked to have helped, but he could do nothing. He had only a bachelor's digs and a surgery. No home to which he could take the kids. And as it was, he was worked off his feet and unable to give Nicholas Hulme more than his fair share of attention.

Any friend, with means or otherwise, upon whom Macil might have called, was out of town at this precise moment. When morning came, after that first, anxious, exhausting night of Nicholas's relapse, it found Macil a wreck. With eyes bunged up through lack of sleep and her whole body aching, she moved about the tiny kitchen making a cup of tea. She felt that sometimes her burden was greater than she could bear. Again and again she had to rush into the spare room into which she had squashed her two small sons and say:

'Oh, be *quiet,* darlings, *do.* Uncle Nicky is awfully ill and he must sleep. *Do* try, darlings!'

Robin, aged six, could try. But Tony, aged three, saw no reason why Uncle Nicky should wish to sleep at this hour of the morning, and thumped the floor with a small, wooden motor-car, repeatedly assuring his mother that the 'woad was wuff' and that was why the car bumped.

Macil, in the kitchen, hid her face in her hands and broke down and wept for the first time since the agonising weeks following her husband's death.

Mr Heslop sent an assistant from Dalbeattie's Ltd. to inquire if Mr Hulme was returning to work that day. Macil sent back the message that Mr Hulme had had a relapse and was seriously ill. That meant he would lose his job. They couldn't keep it open indefinitely, and he had been ill for three weeks now. Macil wondered what in heaven's name they would all do in the future. Her miserable pension was like a drop of water in a sea of small debts. Bills were running up on all sides.

That same morning, Gerry Wayde drove her car up to London to have the carburettors adjusted by Dalbeattie's. It was a Friday. On the Saturday she was going down to Devonshire with her parents for a week. Father wanted a rest from politics and mother was sick of Ponders for the moment, so, rather unwillingly, Gerry had promised to accompany them to Babbacombe Bay.

She had a faint hope that she would see Nicholas at Dalbeattie's. Surely he would be back by now? Then Mr Heslop informed her that Mr Hulme had had a relapse and was dangerously ill.

'One of my assistants saw Mrs Robertson, Hulme's sister, and he told me that he thought from what she said that Hulme had pneumonia and was at death's door,' said Mr Heslop, who was quite harmless but liked to make a dramatic effect.

Gerry went white to the lips and felt as though something clutched at her heart. She felt very sick. And an overwhelming sensation of fear came over her. Fear that

Nicholas was going to die. In the anguish of that moment she felt that she would blame herself even for his death. If he had not left Ponders he would not have become ill. It was because he had been hard up, perhaps denied himself things which he needed, that he was so gravely ill. And *she* was the original cause of it all.

'If he dies,' thought Gerry wildly, 'I shall go mad!'

She was not quite responsible for her actions when she drove away from Dalbeattie's. She became blind and impervious to the conventions, to pride. She only knew that Nicholas was dying and that she must see him before he died and tell him how much he meant to her.

She drove furiously to Golders Green.

Two at a time she leapt up the ugly stone staircase, up to that hot, stuffy top floor. She found the knocker muffled in a duster and sweat broke out on her forehead. The palms of her hands grew moist.

'Oh, God!' she thought. 'He *must* be terribly ill. Oh, God, don't let me find that he's *dead...*'

She rang the bell and stood there, her heart-beats shaking her body.

Macil Robertson opened the door. Gerry stared dumbly at the haggard young woman with the black hair so like Nicholas's, and red-rimmed, tired eyes. And Macil stared back at her. She resented seeing this girl here again, but she was so exhausted physically and so worried that she had not the spirit to show her resentment.

Gerry spoke first. Clutching her throat she said,

'Is he – is he – oh, Mrs Robertson – tell me – how is he?'

'My brother is seriously ill; he had a relapse last night.'

'I know. They told me at Dalbeattie's. I had to come. Is he very bad?'

'Yes, I think so. I'm waiting for the doctor now. If you'll excuse me, Miss Wayde–'

Gerry was panting.

'You – you know who I am?'

'Yes.'

Gerry looked at her wildly for a second, then all her control snapped. She caught at Macil's arm.

'Mrs Robertson – don't send me away. Oh, Mrs Robertson – for God's sake – let me come in a minute. If he – if he's dying – I must see him – I *must*. You don't understand what it means to me – but please, please, I beg you...'

She broke off. She sobbed under her breath. The tears rained down her pale little face. Macil Robertson blinked at her in perplexity. She was thoroughly taken aback. It seemed to her such an extraordinary thing for this girl – so chic, so exquisitely turned out – to be standing there sobbing apparently agonised by the thought that Nicky was ill.

'Please, please, don't make me go away,' repeated Gerry in a choked voice. 'I know you must despise me ... like he does. But I can't go away if he's dying, without seeing him once again.'

Macil said awkwardly, all resentment gone,

'But he isn't dying – at least I trust to God he isn't. He's awfully ill, but we hope he'll pull through.'

'Mr Heslop said he had pneumonia.'

'Mr Heslop exaggerated. My brother has very bad bronchitis. He was bordering on pneumonia last night. Naturally I am frightfully worried – but it isn't as bad as Mr Heslop led you to believe.'

Into Gerry's swimming eyes there flashed such a look of relief that Macil could not fail to see it. Gerry drew a handkerchief from her bag and put it to her quivering lips.

'You must think I'm quite crazy ... but ... you don't know what it means. Perhaps I'm almost out of my mind ... I have been since he left father ... oh, if only you *knew!*'

The real agony in her voice distressed Macil. She was a tender-hearted woman, and although she had hardened that heart against the girl who had been the cause of Nicky's trouble, she could not see such naked agony in the eyes of a fellow creature and not be moved by it.

Impulsively she said,

'Look here. You can't stand out here like this. You'd better come in a moment.'

Gerry followed her into the flat. Macil showed her into the sitting-room. Gerry stared blindly and wretchedly at the roses which she had brought two days ago. She felt a grain of comfort that they had not been spurned and thrown away. Macil, shutting the door behind her, thought:

'This is very weak of me, but the child looks simply ghastly... I suppose she is really sorry for what she did.'

Gerry took off her hat and pushed her hair back from her forehead. She wiped her eyes and cheeks. Macil thought how very lovely she was even though dishevelled with weeping. And how young without her hat ... she looked a mere child. How old was she? – Nick had told her – twenty-one.

'Nine years younger than I am,' thought Macil. 'A mere baby. But it's astonishing what a lot of harm these babies can do when they are as ravishingly pretty as this one.'

'Now,' she said, lifting a box from the table. 'You'd better have a cigarette.'

'Thank you,' whispered Gerry.

She took one and Macil lit it for her. Gerry looked at her through the smoke and added,

'I'm terribly ashamed...'

'There's no need to be,' said Macil.

'But I am. I know I ought not to have come. It was outrageous – especially after what I did – but I went mad when I heard – when I thought he was dying.'

Macil looked at her curiously.

'Why does it matter so much to you? I don't quite understand–'

'No, of course not. You must loathe me. I suppose you know all about – what happened down in my home.'

Macil's tired face flushed slightly.

'I know a bit. Not much.'

'I was a little beast,' said Gerry huskily, staring at the point of her cigarette. 'Worse than that. I was angry because he – wouldn't pay any attention to me. I didn't mean any harm at the time – I swear it – I only wanted a flirtation. Please believe that.'

'Look here – must we discuss it–' began Nicholas's sister, suddenly embarrassed.

'Yes, please – *please* let me tell you!'

'What an intense sort of child,' thought Macil. 'And heavens, no wonder my poor Nicky was swooped off his feet. I've never seen such enormous, appealing eyes...'

'Well, I only wanted a flirtation,' continued Gerry. 'And I still didn't mean any harm when he – when I called him into my room – that night. When my mother found us and my father dismissed him I was

184

horrified at what I had done. I was desperate. Oh, Mrs Robertson, do you know what it's like to feel that you've done someone a hideous wrong and then you can't undo it?...' Her voice broke. She put the cigarette down and buried her face in her hands. 'It's sheer torture. It's been on my mind night and day. I've wanted to make some sort of reparation. Do you understand?'

Macil nodded in silence. She fancied that Geraldine Wayde was sincere in her grief, her remorse for the harm she had done Nicky – whatever else she was or had been.

'He wouldn't believe I was sorry,' continued Gerry, in a muffled voice. 'When I saw him at Dalbeattie's a few weeks ago he didn't believe me – I know he didn't although he said he did. It's worked on my mind so that I've been unable to sleep properly – or eat properly – to do anything.'

'My dear,' said Macil Robertson. 'It isn't any good letting it obsess you to this extent.'

'I know...' Gerry raised her face. Macil was shocked to see the anguish in her eyes. 'But it's been like that – ever since he left. I ... I think I realised when he had gone that I ... I'd lost the friendship and respect of the one man in the world who ... meant anything to me!'

Macil took a cigarette and lit it. She frowned as she shook the burning match and put it out. It was all very difficult and

185

awkward to deal with. Was Geraldine Wayde trying to tell her that she had fallen in love with Nicky? She wondered if the girl was not a bit melodramatic and exaggerated. Yet no – that poor, pale little face, bathed in tears, was the face of one who was suffering badly.

The mother in Macil conquered the sister's sudden jealousy. She said, very gently:

'My dear, if you're as sorry as all that, I'm sure Nicky will forgive you. I'm sure he has forgiven you already. He's really a very kind soul. You must try and forget it.'

'I shall never forget it as long as I live. And I still feel I shall go crazy if I can't make some sort of reparation.'

'I don't know what you can do, now.'

'No, that's the ghastly part of it,' said Gerry.

She walked to the window and stared at the roofs opposite – the flat, uninteresting panorama of the suburbs – grey and grim under a haze of heat. It was cruelly hot and stuffy up here in this flat. It seemed incredibly small and unattractive to Gerry who had been brought up in a home like Ponders. She felt unable to breathe properly. And this was where Nicholas lived … where he lay ill … where his sister lived and worked. She turned back, looked at Macil, and was filled with a sudden, intense liking and respect for her.

'You've been awfully decent to me, Mrs Robertson,' she said huskily. 'I wonder you didn't shut the door in my face.'

'Don't be silly, my dear child,' said Macil. 'And now you must excuse me. I must go to my brother.'

'Are you nursing him yourself?'

'Yes.'

'But you look so tired – you must be worn out.'

'I am a bit fagged.'

'But can't you have a nurse … or send him to a nursing home?' Gerry faltered and stopped. Macil shook her head.

'No. Much too expensive, and Nicky would hate a hospital nurse fussing round him. I like nursing him. The only difficulty is what to do with the children.'

Gerry looked at her in dismay.

'Of course. I remember you have two little boys.'

'Yes, two little devils,' said Macil grimly. 'Absolute pets, but it's not easy to keep small boys of that age quiet – it isn't natural for them to be quiet, poor little brutes.'

Gerry swallowed hard. Then she said huskily:

'Mrs Robertson – will you give me a chance to do something … some little thing for you and … and Mr Hulme?'

'In what way?'

'I mean – I adore children – and generally they like me. Can I stay and help you? I mean just for the day. I'll take the children out – I'll help you in any sort of way.'

Macil was touched, but she shook her head.

'No, no – I can manage. It's quite all right.'

'But please...' Gerry's voice was full of pleading. 'I beg you. Let me help. I won't be in the way. I'll take the little boys out. Now ... in my car ... we'll go to the Zoo. I'll give them some lunch out. I'd love it. Oh, *do* let me!'

Macil thought of Nicholas. What would he say? Wouldn't he be annoyed if she let Miss Wayde have anything to do with Robin and Tony and their private affairs? And yet ... this girl wanted a chance to do some service to them ... wasn't it right that she should have it? She was so sincere and so obviously unhappy, poor child. Macil was human. She was also tired out and she felt what a mercy it would be if somebody could take the boys out – all day.

'Please!' implored Gerry.

Macil gave way. She felt guilty about it, but she was in sore straits, and this offer of Gerry's was a God-send. As for poor old Nicky – he was too ill to know or care.

She took Gerry into the kitchen where Robin and Tony were chattering to Mrs Smithers. They were introduced to Gerry and a little awed by this stranger, but they soon made friends with her. She was young and pretty and smiled at them, and children, like animals, are responsive little creatures. When she mentioned the word 'Zoo' and 'chocolates' they became firm friends with her.

She left the flat with them, a hand in each of theirs. They were in buoyant spirits. And Gerry felt curiously happy – happier than she had been for months. They were *his* nephews and she was doing Macil Robertson a service. That was a great comfort to her...

She was filled with the ardent longing to be of help to these people. The harm she had done Nicholas had, after all, reacted on them.

Macil, thankful for the respite – no midday meal to cook for the children now – returned to her brother's bedside.

Gerry drove the small boys to Fullers and gave them as much lunch as they could eat. She found then an adorable pair. Tony, blue eyed, fair-haired – presumably like his father – chubby and delicious in small blue linen pants and blouse; Robin, taller, a real boy and a ridiculous image of his mother. Incidentally he was very like his uncle Nicky. Gerry, looking at him hungrily, saw the likeness to Nicholas – the same jet-black head and rather narrow, brilliant grey eyes. She immediately adored Robin. When she looked at him, she thought:

'If Nicholas had a son he would be like Robin!'

CHAPTER 15

An unusual number of parcels were delivered during that afternoon. Mrs Smithers thought them mysterious, and her hot face grew hotter and redder each time she answered the door bell. But they were no mystery to Macil. She unwrapped each one that came feeling almost guilty; disloyal to Nicky for accepting them, and greatly embarrassed. They were from Geraldine Wayde, of course.

A box from Fortnums – the finest essences and jellies and invalid foods. A great basket of fruit … hot-house grapes … nectarines … peaches. More flowers. And finally an assortment of toys and books from Hamley's. Robin and Tony had obviously been shopping with their new friend.

Macil realised that Gerry must have spent at least twenty pounds. How wonderful it must be to have money … to be able to spend it like this on others. Wistfully, Macil thought how much she would like to be able to buy these things for her brother and her small sons. And when she felt guilty about accepting the presents she told herself that this was Gerry's way of making amends. It would be brutal to deny her that consolation.

But Nicholas would have to be told some time.

'I suppose I'm a soft-hearted old idiot and I ought to have called the girl a beastly little vamp and told her to get out,' thought Macil.

But she couldn't have done that. She couldn't forget the sight of the tears raining pathetically down Gerry's cheeks; her horror when she thought Nicholas was dying.

When Gerry returned, late that afternoon, with two tired but elated little boys – laden with still more parcels – Macil thanked Gerry, but told her that she should not have done all these things.

Gerry shook her head and said:

'I've done nothing. And nothing I can do will ever be enough.'

'My dear child, I know Nicky wouldn't want–'

'Don't tell him – please,' broke in Gerry passionately. 'He might say I mustn't do it. And I want to come again tomorrow – yes, yes, don't say I can't – I'll take Robin and Tony out again tomorrow, all day. Then you'll have peace and quiet. I adore them. If you'd let me I'd have them down at Ponders, where there's a big garden and horses and dogs. Will you let me take them down with me for the week-end?'

'No, that's impossible!' said Macil.

'Then I'll come up and drive them down to some country place for the day. Yes, you must let me.'

'Oh, mummy – *yes!*' screamed Robin and Tony together.

'Ssh!' said Macil, glancing anxiously at Nicholas's door. 'If he heard...'

'Yes,' repeated the children in chorus.

'They seem to like you,' said Macil with her tired smile.

'I love them,' said Gerry.

Macil weakened and finally gave the permission. Gerry put out her hand and bade her good-bye.

'You do believe in me – believe that I'm sorry for that disastrous business?' she said, before she left.

'Yes, I think I do believe you,' said Macil. 'Now don't worry yourself to death any more.'

'But is he better?'

'Yes. Dr Agnew says he is distinctly better tonight. His temperature has dropped.'

'Thank God for that,' said Gerry.

'No more extravagance tomorrow. You have given us enough – much too much,' said Macil.

'All right, I promise,' said Gerry.

But when the morrow came, Gerry broke that promise. She sent more luxuries – everything that she could think of – that Nicholas or Macil or the boys might need. She drew more money from her account than she had drawn for months. She had let her allowance accumulate, had had no desire to spend while she was fretting about Nicholas down at Ponders. And, unknown to Macil, of course, she upset her mother by refusing to accompany her to Devonshire.

'I don't want to come, Mother. I want to stay at home,' she said, thereby reducing Mrs Wayde to tears. 'I hate Torquay. I hate a crowded hotel. Let me stay at home quietly by myself.'

Mrs Wayde protested but with no success. Finally she and her husband departed in their Rolls for Devonshire. Reluctantly they left their daughter behind.

'*Quelle idée* – staying all by herself. *Mais c'est affreux.* The child has gone mad, and ever since that abominable young man, Mr Hulme, left our house!' Mrs Wayde complained to her husband.

Austin Wayde pooh-poohed this.

'Hulme's got nothing to do with it. I daresay Gerry has had a secret love affair with young Withambury, and they've had a tiff or something. I'm not worrying about her, my dear Désirée. Leave her alone. She'll come round. I thought she was looking distinctly better this morning.'

'Well, as soon as we get back, she's got to pull herself together,' said Mrs Wayde firmly. 'There's that big theatrical party that Lady Prangbourne has asked us to in September. All sorts of well-known theatrical people will be there and I shall insist upon Gerry coming. Lady Prangbourne particularly wants her to meet Julian Barwise.'

'Who the devil is he?' asked Austin Wayde.

'Austin – really!' protested his wife. 'He's the most famous producer in England – and owns two of the biggest theatres in town and three in New York.'

'H'm,' said Mr Wayde. 'I don't like these theatre-fellows.'

'*Tant pis*,' said Mrs Wayde. 'They make fortunes, and they're not so dull as your horrid politicians, Austin, and Mr Barwise is to be knighted in the new year, they say.'

'Very soon they'll knight every policeman who holds up the traffic for the Queen to pass into Buckingham Palace,' growled Austin Wayde, M.P.

'You're feeling very Conservative this morning, *mon cher*,' said his wife sweetly.

'Poof, my dear Désirée,' said Mr Wayde, and ignoring the passing scenery, buried himself in *The Times*.

Up in London, the daughter whom these people imagined to be wandering forlornly round Graylingstone spent another happy day with Macil's children. This time Gerry took a picnic-basket, packed with goodies from Ponders, and drove the boys to Richmond Park. She played hide-and-seek with them, cricket, blind man's buff – every game they demanded. They were a tireless, exhausting pair and they exhausted Gerry. But her patience was unlimited and she could not do enough for them.

It was quite late when she returned them – somewhat grimy, but undeniably happy – to their mother.

Gerry remained in the drawing-room smoking, whilst Macil put the boys to bed. Somehow she could not bring herself to go. Somewhere in this flat … next to this very room … Nicholas was lying. She had an aching longing to see him. Macil said he was making very good progress and once more the danger of pneumonia had been staved off.

Macil came in.

'You *have* been good to the kids. They've been burbling in the bathroom about their marvellous time. They think you're a sort of fairy godmother.'

Gerry flushed and bowed her head. Macil walked up to her and put a hand on her shoulder.

'My dear – you can't go on doing so much. You sent a lot more parcels here today. Honestly – I cannot accept any more. I daren't think what my brother will say.'

Gerry's underlip quivered.

'Don't stop me taking the children out. I want them again tomorrow. It must make things easier for you.'

'It does – it relieves things beyond words.

In fact, I'm sure it's saved me from a break-down, as well as enabled me to look after Nicky properly.'

'Don't you see what that means to me,' whispered Gerry.

A bell tinkled from the adjoining room.

'That's Nick ... wait a moment,' said Macil. 'I think I'll tell him you're here, tonight.'

'Don't – he might send me away,' said Gerry in an agony of nervousness.

'I don't think he will,' said Macil.

She left Gerry alone. Gerry sat down and hid her face in her hands. Her heart was pounding ... pounding ... her thoughts in chaos.

Macil came back.

'Look here,' she said. 'I've told Nicky, and he wants to see you.'

Gerry stood up. Her face flushed scarlet to the roots of her blonde hair. Unbelievingly she said:

'Wants to see *me?*...'

'Yes. I've told him everything. He was angry at first, that you had been allowed to do so much. Then I explained why I'd al-lowed it. He seemed to understand. He isn't quite such a brute as you think, you know. He does understand things...'

'But I hurt him so...' Gerry clenched her hands. 'Oh, Mrs Robertson – can he really want to see me?'

'Yes. Come along.'

Gerry felt much as though some priest of olden days had shriven her for her sins. An enormous burden was lifted from her mind, her heart, when she tip-toed into the bedroom where Nicholas Hulme was lying. Macil did not go with her. She left them alone. She was herself a woman of very great understanding, and she had seen a strange light in her brother's eyes when she had recounted all that Geraldine Wayde had done these last forty-eight hours.

Gerry moved to the bedside. It was dim and shadowy in here. The August sun was still shining outside, but there were green casement curtains drawn across the windows. The atmosphere was cool. Macil had bought and installed an electric fan. There was that faint smell of eau de Cologne which one associates with the sick-room; flowers everywhere and fruit on the table beside the bed. With a heart almost bursting with emotion Gerry saw that they were her flowers and her fruit.

Then she saw Nicholas. He looked gaunt and changed. A white ghost of the Nicholas he had known, lying rather flat in the bed; a long figure outlined under a white bedspread. Everything seemed painfully white ... including his face. His eyes, those eyes which had been so brilliant and eager, were sunken in his head. His lips were a thin line, down-curved, bitter, as she remembered them. Yet there was a new gentleness written in his eyes when he looked up at her. He held out a thin hand.

'I want to – thank you–' he said. His voice sounded weak. 'For all you've done – for the children – for everything.'

Gerry could not answer. There was a great lump in her throat. He continued to look up at her with that kindness in his eyes which she had never seen in them before.

'You – needn't – have – done so much,' he said.

Then something seemed to break in Gerry. All the fever of love that had been burning in her heart for him, all the agony of regret, remorse, rushed over her afresh and made her forget to be calm and natural with him, as she had meant to be. He looked so ill and so spiritualised by his illness. She could not bear it. She went down on her knees by the bed and caught his hand; clung to it; buried her face against the bedspread. She said in a choked voice:

'I've done nothing ... but I did a lot of harm to you ... oh, please, forgive me...'

Nicholas looked down at the bent fair head. There was a peculiarly hot, dry sensation in his throat. It was terribly embarrassing and seemed all wrong for the gay, careless Geraldine Wayde to be kneeling here at his bedside. Poor child! Had she regretted what she had done as much as all that? Macil said she had. He believed it, too, now. He put out his other hand and touched her hair ... that fair, thick wave of hair which he had always thought so beautiful.

'My dear, of course I forgive you. For God's sake let's forget that damnable business,' he said.

He spoke curtly. It was the voice of the old Nicholas who had avoided and eluded her. Yet it was different. And he had said 'My dear.' And she could feel his fingers on her hair.

She wanted to burst out sobbing, but she controlled herself, remembering that he was still a sick man and must not be excited. She clung desperately to his fingers with both hers and laid her forehead against them. Nicholas was horrified to feel something wet and warm fall upon them.

'You mustn't cry,' he said. 'Gerry, don't cry.'

'I'm so sorry.'

'Yes, yes, I know. But you mustn't upset yourself like this.'

'Forgive me – please.'

'Yes, absolutely.'

The word 'absolutely' was balm to her bruised spirit. She felt broken and battered by the old grief and remorse, and yet she was comforted now. For the first time since he had gone away she was comforted and almost at peace.

'You've been awfully decent to my young scamps of nephews,' he said.

'No. I – I like them – immensely...' She tried to smile. She let go of his hand and wiped her eyes.

'Tell me – how is your father?'

'Very well. He and mother have gone to Devonshire for a week.'

'And left you behind?'

'I wanted to be left. I wanted to come up here and take the children out.'

'That was wrong.' Nicholas frowned. 'You mustn't do that sort of thing, you know.'

She stood up and gave a husky little laugh. She looked down at him with wet, glowing eyes.

'I'm not a baby,' she said. 'I'm a thoroughly independent young female and I can look after myself – and do.'

He smiled up at her. The smile went straight to her heart. She remembered how often, down at Ponders, she had tried to make him relax the gravity of his face. But then he would not smile at her. She wished passionately that he was not so fine-drawn, so white.

He felt it was strange and rather sweet to see this girl standing beside him, talking to him in a shy yet friendly way. Gerry Wayde shy ... she, of the many friends! The social light of so many gay parties. Strange and sweet that she had knelt at his bedside and bathed his hand in her tears. Poor child. She had really suffered. He could see it ... see how changed she was. And he had left Ponders despising her.

'I'd better go,' she whispered. 'You mustn't talk any more.'

He was curiously reluctant to let her go. But he looked at her with the old familiar scowl.

'I wonder why you minded so much what happened down at Ponders,' he said suddenly. 'It beats me.'

She said nothing. The burning colour rushed to her cheeks. Long lashes veiled her eyes from him. A sudden flash of understanding enlightened him. His heart gave a great twist. He looked intently at the beautiful fair hair – it was like silver in this dim room – and at the slenderness of her in the green Irish linen dress which she was wearing; a wide belt around her waist and green beads twisted about her neck. He remembered how he had wanted her almost to madness, that night in her room.

He thought:

'Steady on, you fool ... don't lose your head again...'

But she was very close to him, and her sweetness, her new pathetic humility, awoke the old hunger for her which he had tried to stamp on, to kill, down in Graylingstone.

'Gerry,' he said.

She raised her lashes and caught his gaze.

'Gerry,' he said again and held out his arms. 'Come here...'

Her heart pounded so that it seemed to shake her. She sat down blindly, quickly, on the bed. He put his arm around her.

They stayed thus for a moment, cheek to cheek, in silence. Then he turned his lips to her mouth.

His kiss was an almost unbearable ecstasy after the agony she had endured, after the long bitterness between them.

She put her arms about his neck and he held her very close. He kept his lips on hers, not moving. He knew that he loved her. He had loved her ever since that night when he had first kissed her and she had done him such irremediable harm. At last he said:

'My dear – this is all wrong.'

'No,' she answered. 'No. I love you.'

'You can't love me, child.'

'I do. I've been terribly in love with you ever since you went away. It's been torture to me...' she was trembling violently. He soothed and caressed her hair with his right hand.

'Hush, my dear. Don't worry ... don't worry now. It's all right now.'

'It can never be all right, can it?'

'Yes, it is now.'

'It was abominable ... I know it.'

'Ssh – forget it, dear.'

She abandoned herself to the comfort of his arms, of his caressing hands. In an anguish of tenderness she kissed the rough black head which had haunted her visions. She kissed his eyelids and his hollowed cheeks.

'Oh, Nicholas, my darling, my darling,' she whispered again and again. 'Oh, Nicholas, my *darling.*'

He was filled with wonder and amaze and an immense happiness that this girl should love him like this.

'Poor little Gerry,' he said. 'Poor child. You've worried too much. I wasn't worth it.'

She clung to him, mute and passionate. Her love for him filled her whole being.

'I love you,' he said. 'I love you, dear. It's going to be the very devil, as things are – but I love you.'

'Oh, Nicholas,' she said. 'Nicky ... I want to call you Nicky ... like your sister does ... darling Nicky ... I can't believe you love me. It's too wonderful.'

She put up her head and laughed. He thought he had never seen anything so beautiful as Gerry with her big, dark eyes blazing and adoring him; her flushed, tear-wet cheeks; her tumbled, silver-fair hair. She was ardent and glowing and on fire with love for him. And he was suddenly conscious of his inferiority. He was penniless ... sick ... a wreck...

A fit of coughing shook him. He stifled it,

drew her down to him, and put his lips against her throat.

'Darling,' he whispered. 'That's heavenly ... stay like that...'

But Gerry was full of anxiety now for him.

'You're ill – I've excited you – your sister will murder me... I'm going – yes, I'm going now – this moment, Nicky darling.'

'Then come again tomorrow. No, you mustn't. It's all wrong. I oughtn't to have allowed this.'

'But I'm coming tomorrow,' she whispered, and laid her lips upon his. 'And every day – every day, darling.'

'But your father – your mother–' he began feebly.

'We'll talk about it tomorrow. Hold me. Hold me very tightly. I've suffered so. I've wanted you so!'

He wrapped his arms about her. He could feel her trembling. He was mute before the face of her adoration.

She smoothed his hair back from his hot forehead.

'My darling,' she kept saying in a voice of passionate tenderness. 'My darling...'

And he had believed her a heartless coquette – incapable of any real feeling. If he had ever dreamed of a woman loving him it had been of one who would love him like this. He lay back on the pillows and wished that he did not feel so infernally weak.

'For the first time for weeks and weeks I shall go to bed and be glad, glad that I'm alive,' she whispered. 'I'm terribly happy tonight. Good night – Nicky.'

'Good night, my dear,' he whispered back.

She went softly from his room, like one in an ecstatic dream. But some of the ecstasy was dulled when she heard him coughing – coughing. In an agony of anxiety she thought:

'He is still awfully ill. If only I weren't a woman. If only I could do more – with all father's money to back me. But Nicholas wouldn't accept it … he'd be insulted … oh, damn … why can't a woman ever give anything worth while to the man she loves?'

Then she went into the sitting-room and told Nicholas's sister what had happened. And all that wise and charming woman did was to put an arm around her shoulders and say:

'Well, my dear, if that's how things are between you – I'm quite glad. I daresay you'll bring poor Nicky a lot of happiness. But mind you don't ever bring him more of the other thing.'

Then Gerry went down on the hearth-rug beside Macil and buried her face in her lap and said:

'I love him – I worship him – I'd die for him. I'd die before I'd make him unhappy again. You know that.'

'Yes, I think I know,' said Macil.

She put a hand on the girl's silver-fair head. But there was an anxious look on her tired face. She was thinking:

'It may be all right. She's obviously in love with him and I daresay he's in love with her. But he hasn't a bean, my poor old boy, and she's the only daughter of rich people who haven't too good an opinion of him after that rotten affair. How's it all going to end?'

CHAPTER 16

On Sunday morning when Gerry drove up to Golders Green she was met by Macil who, for the first time since Gerry had known her, looked rested and without that pucker of worry between her brows.

'My dear,' she greeted the younger girl. 'You've done wonders to Nicky. He's much better this morning and he slept well, for him, and coughed very little. Incidentally I've had a good night myself.'

'I'm terribly glad!' said Gerry.

Macil smiled at her. 'Go in and see him.'

Gerry walked into Nicholas's room. The sun was streaming in through the wide-open windows. A faint breeze billowed the green curtains. The room was fresh and full of the scent of flowers. Gerry saw Nicholas – only Nicholas. Propped up against his pillows, he looked a different being. His eyes were brighter, not quite so sunken. He was always ivory pale, but his expression was one of eagerness, of excitement. All the gloom, the bitterness, had been wiped away from his face as though by a magic hand.

He put out a hand when Gerry came in. She had dressed expressly to please his eye, and he thought that she was like the incarnation of summer itself in one of those thin, flowered dresses which she favoured; a small straw hat pulled rakishly over the fair, cropped head. The moment she entered the room the hat came off and was thrown recklessly on the floor. She was on her knees by the bed, her arms about his neck.

'Nicky ... Nicky ... hold me tightly ... tell me it's true. I woke up this morning feeling it couldn't be true!'

His arms went round her. He bent forward and laid his cheek against her hair.

'My dear, I was wondering, myself, if it could be true. It's good to see you again ... to feel you close to me.'

She lifted a rapt face – cheeks burning.

'Am I close to you – close in mind as well as body now, Nicky? I've wanted to be – prayed to be.'

'You are, my dear.'

'You do really love me?'

'I'm afraid I do, Gerry.'

'Why afraid?'

'Because there are three thousand difficulties ahead of us, my dear.'

'I wouldn't mind if there were three million.'

He pushed back the big wave of hair from her forehead and looked at her long and earnestly.

'I can't think why you care about me like

this, Gerry. After all, you're young – five years younger than I am – and you're a wealthy young woman with the world at your feet.'

'Don't go on,' she broke in. She caught the hand that smoothed her hair and put her lips to it. 'I simply adore you – that's all – and I'm not ashamed to say it. I discovered it directly you left Ponders. Day after day, night after night, I thought about you. I was tortured. I nearly went mad. You can't think what it means to me to know that you care a bit for me and don't despise me any more.'

'Gerry, I didn't know the real you. I'm sorry if I was a beast to you.'

'I deserved it. *I* was much more beastly, Nicky. When did you begin to love me?'

'I don't know, dear.'

'Men never know.'

'You're right. Men are generally fools about love. Just blind fools. Women have all the vision. Sit on my bed, nearer me, sweetheart.'

She rose and sat on the bed. He pulled her down to him.

'I love you – like this – Gerry–'

Her heart raced. Her eyelids closed for a dizzying moment as she felt the hard pressure of his lips on her mouth. They stayed like that for a little while … until suddenly Nicholas relaxed his hold of her and said:

'I love you much more than is good for me. Give me a cigarette, darling, and let's talk.'

Gerry, shaken to the depths of her being,

came back to earth. She found and lit the cigarette for him. He began to cough at once and she took the cigarette away.

'Nicky – you mustn't – see what it does to you.'

'I know, but I must have something to calm down my nerves, child. You're much too attractive.'

'Oh, I'm glad if I am – to you,' she whispered.

'Now, listen, Gerry,' he said. 'We must be sensible and face facts. This is all mad and glorious but – my dear – it's been wrong and weak of me to let it happen.'

'Why?' She sat straight up, tilting her head.

'You know why. I love you, Gerry. I'm madly in love with you but–'

'Well–' Her heart was sinking.

'Well – how can I do what I want – which is to ask you to marry me – when you are Geraldine Wayde and I am Nicholas Hulme without a bean, without even a job? I've been ill with this infernal bronchitis so long now, I shan't even get my job back at Dalbeattie's.'

'That may be. It can't alter the fact that I worship you, Nicky.'

'You're very sweet, my dear...' He took her hand and kissed it. 'But I'm not going to allow it.'

'Nicky – you can't go back now–' her eyes looked into his with sudden terror.

'Oh, sweetheart,' he said, 'don't look at me

like that. You make me feel an absolute brute. I've got to be fair. Help me, please. It wouldn't be fair of me to ask you to marry me – under such conditions.'

'You mean – because I happen to be the daughter of people with a lot of money and you're hard up – we can't belong to each other?'

'That's what it means, my dear.'

'Then I shall leave home at once for good and chuck up the money.'

'I believe you would,' he said. His eyes were very tender. 'I know you would. I'm just beginning to realise what a generous person you are – what a generous lover, my dear. But I'm afraid what you suggest is out of the question. It's all right in novels and plays. It won't work in everyday life. Literally, Gerry – I haven't a bean. I've got to find a job. My sister and the kids depend largely on me for support. Macil would howl that down and say she could manage on her pension, but she couldn't. She leads a hell of a life as it is and is a perfect angel. She's my first thought – got to be. I was very fond of Tom, her husband. I promised him when he died, poor chap, that I'd do my best for Macil and the boys. I want Robin to go into the Navy. It's a poor look-out at the moment, but my dear, you see that marriage is impossible for me under these conditions.'

Gerry was silent. She allowed this speech

to sink in. She was sensible enough to realise at once that every word he said was true. However much she loved him, however much he loved her, marriage was out of the question. Of course – his first duty was to his sister and his nephews. It seemed frightfully hard. But he could not desert them. Macil had been wonderful to him. He must consider her now. And she, Gerry, if she left home, would be without means. She could plainly foresee trouble in that quarter if she announced her intention of marrying Nicholas Hulme. It would antagonise her father. It would break her mother's heart. Poor, foolish old 'Désirée duck,' who yearned after a fortune and a title for her.

Nicholas saw her face gradually lose its radiance. The brilliant colour faded until she became quite pale. She looked down at him with large, mournful eyes.

'I suppose you are right.'

'I know I am, my dear.'

'But I could ask father – he might–'

'No!' broke in Nicholas. It was the old, curt voice – the old stubborn Nicholas. 'No, my dear. I'll never consent to that as long as I live. Nothing – not even my love for you – will make me accept a thing from your father. Either I go to him with an income of my own and prospects and say I feel justified in marrying you – or I don't marry you at all. Never shall it be said that I wormed my way into the affections of his young daughter for the sake of money, etc., etc.'

'Nicky!' The name broke from Gerry in pained protest. 'How can you say things like that. *You* – worming your way into *my* affections – when it's the other way about!'

He laughed and suddenly squeezed her hand.

'My darling! That's not the point, anyhow. I was ragging. But ragging apart – you see what I mean. I can't in my present position ask you to be my wife.'

'No – I understand,' she said in a low voice.

'Neither can I dream of asking you to wait until *I am* in a better position.' He added: 'God knows when that will be.'

She sat very still and silent for a moment, staring at the floor. Nicholas looked at the fair, bowed head, and there was hunger in his eyes and gnawing pain in his heart. She had grown so suddenly, unbelievably dear. And although the love which had blossomed between them was a thing of rapture, he knew that nothing but pain and bitterness could evolve from it. Renunciation. As friends they might remain. As lovers they would have to renounce each other because of the disparity in their positions. It was the old, sordid tale … lack of means.

'Lord – what a power money is,' Nicholas thought. 'What a brutal power. What can anything mean – even love – without money?

The lack of it is the root of half the trouble in this confounded world.'

Then he saw that Gerry was crying. The tears were chasing down her cheeks. He put his arms swiftly about her.

'Darling, darling, don't ... don't, please!'

She clung to him and pressed her cheek to his.

'Nicky, I can't bear it... I can't. I've only just found you. We've only just found each other – like this. I can't give you up.'

'I know, dear. It's damnable. But we have no choice.'

'Don't you see how it agonises me?' she wailed. 'It's my fault. *My fault!*'

'No – that's rubbish.'

'But it is. If you'd stayed with father – you'd have had every chance of doing well with him in politics. And if you'd left him, ordinarily, you'd have had more chance – he'd have helped you. It's coming back on me now. To love you so much and to know what harm I've done you!'

He felt her slim body shuddering with sobs. Her tears drenched his cheek. He held her tightly and tried to comfort her.

'My dear, don't ... don't reproach yourself ... don't – you're hurting yourself and me – unnecessarily – honestly, Gerry. You mustn't go on saying you ruined me.'

'But you know it's true,' she said in a desperate little voice. 'And now – even though you love me, Nicky, my punishment is going on and on. We can't be engaged or married or anything … because of your position. I've helped to drag you down, instead of helping you up. And I'd give my life to help you.'

'I know, dear. Dearest – don't cry like this. I can't stand it.'

'Oh, Nicky,' she whispered. 'Oh, my darling, if only I'd known … if only I'd seen ahead. You might be down there with father, now, and we might have found out that we cared for each other and everything would have been all right.'

He stroked her hair.

'I don't know that that's true, my dear. If I'd stayed at Ponders in the normal way we might never have found out that we cared. In fact, I doubt if I would have discovered it. I admired your beauty – I was attracted by you, physically, but I wasn't in the least in love with you, frankly speaking.'

Gerry swallowed that.

'Then why do you care for me now?'

'Because I realised that, in spite of the fact that you did hurt me, I couldn't forget you or stop wanting you. Then when I knew how *you'd* suffered and I got to know the real, generous, sweet thing that you are – it just decided me that you were the only woman in the world for me. You are, Gerry. But I'm afraid we're up against a brick wall.'

She dried her eyes and sat up. Her spirits

which had been so bright when she rushed into the room were at zero. She walked to his dressing-table; smoothed her hair and powdered her nose. She was trying not to be a coward – for his sake, when he was still so weak and ill.

'It's damnable, Nicky.'

'Damnable,' he agreed.

'Can't anything be done?'

'Not much, my dear, unless I turn out a really good play and make a fortune, and I've precious little hope of that.'

She walked back to the bed.

'Oh, if only you could! You will – I know you will write a big play one day.'

'It isn't easy to get a producer even to read a play when one's written it,' he said grimly.

'Nick, something must happen or I shall go mad. I can't face life without you.'

'I don't want to face it without you, Gerry. But God knows, dear…'

'There'll never be anybody else – never – never!' she broke in passionately. 'If I don't marry you, Nicky, I shall die an old maid. On my oath!'

'My dear,' he said very tenderly. He held out his arms to her.

'Wonderful of you. But I'm not going to let you make any oaths of that sort. It would be most unfair.'

She surrendered to his embrace.

'But I've made it… I'll make it again.

There'll never be anyone else.'

'God bless you, darling. But I refuse to accept that oath. You never know whom you may meet, and you're a very attractive, popular young woman.'

She looked at him almost angrily.

'Do you *want* me to marry someone else?'

'No – I think it'd be a knock-out blow to me,' he admitted. 'But I won't allow you to bind yourself to me; you're much too young.'

'That's rot. I know my own mind. You're the first lover I've had, Nicky, and you'll be the last.'

He sighed painfully.

'It's all cruel and difficult, my dear. And I oughtn't to let you–'

She stopped his words; pressing her lips against his.

'I love you, Nicky – love you. I don't care if we aren't engaged, if we never marry. I shall never stop loving you and you must see me when you can. I shan't say a word at home. But something can be managed, somehow.'

'It's wrong, Gerry…'

'Do you love me?'

'Yes,' he said weakly.

'Then don't drive me to despair by hinting that you won't see me any more.'

'Gerry,' he said, 'if you kiss me like this we shan't be able to see each other very often. I couldn't stand it. I'm too much in love with you, my dear.'

She was triumphant, glowing again. Woman-like, she staved off the recollection of the difficulties, of everything but their mutual passion.

'Thank God you *are* in love with me, Nicky,' she whispered.

'But we must be sensible, sweetheart. Honestly we must. If we are to go on meeting – we must try to be friends.'

'We are friends, but we're lovers, too.'

'Darling, you *must* help me...'

'I will,' she said, relenting. She took his face between her hands and kissed his eyes and his black, ruffled head. 'I'll do anything ... anything you say ... except stop loving you.'

'All right, darling, and you can be sure I won't stop loving you. And now ... to get fit and make money ... *somehow*...'

'I shall help you make it. I know people – men in good positions. Leaving father out of it, I shall try and get you something.'

'No, you can't do that. I must get back on my own feet.'

That hurt her. She could not forget that she had been the original cause of his present impecunious position; of the hardships Macil Robertson was enduring. She thought:

'I shan't tell him. But I must help. I *will*. I *must!*'

A thought suddenly flashed through her mind. Before leaving home her mother had told her that she must go with her as Lady

Prangbourne's guest to a big theatrical party in September. Gerry remembered that she had only half-heartedly agreed to go.

Now there was a new complexion on it; she attached an altogether new importance to it. Wasn't Julian Barwise, the famous producer, to be present? Wasn't he a special friend of the Prangbournes? Yes. Mother had said that Vera Prangbourne was going to introduce them to Julian Barwise. He had produced two big successes this spring. He was to be knighted in the new year because he had done good service to the country in the War – arranging entertainments for the Tommies at the front. And he had organised various big charity matinees. He was a man of considerable importance these days – not only in London, but in New York.

If she could only show Mr Barwise a finished play that Nicholas had written and ask him to read it – he would probably do so. She would try, anyhow.

She grew suddenly, wildly excited. The colour came back to her cheeks. But she must keep it a secret – from Nicholas. She wouldn't tell him anything – yet.

'Nicky,' she said casually. 'You told me the other day that you had written another play after you left Ponders.'

'Yes, that's so, my dear.'

'May I read it?'

'Oh, my dear – it isn't even typed – I

haven't been able to afford–'

'That doesn't matter,' she interrupted. 'I want to read it. Please let me.'

'Oh, all right…' he gave a short laugh. 'It's in the top drawer of my chest-of-drawers – over there.'

Gerry found the manuscript. She glanced at one or two of the closely written sheets of foolscap … blue-pencilled … corrected … untidy. Her heart ached with remembrance of that other torn manuscript which she had pieced together. She was so familiar with his writing now. She could decipher it easily.

'I'd like to glance through it,' she said. And her heart beat swiftly with her secret thoughts of Julian Barwise.

'It's charming of you, my dear. I'd like to know what you think of it, Macil quite liked it, but I daresay it'll find a place on the fire like most of my other ambitious creations.

'Oh – will it!' thought Gerry. 'We shall see!' She pressed the manuscript tightly to her breast and decided to have it typed tomorrow without telling Nicholas. She knew a girl in Graylingstone, in the village, with a machine. She was a cripple who took in typing for authors. She could probably type the play at once. The theatrical party was not until September 5th. Another week. Her hopes soared high at the thought of Julian Barwise. Never had she thought the name of Mr Barwise would assume such importance to her.

'I haven't got a title for it yet,' said Nicholas gloomily. 'I don't think I'm much good as a dramatist, darling. Perhaps selling cars if more in my line.'

'Rot,' said Gerry. 'Absolute rot. I shall choose a title when I've read it.'

'So you shall, sweetheart.'

He leaned back on his pillows, feeling suddenly tired and dispirited. He laced his fingers behind his head and stared up at the ceiling, where a patch of sunlight flickered and whirled with a million specks of dust.

'Oh, Gerry!' he said. 'If only I could make money and my name. For you, my dear … for Macil … for the kids. It'll break me up if I turn out a failure and achieve nothing. For their sakes particularly. I gave old Tom my word…'

'Darling,' she said, kneeling beside him. 'I never knew Tom, but I'm sure he must know how hard you've tried already and be satisfied. You will achieve something. I *know* you will!'

He looked at her and touched her hair with thin, nervous fingers.

'You're very comforting, my dear.'

She leaned her cheek against his hand. She thought with the most passionate love for him surging over her:

'You *will* achieve something … and through me. It's got to happen … I owe you a big debt, and oh, my darling, it's got to be paid!'

221

CHAPTER 17

Désirée Wayde considered herself a woman of wits and judgment, and she thought that she knew her own daughter. But she was baffled by the sudden and complete change which she found in Gerry when she returned with Austin from Devonshire.

They had left a pale, melancholy girl who took little interest in life. They found a transformation. Gerry was full of spirits. She looked well. She had got back her colour. She ate her food with more zest. She went about the place with a little secret smile on her lips as though her thoughts were continually pleasing her.

Mrs Wayde, ever suspicious, questioned her the first night she got home.

'I'm delighted, *chérie*, that you've cheered up again, but 'pon my soul, you make me wonder what secret you are keeping from me.'

'Why should I be keeping a secret?' said Gerry rather guiltily.

'Anybody would think you had fallen in love,' said her mother unconsciously hitting the mark.

'H'm,' said Gerry. 'Well now, what I want to

talk about is the dress I'm going to wear for the party Lady Prangbourne is taking us to, so turn your attention to that, Désirée duck!'

Mrs Wayde's fat face expressed relief and pleasure, and she was put right off the scent, which was what Gerry had contrived. She was so pleased that her daughter should address her by the old pet name which she had not heard for a couple of months, and which meant that Gerry was happy, and so glad that Gerry was taking an interest in clothes again, that she questioned her no further.

'We shall go up to town together early next week, *petit chou*,' she said. 'You must have a marvellous dress. It will be a very big affair and you must make a good impression on Julian Barwise. Vera tells me he is quite the most engaging person.'

Mrs Wayde rattled on about clothes, material, style, modistes, for the next half-hour with long-drawn breaths, gesticulations, and a great deal of French. Gerry bore with it patiently. The name 'Julian Barwise' had set her pulses racing. She thought of a play – now beautifully typed – reposing in a locked drawer in her bedroom. She had chosen a title for it. *Our Discovery*. But she hadn't even told Nicholas that. The title could be altered, anyhow.

Our Discovery was a great play, Gerry thought – full of wit. Nicholas was a genius. His epigrams sparkled. The story made one laugh and then cry. She was certain that Julian Barwise would like it and take it. And yet – deep down in her – she preferred *At Boiling Point*. But, alas, that wasn't finished. And one couldn't give a producer two acts and a half to read.

She had thought of nothing else but Nicholas and his play for the last week. It had been an amazingly full, happy week. Happy in spite of the apparently hopeless barrier between herself and Nicholas. She had fetched some luggage from Ponders and gone back to London to an hotel, and stayed there until her parents came home. She had had to lie about it. She had said she was staying with Phyllis Crozier. Phyllis wouldn't give her away. She was herself always involved in some complicated affair, and Gerry had been her alibi on many an occasion.

It had been an innocent week in all conscience. She had stayed in town just so as to be near Nicholas and Macil. Every day she had seen her lover, and she felt, with deep thankfulness, that he was, now, more than ever her lover. Every day she had helped Macil by taking Robin and Tony out. Never had the children had such a time. She had spent money recklessly. Most of her quarter's allowance. That didn't matter. There was more money due this very week. And she was happy to spend it on the little boys and to

send Nicholas and Macil luxuries. They protested and reproached her in vain.

Now that her parents were back Gerry
chafed at being tied. It wasn't going to be
easy to get up to town and go to the flat.
That flat and its inmates which had grown
so incredibly dear to her. Her mother nearly
always insisted upon accompanying her
when she went up to town. Gerry had to
content herself with letters. She wrote every
day to Nicholas – poured out her heart to
him. He wrote back, printing her name on
the envelope lest the Waydes saw and recognised his hand-writing. But he was not
happy about it. He wrote on one occasion:

*'I've no earthly right to carry on a clandestine
affair with you in my present position. I wish I
didn't love you so much, my dear...'*

Gerry wrote back:

*'It doesn't matter. We're not harming anybody,
and one day you will be able to love me openly,
darling, you will see!'*

He was not so sure as she was. He was
gloomy and depressed. The natural depression, more a physical than a mental thing,
which cloaks one after a serious illness.
When he was up and out again he was a
lean, hollow-eyed ghost of himself. But he

had something to be thankful for. Dalbeattie's – through the influence of Nicholas's old school friend who was a director – had kept his post open. He returned to work at the show-room on the 4th of September.

On the 4th of September Gerry was in a state of subdued excitement. Tomorrow she was going up to town with her mother for the theatrical party. They were lunching with Lady Prangbourne in Pont Street and then going on to Mrs Chetwynd-Lacey's house in Eton Square where the party was to be held. The Chetwynd-Laceys, as a family, were mixed up with the theatre, and Irene Chetwynd-Lacey – a rich American – financed a great many of the plays which Julian Barwise produced. Gerry had got all this information from her mother and stored it up. There was so much at stake. She was going to that party with such high, secret hopes. She would meet all these influential people – people who could open the door to success for Nicholas. She felt that she would be no earthly use if she failed to do something for him now.

She had told herself grimly that this was an occasion when she must really do a little 'vamping.' She knew that she was good to look at and that men found her attractive. Well, it was up to her to use some of that attraction upon Julian Barwise and make him read Nicholas's play.

The difficulty was to carry the big envelope containing *Our Discovery* without arousing her mother's curiosity. That remained a problem till the last hour. Then – although Mrs Wayde bemoaned the fact – it poured with rain. The 5th of September was a day of incessant, drenching rain and it turned cold. The beautiful, delicate frocks chosen for the party had to be well covered. Gerry wore her fur coat – pale golden wool with a great fox collar. And the coat proved a blessing because it had a huge pocket in the satin lining, and into this lining Gerry folded and stuffed Nicholas's manuscript.

Driving up to London in the Rolls limousine with her mother, Gerry inwardly prayed as she had not prayed since she was a child.

'God, let me do something for Nicky ... let me succeed ... because he's suffering now through me and I *must* make reparation. Please, God ... let me succeed!'

Mrs Wayde was in excellent humour. She looked large and magnificent in coffee-coloured lace and a coat of Persian lamb. Her plump face was well powdered and painted. She gazed through her lorgnettes at her daughter and was satisfied.

'You look *ravissante,* my darling. That frock is divine, *Merveillieux!* You'll make a great stir, and I shall be surprised if Mr Barwise doesn't want you to be the leading lady in his next play.'

She chuckled at her little joke. Gerry smiled her new, secret smile. Her cheeks were flushed and her eyes very bright. She wanted to make a stir – with Julian Barwise. Close to her fast-beating heart was Nicky's play ... and for his sake she *must* make a stir.

If Mrs Wayde wanted a success for her daughter, she had it that afternoon. At the Chetwynd-Lacys' party there was no prettier girl than Geraldine Wayde and none more admired.

The dress which had been chosen for her with such care was palest primrose chiffon with little gold flowers stamped on it. The irregular skirt, long at the back, made her look tall and very slim. The long satin coat, to match, had a collar, and deep, huge cuffs of soft, pale sable. Her hat was of the same shade of primrose and gold. She wore gold jewellery.

The whole effect was charming. She was like a figure of English spring in the somewhat Oriental atmosphere of Mrs Chetwynd-Lacey's drawing-room, which was full of Chinese lacquer and sombre colours.

Everybody – men and women alike – turned to look again at the slender girl in yellow with her beautiful fair hair and dark, luminous eyes.

One man in particular, who stood in a circle of friends, followed Gerry with his gaze wherever she went, while he kept up a running flow of chatter with his companions. The big room was crowded with exquisitely dressed women, old and young; many well-known stage folk. And he was the lion amongst them. But he would have been bored if it had not been for the girl in yellow.

Finally he moved to the side of his hostess. Irene Chetwynd-Lacey was an intimate friend of his, and they had been hand in glove, producing plays, for the last three or four years.

'Irene,' he said, 'who's that girl in yellow?'

Mrs Chetwynd-Lacey, a tall American woman with horn-rimmed glasses and a beautiful figure, looked at the girl he indicated.

'Oh – nobody in particular. Rather pretty, though, isn't she, Julian?'

'Pretty? My dear Irene – she's ravishing.'

'Don't tell me you've fallen for a blonde, my dear Julian! Say – she's only about nineteen or twenty.'

'I like 'em young, my dear Irene. Introduce me.'

'Why, you're just too disgusting!' said Mrs Chetwynd-Lacey. 'Very well. Come along. Her name's Geraldine Wayde. She's a little friend of Vera Prangbourne's.'

'Geraldine Wayde,' said Julian Barwise softly. 'But she's charming – charming!'

'And you're just incorrigible, my dear Julian. You're the finest producer of plays either this side of the herring pond or the other, but I guess you're the most immoral man I know. I thought you were going to marry Beatrice.'

'My dear Irene, Beatrice is the cleverest leading lady we have in town, but I'm not going to marry her. I don't suppose I shall ever marry. All the same, introduce me to the golden girl. She's got the eyes of a Madonna – I love dark brown eyes. And the lips of an *amoureuse*. She interests me.'

And so Gerry found herself being introduced to the big man whom she had wanted to meet for so many vital and important reasons.

She gave Julian Barwise her most charming smile, without being in the least conscious that he had been staring at her for the last half-hour.

He looked quite a pleasant man, although he was not the type that she cared for. He was very tall and built on massive lines. A conspicuous figure in a light grey suit, with a white flower in the buttonhole. He had a square, rather brutal jaw; a pair of dark blue eyes with drooping lids which gave him a lazy, secretive look. But there was not much going on around him that Julian Barwise did not see. He had full, red lips, and when he smiled he showed strong, white teeth. Women liked him. He was an adept flatterer. He could make love easily and lightly to any woman so long as she was not physically repulsive. But he knew women and how to manage them, and it was a generally accepted fact, both on the stage and off it, that Julian Barwise was a tough nut to crack. Nobody – not even Beatrice Philoman herself – had got him to propose to her yet.

Gerry disliked his full lips and his curly hair, but he had a charming, easy manner and she found him agreeable to talk to.

'This sort of entertainment is very boring, don't you think so, Miss Wayde?' he said. 'Come and find a quiet corner and let me give you some tea.'

Gerry went with him to the quietest corner they could find. He gave her tea and tiny *pâté* sandwiches. They talked about nothing in particular for a few minutes. Julian Barwise pointed out the interesting people. That tall man with the monocle was Hervey Bright, who made such a success in the revival of a Sheridan play last January. The thin, red-haired girl with slanting, wicked-looking eyes and scarlet lips was Monica Storme, who was playing lead in *Let's Try* which was running at the Propinquity Theatre in town at this moment.

Gerry listened attentively to all that Mr Barwise had to say. And everything – every detail about theatres or actors and actresses – assumed peculiar importance to her. She could see what a big man Julian Barwise was. A man on the top rung of the ladder of theatrical success. And he could do anything … everything … for Nicholas.

'Didn't you produce *Let's Try?*' she asked.

'Yes.' He smiled at her benignly. 'I did. For Mrs Chetwynd-Lacey. She financed it and it was a capital deal. A most amusing show. First-rate comedy. Have you seen it?'

'No.'

'Any time you'd like to, phone me up … my office at the Propinquity. I'll give you a box.'

'Thank you so much.'

'Monica Storme is very good as the typist in it. She can get across the footlights that girl … one of the best light comedy actresses we've got in England at the present moment.'

Gerry stirred her tea and looked across the crowded room at Monica Storme's red head.

'And who's the best actress today for a dramatic part?' she asked breathlessly.

She was remembering *Our Discovery* … Nicky's drama … the strong woman's role in it .. the wife who has to divorce the husband she adores because he has run away with her best friend.

'Oh, for strong, dramatic parts, I suppose Beatrice Philoman,' said Barwise thoughtfully.

'Oh, yes, I've seen her. She's wonderful. She has wonderful black hair and dark eyes. Is she English? She doesn't look it?'

'There's Spanish blood somewhere, I fancy. Did you see her in *Man to Man* when it was running?'

'Yes, I did. You produced that, didn't you?'

'I did. How charming of you to remember.'

He smiled down at her. She was suddenly conscious of a spark of admiration in his eyes. When he took her empty cup he deliberately touched her fingers with his. She knew that he was attracted by her. She felt a sudden distaste for him – big and successful man though he was. But Nicky's manuscript, clasped against her breast, urged her to go ahead ... to make the most of her opportunities if Barwise admired her.

'You *are* a vamp, Gerry Wayde,' she admonished herself. 'But this time it's for Nicky ... so carry on.'

'Of course I remember that you produced *Man to Man*,' she told Barwise. 'Everybody was talking about you.'

'I have never been so conscious of my triumph as now when I hear it from your lips,' he said with a graceful bow. 'In spirit, I "kiss your little hand, madame."'

'Idiot,' she thought.

One couldn't believe a word these people in the theatrical world said to one. Insincere, fulsome flatterers, all of them. But for Nicky's sake ... go ahead!

It was a great success,' she said. 'And Beatrice Philoman was wonderful. She reduced me to tears.'

'I shall tell her that she brought tears into

the loveliest eyes I have ever seen,' said Barwise.

Gerry gulped and said quickly,

'She isn't playing in anything now, is she?'

'The divine Beatrice? No. We're looking for something for the winter. She's got a three-years' contract with us.'

Gerry's heart beat fast. So they were looking for a play for Beatrice Philoman ... now ... oh, what a chance!

'Shall I write you one?' she asked in a joking voice, looking at him through her long lashes.

Julian Barwise was not impervious to the length of those lashes; neither was he blind to the fact that they were naturally dark and had no need of artificial blackening. He was fascinated by the darkness of this girl's eyes and the silver sheen of her head. He wanted to take her hat off and see her hair properly. He found her altogether adorable.

'You aren't by way of being a dramatist, are you?' he smiled, at her. 'But, how wonderful! I shall most certainly produce everything you write.'

'Is that a promise?'

'If you'll sit next to me at all the rehearsals.'

Gerry bit her lip. There was nothing serious about this conversation and she knew it. He was treating the whole thing as a jest... But go ahead ... go ahead ... for Nicky...

'Do you really want a new play for Beatrice Philoman?' she asked.

'Yes, and not only for Beatrice. Irene – that's Mrs Chetwynd-Lacey – and I are constantly on the look-out for good stuff. We want new talent. Now tell me that you are as talented as you are fair and I shall feel myself the discoverer of the world's most beautiful genius.'

'Oh, you are silly,' she laughed. But her cheeks grew warm and pink. That word 'discoverer' … how like the title she had given Nicholas's play. Her heart beat a little faster. 'As a matter of fact, I don't write myself,' she added. 'I'm not at all clever.'

'I can't believe that.'

'It's quite true. I can do nothing but ride a horse and dance all night without getting tired.'

'Two amazingly good achievements.'

'Useless ones.'

'I like to see a woman ride well.'

'Do you ride?'

'I get very little opportunity.'

'I'm sure my father would be delighted for you to come down one week-end to Ponders … our place in Graylingstone. We have one or two really nice mounts. Deirdre, my little mare, is a beauty.'

'I'd like to come down and see your home – and more of you,' he said boldly.

Julian Barwise prided himself upon 'working fast' with the fair sex.

Gerry turned the conversation to plays.

'What about making me your agent,' she said chaffingly.

'Agent … for what?'

'Plays. I read tremendously. I'll find a marvellous play for Miss Philoman.'

He found her charmingly young and naïve for the modern girl. He was enchanted.

'Anything you told me was good would be good, I'm positive.'

'I have a friend … who writes plays.'

He knew that was coming. He distrusted the taste of people outside the theatre. But with a girl so adorably pretty as this one, Julian Barwise could be tolerant. He smiled down at her vivid face, took a cigar from his pocket, and removed its gold band.

'Has this friend ever had a play produced?'

'No. Never.'

'Has she tried?'

'It's a – a "he".'

Julian Barwise was not so pleased. But he continued to smile.

'And he's written what you think a good play, eh?'

'Yes. Awfully good. I think so, really.'

'What's it called? What's it about?'

'It's called *Our Discovery* – it's about divorce.'

'Not an original subject.'

'But an awfully popular one.'

Barwise laughed.

'How true! And has this play on divorce got a big woman's part in it for Beatrice?'

'Yes. That's what I was thinking of.'

'Well, I must read it.'

The colour rushed to her cheeks. Her eyes blazed with excitement. Barwise, who had lit his cigar, blew a cloud of fragrant smoke into the air, then put the cigar back into his mouth. His full lips rolled it round. His eyes narrowed. The little lady was very eager to talk to him about this play. Was the author her lover? He decided that a man might be damn glad to be her lover.

'Would you really read it? Oh, would you?' she exclaimed.

'To please you – yes.'

'It would be most awfully nice of you.'

'Send it to me,' he said casually. 'My office – the Julian Barwise Office, Propinquity Theatre, W.'

She thought:

'Yes, I'd better send it. It will look too frightful if I give it to him ... let him see that I came to town with the idea of giving it to him.'

She said:

'Thanks most awfully.'

'Who is this young genius?' He continued to be amused by her eagerness; tolerant. 'A particular boy friend of yours?'

Gerry looked round quickly; terrified that her mother might be within earshot. But

Mrs Wayde was at the other side of the room, her large, black hat well on the side of her auburn head, talking volubly to a young actor who looked bored to death. Her succulent voice, with its French inflexions, wafted across to Gerry.

'N-no,' Gerry hesitated over the lie. 'O-only a friend. I say, Mr Barwise, don't say anything to my mother if you meet her, please. It's a secret.'

'Ah ha!' he said, shaking his head. 'My new agent, Miss Geraldine Wayde, works in secret and in the dark.'

She laughed, embarrassed. The thought of Nicky made her feel guilty. But it was a delicious, warm feeling ... the remembrance of the secret love between them.

'I won't say a word,' Barwise assured her. 'You send me this play, and if I think there's anything in it, I'll get into touch with my new and beautiful agent.'

'Thanks awfully,' she smiled up at him.

Barwise regarded the fine, pale ash of his cigar, then he drew a little nearer to her.

'How about lunching with me ... one day next week. We might talk this play over.'

Gerry – wildly enthusiastic on Nicholas's behalf – did not shy at this, though under ordinary circumstances she would have done so.

'Thanks very much. That would be lovely.'

'What day will you be in town? You stay in

the country as much as you can this hot weather, no doubt.'

'Yes. But we come up to shop... I've got a new car. I like an excuse to drive it.'

'Then what about next Wednesday?'

'Yes.'

'Have you a favourite place for food?'

'I don't think so.'

'Then say the Savoy Grill – 1.30.'

'The Savoy Grill, 1.30. Thanks so very much, Mr Barwise. I shall look forward to it.'

'*I* shall.' He was so close to her now that their arms were touching. The heavy lids of his eyes had drooped so that she could scarcely see his eyes. She suddenly disliked the famous Julian Barwise exceedingly. She wanted to tell him that she wouldn't lunch with him on Wednesday. But that would be crazy ... when he was going to read Nicky's play ... when he was interested.

Barwise looked at the charming, slim figure in the yellow dress and drew a breath of satisfaction. He was going to look forward to that lunch at the Berkeley next week and to seeing quite a lot of Geraldine Wayde in the future. She was a mere child ... but an adorable one ... and he was sick of the ripe charms and the smart cynicism of an experienced woman and actress like Beatrice Philoman. Or of the immoral and tantalising Monica Storme, who boasted that she had had a lover of every nationality.

The freshness of this girl, Geraldine, who was of good family, not of the theatrical crowd, was a stimulus to Barwise's jaded senses. He was forty-one and blasé, and just of the type and at the age to fall for a mere child. He had not felt so attracted by any woman for years. He decided that he would like to marry a girl like this ... take her to Paris and spend a fortune on her clothes ... take her over to New York ... they'd be crazy about her ... all his pals in the theatre over there.

Irene Chetwynd-Lacey came up to them.

'Julian, you must come and talk to the old Princess Marie-Silveta. She wants to congratulate you on the production of *Let's Try*... There she is – talking to Monica Storme.'

Julian immediately looked bored, and regarded the figure of the Princess Marie-Silveta with gloom. She was a fat old woman with bulging eyes and a bubolic face. She wore a flaxen wig and glittered with jewels worth a fortune.

'I hate Ruritanian princesses who admire my productions,' he said. 'And I want to go on talking to Miss Wayde. Have a heart, Irene.'

'Now, say, Julian, don't be tiresome,' said Mrs Chetwynd-Lacey. 'The old lady's a guest of honour. You must talk to her.'

Barwise heaved a sigh and turned to Gerry with an expression of regret on his face.

'I'm afraid I must leave you...'

'That's quite all right,' murmured Gerry.

'Next Wednesday, then.'

'Thank you – yes.'

Julian Barwise moved away with his hostess. Gerry looked after him, her heart beating high with hope. What would he tell her next Wednesday about the play – Nicky's play? Would he read it? Yes, surely. Would he like it? She could almost go down on her bended knees and pray that he would.

She watched him bow to the Princess and kiss her hand. Gerry thought that the Princess with her fat, comic face and bulging eyes looked rather like a Pekinese. But Julian Barwise, in his facile way, was bending over her, talking to her as though she were young and pretty.

'How frightfully insincere he is,' Gerry thought with some scorn.

She grimaced at the thought of lunching with him next week; of having to listen to his fulsome flattery. But it was for Nicky ... and that made it tolerable.

Mrs Wayde let the young actor with whom she had been conversing out of her clutches, and hurried up to her daughter.

'*Mais, c'est merveilleux* – it's marvellous – this amusing party, darling. I've been talking to such a charming young man. And what has that fascinating Mr Barwise been saying to you?'

'I don't call him fascinating,' said Gerry.

'I thought he was most delightful.'

'He poodle-fakes,' said Gerry.

'What a word, *chérie*,' said Mrs Wayde. 'But I hope you were nice to him. He is the most important man in the theatre today.'

'I'm lunching with him at the Savoy next week, if that's any consolation to you, duck,' said Gerry, lifting one eyebrow and grinning like a boy at her mother.

'Lunching with him! He asked you to lunch!'

'Yes.'

'He must be attracted...'

'Bah!' said Gerry.

Her mother shook her head.

'Really, my darling, you can't turn your nose up at *every* man who is attracted by you!'

'You old match-making Martha,' said Gerry disrespectfully, and to stop the conversation pointed out the famous Monica Storme and told her mother all that Julian Barwise had had to say about her.

Secretly Gerry turned her thoughts to Nicholas.

'I don't turn up my nose at you, do I, my darling? But if mother knew, how furious she'd be! Heigh-ho! I must wait for the success of *Our Discovery*, and then perhaps you will let me tell the world how much I love you!'

CHAPTER 18

The lunch between Gerry and Julian Barwise at the Savoy Grill, that following Wednesday, was an event teeming with excitement for Gerry – an excitement born of her secret hopes for Nicholas.

She was like a child, bubbling with eager spirits, when she took her place opposite the big theatrical man in the grill room. The head waiter knew Mr Barwise and his little foibles and fancies, and had given him a corner table, special flowers, and a spray of creamy camellias for 'mademoiselle.'

Gerry pinned the camellias on her dress. She was in thinnest black silk today, with a white hat, gloves and bag, and Julian Barwise found her more than ever enchanting. What a pretty child she was, he thought. The camellias were not a paler cream than her throat and her slim hands.

'It was charming of you to come up – specially to lunch with me,' he said.

'Not at all,' said Gerry. There seemed no other reply possible. She had to be polite. Inwardly she was chafing to get the preliminaries over and done with. She wanted to burst out with the one burning question:

'Have you read the play?'

It seemed an interminable time before she could turn the conversation to Nicholas's play. There was the question of food to be discussed. Julian Barwise considered himself a connoisseur in food. He consulted the *carte* with a seriousness which bored Gerry. He kept asking her what she would like. She kept saying:

'Anything! You choose.'

Three sleek, suave waiters hovered round; the *maître d'hôtel* in the background with his wine-list; waiters, old and young, of varying degrees of importance; all very important, very intense about nothing at all. This food business was a sacred rite and they were the officiating priests. Mr Barwise came very often to the grill room. Always with a beautiful lady. Rarely with the same one. But he invariably ordered special dishes and gave special tips.

Mr Barwise finally decided on iced cantaloupe, cold *consommé truite au bleu,* young partridges, and salad. A choice meal for a warm September day. And, of course, champagne.

Gerry paid little attention to what was ordered, and when it was brought to her, ate very little. She listened patiently while Julian Barwise told her that she looked enchanting in black and that she was a little like Greta Garbo and that she must go with him one day to the film studio and be 'shot.' She had to murmur a few replies; smile at him; answer his toast when he raised his cool, sparkling goblet of champagne and drank to her *'beaux yeux.'* Then, when they had reached the trout stage, she put the all-important question – her heart pounding in her breast.

'Well, Mr Barwise, and did you – did you read the play?'

He leaned back in his chair and wiped his full lips delicately with a napkin.

'Ah, the play! Well, now...'

'Well?' Gerry was on tenterhooks; her big eyes riveted on him.

'It reached my office on Monday.'

'Yes.'

'I kept my promise to you and I read it at once. A compliment, I assure you. I read one out of a hundred plays that are sent to me.'

'Thanks awfully. Tell me – did you like it?'

'Yes, I liked it.'

The blood crimsoned her cheeks. The man, watching her, frowned. He did not want to dwell on the thought that the author of this play meant a great deal to this pretty child. But it was obvious. She was not adept at hiding her emotions. She was very young and very transparent. That intrigued him. He was weary of the subtleties and hidden motives of the women in his particular world.

'You think it – it was really good?' Gerry persisted.

'Distinctly. The third act is, perhaps, on the weak side. That's the act on which authors generally fail. But the first act's a corker and the construction is excellent.'

Gerry leaned across the table.

'Is it – is it good enough to produce?'

He smiled at her in the tolerant way that annoyed yet encouraged her.

'It might be done.'

'Really and truly!'

'Yes ... if Beatrice Philoman likes the part of the woman ... what's her name...?'

'Jean Strange,' said Gerry quickly.

'That's it. Well, the rôle of Jean Strange might well suit Beatrice. It's very strong and emotional. She wants that.'

'Oh – if only she would like it!'

'If she does, I daresay I could get Irene to finance it with me. She and I generally produce these shows together. As a matter of fact, if I tell Irene it's a good play she'll do it at once.'

'Will you tell her that?' asked Gerry breathlessly.

She was thinking:

'Oh, Nicky ... Nicky ... he likes it ... there's a big chance ... at last!'

Barwise took a draught of his champagne. He looked at Gerry through half-shut eyes. Then he said:

'You're very anxious to get this play on for this friend of yours, aren't you, little lady?'

'Yes,' she said frankly. 'I am.'

'Well, let me tell you something. I'm very anxious to do something to please *you*.'

Gerry dropped her gaze nervously. She crumbled a piece of roll in her fingers.

'But I want to know more about the author,' continued Barwise. 'Who is he? What is he to you?'

Gerry looked up. Her cheeks were burning.

'Does that … does that matter?'

'I think I'd like to know – yes.'

'He's a – a very great friend of mine.'

'A friend, eh? Not more?'

'Oh!' exclaimed Gerry. 'Why should you–'

'You don't like my being so inquisitive,' he cut in, smiling at her. His eyes were still half shut, and Gerry thought that he looked rather like a big, fat satyr, grinning over some lewd thought. He was horrid. She hated him.

'I don't see that it can matter much to you,' she said.

He put his tongue in his cheek. So the little lady was going to snub him. He wasn't used to it. But it appealed to his sense of humour and whetted his appetite.

'Look here,' he said. 'You asked me to read that play and I promised that I would. I thought it meant we would be – er – pals, shall I say?'

She was suddenly afraid that she had offended him. For Nicky's sake she mustn't do that. She broke into a smile.

'Of course. It was awfully decent of you to read the play.'

'Not at all. But I want a little more information about this unknown author you're befriending. You asked me to keep it a secret from your mother if I met her. That means only one thing, my dear.'

'W-what?' she stammered.

'You and this – what's-his-name – Hulme – are having a little affair, eh?'

He was smiling broadly. She wanted to get up and march out of the grill room. He was hateful ... with his satyr-like face and his caressing voice and eyes and that easy familiarity of the theatrical crowd. 'My dear,' indeed! And he'd only met her once before today.

'Come, don't look so cross, baby,' he said. 'I assure you I'm a very broad-minded person and it doesn't matter to me if you're having a little secret affair with your author. But I'm not over keen about taking a lot of trouble over this play... I mean, I can induce Beatrice to play in it, if I try, and I can get Irene Chetwynd-Lacey to come in with me and we might produce it this winter at the Propinquity. But if it's just for some fellow you're keen about – it stops me being so keen. I never was a philanthropist. Quite frankly, I'm a selfish being, and if I do something for you – it'll be because I, personally, am going to get something out of it, too...'

All Gerry's colour faded. She grew quite pale. She knew exactly what she had to deal with now. She might have known it. The great Julian Barwise held this reputation. Well – certainly he was frank about it.

She left untouched the wing of partridge placed before her, and the delicately arranged salad. She stared into space.

'I'm being quite frank,' said Barwise. 'I give this play quite a few marks. It's a bit amateurish but it can be polished up. I could see the author and get him to make one or two alterations in Act III. And provided Beatrice likes the part of Jean Strange – it might make a lot of money.'

'Well – you – you'd make a lot of money, too, wouldn't you?' said Gerry in a small voice.

'My dear, I'm always keen to make money, but I've got a nice bit already. There's something else I'd prefer.'

'I don't know what you mean,' she said, suddenly afraid of him.

He leaned across the table and touched her hand.

'I'd prefer that you should be nice to me, you pretty thing ... than that I should make a pile out of a new play.'

She drew her hand away and swallowed hard.

'I ... I see.'

'You may say I've only just met you and

that I'm a queer brute. Maybe I am. But generally I know what I want when I come up against it. You're the sweetest thing I've seen for a long time. I'd like to be very great friends with you.'

The palms of her hands felt moist. She doubled them in her lap. She felt sick with disappointment. What beasts men were! What a beast this man was. He'd produce Nicky's play ... he'd do something for her ... but only if he got what he wanted out of it. And she had hoped he would take an interest in the play, impartially; leaving her out of it.

'Aren't you being rather – previous?' she said suddenly; angrily.

He fingered his champagne glass with one hand and put the other in his pocket. He continued to smile.

'Oh, my dear – you misunderstand me.'

'Perhaps I do.'

'When I suggest that you should be very nice ... I mean just – very nice. My intentions are strictly honourable ... isn't that what they say in the best circles?'

'Strictly – honourable!' she repeated the words and her lips twisted into a wry smile. 'I see.'

'I mean ... if you are just pals with Hulme – I'm quite willing to go ahead. But not if he's your boy friend. Is he – boy friend?'

Silence a moment. Gerry felt sick again.

But she managed to answer:

'N-no. Not in the way you mean. That is ... I... We're not engaged or anything.'

'He hasn't a bean?'

'No.'

'Your people wouldn't permit a match?'

'No...'

'Quite so,' said Barwise in a satisfied voice.

'What does it matter?'

'I've already explained. I'm not prepared to go to the infinite pains of getting this young man's play produced to please *him*. To please you – yes – if you'll promise that there won't be any engagement between you.'

Gerry gasped.

'But, Mr Barwise–'

'I'm trying to tell you,' he interrupted, 'that I'm in love with you.'

'You can't be. We've only just met.'

'I fell in love with you at Irene's party, my dear. Something in you appeals vastly to me. Now that I see you again I am still more in love. And I want to see a lot of you.'

'Oh!' she said lamely, fiery red.

'Believe me,' he added. 'I'm not insulting you. I've never felt about any girl what I feel about you. I may be crazy – probably am. I've been crazy ever since I first saw you. I picked you out in that room from all the other women. You're different ... adorable. I'm in the mood to marry and settle down. Well – now you know all about it.'

In the mood to marry and settle down. Gerry swallowed this; too staggered to speak. But she realised that he was not insulting her. He was suggesting that he might want to marry her. He had fallen in love with her at first sight.

Of course, it was ridiculous and impossible. She disliked him and men of his type. She wouldn't dream of marrying him. Yet she saw plainly that if she told him that, here and now, Nicky's play would be handed back to her.

How unfair. How damnably unfair!

'Have some more champagne and cheer up, honey baby,' said Julian Barwise in his most caressing voice. 'I'm not such a detestable fellow – am I?'

She wanted to say:

'Yes – you are – *detestable!*'

But she kept silent. She would have got up and walked out of the grill room long ago and never seen Mr Barwise again, but for the thought of the man she loved … his play … her burning desire to achieve something for him … the money, the success he deserved.

A waiter filled up her glass. She drank some of the cool liquid, thirstily. Her throat felt hot and dry. Julian Barwise looked at her and at the fair sheen of her beautiful hair under the white hat, touched by the sunlight that slanted through the windows behind her. His pulses stirred as they had not stirred for years. Bored and sated with women, he was now in the throes of a more absorbing passion than he had ever known. A real passion for this fresh, charming girl. He wanted her. He was prepared to pay even the price of marriage for her. And he had for years eluded marriage and the various actresses who had hounded him.

He was forty-one, and, well – that was the commencement of the dangerous age in the life of a man of his sort. To marry a girl like Geraldine Wayde would be a triumph. He had made up his mind to marry her, this very day, when he saw her again. He was not a very scrupulous man where affairs of the heart were concerned. Up till now he had managed to get the maximum of satisfaction out of his physical relationships to women with the minimum of trouble, and a complete absence of responsibility.

In this case he was willing to accept a certain amount of responsibility. To take a wife, in fact. He wanted to possess Geraldine Wayde completely. To achieve this end he was prepared to behave like a blackguard. She was in love with this unknown young playwright. To use her love for this fellow as a means toward getting her for himself would be blackguardly – low. But from a boy, Julian Barwise had believed in but one creed: 'The end justifies the means.' He wanted to marry this girl. That end justified the means he used in order to win her.

'Look here, pretty one,' he said in his silky voice, 'don't worry yourself about anything just now. Think it over. Come out with me again. We'll dine ... dance ... go to a show ... anything you want. Or perhaps I'll take advantage of that sweet suggestion you made that I might run down to your place for a week-end. We can see more of each other and discuss this play again.'

Gerry's hands shook in her lap. She laced the fingers tightly together. She regretted that she had made that suggestion to Mr Barwise. She knew she had vamped him. It had been for Nicholas. But she had not dreamed it would create this havoc. How dreadful – how perfectly dreadful – that Julian Barwise should have fallen in love with her. The fact that he was wealthy and famous and about to be knighted held no thrills for her. It was Nicky she loved. Her poor and unknown Nicky!

She sat there, irresolute. Several times she meant to tell him directly that she did not wish to see him again. But she could not easily put an end to all those glorious hopes for Nicholas.

'Don't say anything about me to this pal of yours – at least, not just yet,' said Barwise. 'Let's wait and see what happens.'

'Yes,' she said.

'Meanwhile,' he said, 'I'll get Beatrice to read the play and I'll phone you up and tell you if she likes the part.'

Gerry cheered up.

'Thank you.'

He leaned closer to her.

'But you will be kind to me, won't you?'

'I – I don't know.'

'Of course you will. I want to come down to Hampshire and ride with you. I want to see you on horseback. I know you'll look adorable.'

She was speechless; vacillating between her longing to be rude to him and to do something for her lover.

'If *Our Discovery* is produced – say in December,' added Barwise. 'We'll try and give Hulme a good contract. Two hundred advance and a decent royalty…'

Gerry's heart leaped, but only for an instant. Then came the dark thought:

'And if I snub him the play'll come back. Oh, it's *damnable*…'

She parted from Julian Barwise on that unsatisfactory note. He was, however, in excellent humour. He kissed her hand, smiled into her eyes, and whispered:

'Don't forget. I'm very much in love with you, little lady. It's up to you to decide. Beatrice shall read the play and then I'll phone you up. Not a word to the author, remember! Bye-bye!'

She left the Savoy, shivering, in spite of the warm September sunlight. She had come up by train today. She hailed a taxi and drove to Golders Green. She was going to have tea with Nicky and Macil and catch the 6.49 down to Graylingstone.

For a whole week she had not seen Nicholas. All day, every day, and most of the nights, she had thought of their next meeting and hungered for it. But it was with a heart like lead that she drove to Macil's flat that afternoon.

In a measure she had triumphed with Julian Barwise. Yet she felt that she had failed. How could she 'be nice to him' – in the way he wanted? It was asking too much – too big a price to pay for the sake of getting Nicky's play produced. She could imagine how furious Nicky would be. He would want to knock Julian Barwise's head off. Not for an instant would he allow her to 'be nice' to Barwise. He would prefer to see the play burned and finished with. Gerry knew all that. Yet she could not decide to abandon her hopes definitely. She owed Nicholas so much. She must pay her debt somehow … or know no peace of mind.

CHAPTER 19

When she reached Golders Green, and the little flat, she found that Macil and the children were out. But Nicholas was there waiting for her. He opened the door of the flat. One quick look at him decided her that he was better. His face was not quite so drawn. He had his pipe in his mouth. That looked good. He gave up his pipe during his illness.

The pipe was speedily put in his pocket. He took Gerry's arm and drew her into the sitting-room. Off came the smart black hat. It was hurled on to a chair. What did she care if she ruined it? She was in Nicholas's arms, pressing her cheek close to his, her arms about his neck.

'Darling, darling Nicky!'

'My dear!'

He held her tightly and wished she did not mean so much to him. She had grown amazingly dear and precious since their reconciliation which had ended in this passionate love. And the chances of asking her to marry him seemed to be slipping further and further away every day.

For a few moments they did not speak. Inarticulate, after the fashion of lovers, they stood there in each other's arms. With his lips against hers like this, Gerry shut her eyes and felt that the end of the world could come for all she cared.

At last he ruffled her hair gently with his fingers and drew her to the sofa.

'Come and sit down and talk to me, sweetheart.'

'How are you, Nicky?'

'In health – better. In mind – extremely worried.'

'Oh, Nicky, aren't things any better?'

'They're worse.'

'Worse? Why? Tell me.'

'I'll tell you in a moment. First of all I want to tell you how nice you look in black.'

She smiled at that. She leaned back against the cushions, his arm about her shoulders.

'You've seen me in black before.'

'But I've never told you before how nice you look in it.'

'No – that's true.'

He touched the camellias on her shoulder.

'How smart we are! Who gave you the flowers? I've crushed the poor things.'

Her smile faded. She unpinned the camellias and looked almost angrily at the bruised petals which had turned brown in streaks. She tossed the spray on to a chair opposite. Ugh! They reminded her of Julian Barwise.

'Why did you do that, darling?' asked

Nicholas. 'I thought they looked awfully nice with your black dress and your pearls.'

'I don't want them,' she said. 'Nicky, I'm worried about you. Why are things worse?'

'Because, my child, I've lost my job.'

'*Nicky!*'

'Yep – rotten, isn't it?' He laughed, but behind the gay courage of that laugh was a dismal ring which Gerry was quick to hear.

'But it's awful!' she exclaimed. 'Why?'

'Heslop said he was sorry, but even to please one of the directors, he couldn't keep me on. They're cutting down the staff. Business is at a standstill all over the country. This heavy taxation is sapping the resources of the people who usually buy expensive cars and there's nothing like the normal turnover in the firm. Prices are being cut … and there you are…' He shrugged his shoulders, pulled his pipe from his pocket, and stuck it between his teeth again. 'They only want one salesman in the showroom, now, and Heslop himself is going to do the job. I quite understand it. I know business is bad. You hear it from all quarters.'

Gerry looked at him in dismay.

'And what will you do now?'

'The Lord only knows, my dear. Answer a few hundred advertisements without any success; tout round my influential pals again. I'm a wash-out – and I feel it!'

'You're not. Nicky – you're *not!*'

259

He laughed and kissed her hand.

'Oh, I'll get something in time. I won't be beaten.'

She was silent. She looked at him with large, intent eyes. Her under lip quivered. She could see how worried, how harassed he was. Of course – there were Macil and the boys to think of. It was of the utmost importance that he should find a decent job. Not a job as a motor-car salesman. He was too good for that, with his brain, his personality. A wash-out! That was what he called himself. Yet a few months ago he had been her father's secretary and settled in a first-rate job with a good salary and in an atmosphere that suited him.

Gerry's heart sank low. She was smitten with the old torment of remorse; of regret. The old, wretched feeling that she was responsible for this present failure and hardship rushed over her – overwhelming her.

'Oh, God, is my punishment never going to end?' she cried inwardly, and the tears sprang to her eyes.

She loved him with all her heart and soul, and he loved her now. But she had brought him nothing but distress. Him and brave, dear old Macil.

Nicholas hugged her to his side.

'Cheer up, my dear. Never say die. Something will come along.'

'But meanwhile you and Macil will have a

perfectly rotten time,' she said, her lips trembling.

'I must say I wish to God it hadn't happened for Macil's sake. She's so done up, poor old girl. And I wanted the kids to have a change. I'm really not much use, Gerry. My plays are so much scrap-paper.'

Her heart seemed to turn over at the thought of that play of his which was now in Julian Barwise's possession. The play which he was sending to Beatrice Philoman to-night. It was on the tip of her tongue to tell Nicholas about it – tell him that Julian Barwise liked it and would possibly produce it in December. That would show him that he was not the wash-out he imagined. But she dared not tell him. It was such delicate ground to tread on. Whatever she did she must not rush headlong into a confession about Julian Barwise and, perhaps, ruin all chance of a production. But it seemed to her absolutely essential that Barwise *should* produce it. Two hundred pounds in advance, he had said he might give the author. How terribly Nicky needed that two hundred – for Macil and the boys and himself!

Gerry drew away from Nicholas's encircling arm. She walked to the window and stared blankly at the chimney tops and a sky that was clouding over and suggestive of rain. She thought:

'What ought I to do? I ruined him. Now I

261

have a chance to set him on his feet –
oughtn't I to take it – at any cost?'

But not at the cost of losing him and his
love. That would be too frightful. She
clenched her hands at her sides at the
thought of it.

'What's the matter, my dear?' Nicholas's
voice reached her.

She turned to him.

'Nicky, I suppose if one of your plays was
to be put on now and make money for you
it would mean more to you than anything
on earth, wouldn't it?'

'Yes, my dear, *if...*' He laughed and
knocked the bowl of his pipe against his
heel. 'But such miracles do not occur in our
workaday world.'

She swallowed hard.

'Nicky, would it mean more to you than …
than I do … than my love does?'

He looked up at her quickly, then smiled.

'Silly old thing – no, of course not. I value
you and your love more highly than
anything in the world. But – I don't want
this to hurt you, sweetheart – I'm afraid I'm
more practical than you are. Love and
romance are the most wonderful things on
earth. But one must have daily bread … one
must live. And when one comes down to
brass tacks, I suppose one's daily bread is
the primary consideration.'

She nodded in silence. Something in her

heart hurt horribly. Woman-like, she was first and foremost a romanticist. But she saw the truth in what Nicholas said. He did love her. He did prize her love. But 'one must live' … how terribly true! … it was, inevitably of primary importance at this moment for him to get a job to support himself and his sister and those children. Of more importance than her love.

He held out a hand to her.

'Darling child – you're not misunder-standing me, are you? Come here. I love you. I love you more than I've ever loved any woman in my life. But it's all so damnably hopeless and impossible – with the wolf, so to speak, at the door.'

'I know,' she said under her breath. 'Oh, I know!'

He pulled her down beside him again, and taking her hand, kissed it many times.

'My little love, I couldn't do without you,' he said. 'You know that.'

She looked at him piteously.

'But you can't do without money, either.'

'I know. But what has one to do with the other, my dear? They're separate – apart.'

She kept silence. But she knew that the two things were far from separate and apart at the moment. It was a serious question now … a terrible problem for her to solve … which mattered to him most. Money … or her and her love. By depriving him of one she could give him the other.

'Queer thing,' said Nicholas, 'how the question of money destroys the romance in this world.'

'Why shouldn't it *make* romance?' said Gerry, sudden passion vibrating in her voice. She turned to him and locked her arms behind his neck. 'Nicky, why won't you let me tell father about our love? He'd get over the shock in time and then find his future son-in-law a decent job. He's got such a lot of money. Oh, Nicky...'

She paused, breathless, her cheeks hot and pink, her eyes beseeching him. Nicholas put down his pipe and hugged her against him for an instant. Then he shook his head.

'No, my dear. A thousand "noes." It's quite impossible.'

'Nicky, if you love me–'

'I do love you. But I'm not going to trade on that or your affection for me and get money or a job *that* way. Can you see me being led by the hand by you to Mr Wayde – bleating that I want to marry you, and when your father very rightly says: "What have you got to offer her?" I say: "Not a damn thing, but I want you to offer me something!" No, by God, no, Gerry. I haven't a bean, my dear, but I've got some pride, I hope!'

His voice was curt, almost angry. Gerry's heart jerked wretchedly. She let her arms fall away from his neck. She sat with her shoulders drooping and her face a picture of misery.

'Now I've made you cross with me,' she said.

He took her hand and pressed it.

'Darling child, you're absolutely wrong. I'm not in the least cross with you. But don't ask me to crawl to your parents – down and out as I am – and inform them that I intend to marry you – their heiress!'

She dragged her fingers away from his. She felt suddenly tormented beyond endurance. She hid her face in her hands.

'Oh, *God*, how I hate being rich. How I *loathe* being in any different position from you! If I hadn't a bean, I suppose you'd let me be engaged to you – let me share your struggle. And I would! I would! Nicky, don't you realise that the luxuries down at home and my car and my dresses and allowance and all the rest of it doesn't matter an atom to me any more? Nothing matters – except you!'

He looked at her with eyes grown infinitely tender. He put out a hand and touched the fair, shining head.

'My dear, it's very wonderful of you, but–'

'Always a "but,"' she broke in huskily. 'Oh, it's killing me, Nicky. I love you so dreadfully and I feel a thousand miles away from you.'

'We're very close, really, darling.'

'We may be mentally – but when are we ever going to be really together?'

'Ah – when indeed!' he said with a deep sigh.

'Must the money come into it?'

'It must, Gerry, dear. The money, the position, Macil, the kids – a devil of a lot to separate us – for the time being, anyhow. I love you a great deal more than you imagine, my dear, but I feel I ought to cut it out – for your sake. My first duty is to Macil, and what right have I got to let you care for me and drag out this sort of unsatisfactory show?'

She looked up quickly. Her lips were twisted with pain and her eyes brilliant with tears.

'Oh, *Nicky!*'

'Well, I haven't any right – have I?'

'Every right. Do you think I ever forget for a moment that it was through me–'

'Ssh – don't talk about that.'

She flung herself into his arms, weeping wildly.

'Nicky, I love you so. And I've brought you no happiness – nothing but difficulties. Oh, darling, darling Nicky. I shall always love you. There'll never be anybody else in my life – never could be!'

He held her close and kissed the top of her head; caressed and soothed her.

'Don't cry, sweetheart. Darling, don't – it

hurts me. I know you love me. I love you. It's a tremendous thing in my life. A tremendous comfort. You're a wonderful, loyal child. I know you don't care about the money. But I've got to consider it. I *must* do something for poor old Macil and the boys!'

She lay against him, her wet, anguished face pressed against his shoulder, her whole body shaken with sobs. She loved him more intensely in that moment than ever before. She knew, indisputably, that there could never be another man in her heart. But she saw only too plainly the tragic hopelessness of her love which could bring nothing to this man that he wanted. He was not a weak sentimentalist who could be content with a successful passion – and financial failure. He was essentially a man with strength of character, with pride, with a purpose in life. His work and his devotion for his sister came first. The knowledge of that could only increase Gerry's love and respect for him. But today, when he told her that he had lost his job at Dalbeattie's, seemed to mark an end to her happiness with him. An end to him as her lover.

Once she had hurt and ruined him. Now it was up to her to make reparation. Hadn't she prayed on her bended knees, night after night, for the chance to make amends to him? That chance had come. She must take it, no matter how bitter the sacrifice entailed. And it *would* be bitter! To put an end to their love; to say good-bye to him finally. To go to Julian Barwise and say to him: 'I'll do anything you ask of me, only produce this play and make a success of it!'

She would have to keep the truth from Nicholas. She would have to act a difficult and painful part. And it would be a perpetual sacrifice ... marriage to a man she did not like. She would have to go on and on bearing it; playing her part; in case Nicholas ever found out.

For a moment Gerry clung to Nicholas with her face hidden; her whole body strained against his. He could feel how she trembled, and he kept kissing her hair and trying to comfort her with great tenderness. How could he know that she was on the brink of a tremendous sacrifice for him? He could not and did not guess. But, perhaps, in this hour, Gerry came as near to being great as she ever would again in her life. It was a drastic and desperate thing she meant to do for him. A thing he would have deplored and prevented had he known. But she looked upon it as her duty; as the one method of atonement for all the harm she had done him, months ago.

Once she had made up her mind to do this, a sort of false calm and courage came to her. She ceased weeping. She told herself that this would, in all probability, be the last time she would feel his arms about her. The last hour when she would feel him – his spiritual as well as his physical presence – so exquisitely close. She had better make the most of it.

'Silly old thing, crying like that and spoiling all your pretty eyes,' murmured Nicholas, unconscious of the mental strain and agony through which she was passing.

Gerry managed to smile at him.

'Yes, I expect I look a wreck.'

'You look sweet,' he said. 'I like your dear little face like a kid's – all tear-stained and natural. Gerry darling, do you know I've noticed that you use very little lip-stick or rouge and I'm damn glad. I hated it. You're pretty enough without it.'

She wiped her face with an absurd wisp of pastel chiffon handkerchief.

'I knew you hated it. That's why I gave it up.'

'You're a darling,' he said.

'How you must have hated *me* in those days at home,' she whispered.

'No – never. But I hadn't much use for you then, I admit... There I am – being my brutally frank self again, sweetheart.'

'I like you to be frank. And I like to know that you *have* got some use for me now,' she said wistfully.

'All the use in the world, dear. You mean the devil of a lot.'

'I'm glad.'

She stared in front of her, twisting the handkerchief about her nervous fingers. She thought desolately:

'And soon he won't have any use for me again. But I shall know that I *have* done something for him!'

He played with her lovely hair for a moment. He was very tired and depressed. The thought of the future filled him with gloom. But it was amazingly soothing to have Gerry here with him; to be able to look at her; touch her; feel how much she loved him. There was something very satisfying to a man to absorb the intense and unashamed passion that she gave out to him.

'I wonder,' he said, 'that you never cared for any other man, Gerry – that you weren't engaged when I met you.'

'I just didn't fall in love. I didn't know what love was – till you came, Nicky...'

'I'm rather glad of that now.'

'And you,' she said, with an aching heart, 'why wasn't there a woman in your life, darling?'

'My work came first. Besides, I've always preferred men pals. I don't like women – speaking collectively, I mean. I thought my sister the finest woman I knew. But on the whole I've found men more dependable and trustworthy. I think you're different, Gerry – that one can depend on you. But, then, you're different in every way, and I love you.'

She pressed his hand to her cheek. Her eyes swam with tears again. She was treasuring, storing up every little tender thing he said. Only too soon he would be misunderstanding and misconstruing her actions. And then he would place her in the rank of the untrustworthy and undependable women. That hurt – horribly.

There was a sudden commotion in the hall. The drawing-room door burst open. Two small figures rushed across the room and flung themselves upon Gerry with screams of delight.

'It's Auntie Gerry! Auntie Gerry!'

Gerry was covered with kisses and clutched at by two grubby, hot little pairs of hands. Her delicate, black dress suffered in consequence, but she did not care.

'Dear old Robin – dear old Tony,' she murmured.

She felt her heart warm at the adoration she received from Macil's boys.

Then Macil came in, looking so pale, so exhausted, it troubled Gerry to see her. Certainly she was badly in need of a holiday; of all that money could buy for her. But she was, as usual, smiling and full of that gay courage which seemed to Gerry so wonderful and so like Nicholas.

'Hello, Gerry,' said Macil. 'How are you, my dear? It's nice to see you. Robin, Tony, stop tearing your aunt's pretty dress to ribbons. Imps of Satan – go and take your things off and wash your hands. I'm just coming.'

She took off her hat and pushed back her untidy, badly cut hair.

'Lord, I'm tired. It's a most exhausting effort, walking the streets of this benighted suburb with my brats. Gerry, you're staying to tea, aren't you?'

'I'd love to, Macil.'

'You look a bit shattered, dear. What's wrong?'

'She's been weeping over our troubles, bless her,' said Nicholas, with an arm about Gerry's shoulders. 'Take her into your room and make her cheer up, Macil. I've told her I'm amongst the unemployed again, but that we'll pull the fallen fortunes of the family together, somehow.'

'Of course we will!' said Macil. 'Silly old thing, Gerry. Come along!'

Gerry went with her dumbly. And the courage of these two, who were so hard pressed, cut her like a knife. How bitterly she blamed herself for everything – even though she had made her peace with them; even though the man she had harmed had become her lover. She knew that she would accept Julian Barwise's proposal if Beatrice Philoman liked the part. Nicholas and Macil should have their chance … at any price that she might be called upon to pay.

CHAPTER 20

For about two days after that, Gerry, at home, relapsed into that feverish and restless state in which she had existed for so many weeks following her father's dismissal of Nicholas.

Mrs Wayde was much perturbed. Gerry had seemed so fit and in such good spirits – especially at the Chetwynd-Laceys' party. Now she was white and big-eyed and living on her nerves again.

'What *is* wrong with you, *grande chérie?*' Gerry's mother asked her a dozen times a day. 'You look as though something dreadful had happened to you. Surely you'd tell your mother–'

'Nothing's wrong,' was Gerry's reply.

'Ever since you went up to lunch with Mr Barwise. I'm sure something has happened!' said Mrs Wayde.

'Not a thing, duck. You're dreaming,' said Gerry.

And that was all that Mrs Wayde, pained and troubled, could extract from her daughter.

The Withamburys returned from Spain. Ivor Withambury drove over to Ponders at once to see Gerry. But he found her so distrait and disinclined to flirt or dance or behave like the old Gerry, he grew bored and drove away again. He decided that 'Gerry wasn't any fun these days.'

Phyllis Crozier wrote from town in a state of excitement to tell Gerry that she had decided to marry her Naval Commander on the 1st of October. She asked Gerry to be a bridesmaid.

Mrs Wayde was all in favour of this. A pretty bridesmaid invariably met her fate at a wedding. She was more anxious than ever, now, to see Gerry safely married. The girl's difficult and incomprehensible moods worried her.

Phyllis was to be married in orange – orange satin – transparent orange veil – and she would carry tiger lilies. The bridesmaids would wear orange dresses with black hats. It all sounded bizarre and so like Phyllis, who could not resist the chance to be *outré*, even on her wedding day. Mrs Wayde thought the colour scheme unsuitable for a bridal but told Gerry she must accept.

'You'll look charming, *chérie*, in orange and black – it will be a lovely wedding – at St Margaret's, Westminster. Dear Edward Harrage has a lot of money and it should be a big show.'

'No, thanks,' said Gerry. 'Sorry, mother, but I don't want to be anybody's bridesmaid. Phyllis has crowds of friends. She can get on quite well without me.'

'Upon my soul, you're quite impossible. What is wrong with you!' exclaimed Gerry's disappointed mother.

'Nothing, darling, except that I have no particular wish to be dressed in orange and black and to stand sedately in the aisle and watch Eddy Harrage joined in holy matrimony to his tiger-lily.'

She spoke flippantly, but away from her mother she was anything but flippant. A wedding was the last thing she wished to attend … the last thing she wished to think about.

For the last forty-eight hours she had thought of nothing but Nicky's play, and had waited for Julian Barwise to telephone to her.

Yesterday had brought her a letter from Nicholas.

'I've begun the search for work again. Hope something will turn up. Darling, you might let me have back the play which I lent you to read…'

Gerry had sent back the original manuscript and with it a confession of what she had done. She thought it better to pave the way – to let him know that she was in contact with Barwise – otherwise he would think it all so peculiar if she suddenly broke the news that she had sold his play and was engaged to the producer!

She wrote a long letter, telling him that she had taken it upon herself to call the play *Our Discovery*. That she had had it typed and given it to Julian Barwise whom she had met at a theatrical party. Then she added that Barwise had read it and liked it. That Beatrice Philoman, the actress, was now reading it, and that if she liked the rôle of Jean Strange, the play would be put on.

'I do hope you're as pleased and excited about this as I am, Nicky,' Gerry finished her letter, trying to be quite ordinary. *'And I hope I shall have tremendous news for you soon. Aren't you surprised?'*

To say that Nicholas was surprised when he received this letter from Gerry was to put it mildly. He could scarcely believe his eyes when he saw what she had written. It came at the end of a disappointing and tiring day's search for the all-elusive job. With the letter in his hand he rushed into the kitchen where Macil was preparing supper.

'Macil! The most amazing news!'

'What, Nicky?' she asked, looking up from the cooker on which she was scrambling eggs.

'Read that!' he said.

He thrust Gerry's letter into her hand. His face was flushed. His eyes alight. His whole face was transfigured with the expression of one who is raised from despair to the heights of hope.

Macil scanned the letter. Her own cheeks grew hot.

'*Nicky!* My dear, what a miracle!'

'But just imagine, that little thing, doing all this on her own.'

'And not telling you a single word about it!'

'No – keeping it a secret. Macil, it's splendid of her. She had it typed, my dear, think of it – and made Barwise read it. Good Lord – Barwise's one of the biggest men in the country. If he likes it – I'm made!'

'And if Beatrice Philoman likes it – oh, how perfectly splendid, Nicky!'

Macil removed the saucepan from the fire and followed her brother into the drawing-room. She was too excited to continue with the cooking. She lit a cigarette with fingers that shook.

'Nicky, you've got your chance – at last, old boy.'

'I know,' said Nicholas in a hushed voice.

He read Gerry's letter again. His throat felt dry. All his former enthusiasm to launch a successful play, all the old excitement about his literary work, returned in full force.

'Barwise likes it. That shows I'm not such

a failure after all, Macil.'

'You never were, darling.'

'Well, I thought so. What a lot I owe to Gerry! God bless her. It was a wonderful thing for her to do. But, Lord, shan't I be cross with her when I see her – for not telling me–' he flung back his head and laughed. It was the first really happy laugh Macil had heard from her brother for months.

'Dear old boy,' she said.

'And what about dear old Gerry!'

'Yes, if the play goes on we'll owe her something, Nicky.'

'Bless the child,' said Nicholas. 'Calling it *Our Discovery* and doing the whole thing all on her own. Not a bad title, either.'

'When do you think we'll hear what Beatrice Philoman says?'

'I don't know.'

'I can hardly wait,' said Macil. 'Nicky, I remember seeing Beatrice Philoman in a play we all went to from home, before poor father died.'

'I remember, too,' said Nicholas. 'She was wonderful.'

'And if she plays Jean Strange–!'

'Don't!' said Nicholas huskily. 'It all sounds too good to be true.'

He felt for his beloved pipe. He wanted to smoke in order to calm his nerves. They were jumping wildly with the unexpected excitement. He was filled with a tremendous desire to see Gerry; to hold her close; to tell her what a colossal thing she had done for him.

'Such is personal influence,' said Macil. 'A man like Barwise wouldn't look at the play if an unknown author sent it up. But Gerry met him and there you are.'

'Used those big, brown eyes of hers on him, eh!' Nicholas put his pipe between his teeth and grinned.

'She certainly does love you, old boy,' said Macil. 'She's made up for everything, now.'

'She certainly has,' said Nicholas.

At that very moment, down in Ponders, alone in her father's study, Gerry was talking on the telephone to Julian Barwise. Not in the least the pleased and contented Gerry that Nicholas Hulme visualised. But a pale-faced, shivering girl who had to grip the desk very tightly in order to prevent herself from breaking down.

'So Beatrice Philoman likes the part,' she was saying.

'Yes,' came Barwise's voice – a trifle thin and faint on the trunk line. 'Likes the part of Jean Strange and is quite willing to play it if I choose to produce it.'

Gerry's heart beat frantically fast.

'That would mean certain production?'

'Yes, it would – in December.'

'And you think it would be a success?'

'Pretty well a certainty, as far as one can

say anything's a certainty in the theatre today. It's a play the public ought to like. And Beatrice is a draw. The gallery like her as well as the stalls.'

Gerry closed her eyes tightly.

Certain production for Nicky ... almost certain success. And now...

'But you understand what I told you at the Savoy, don't you,' came from Barwise.

'Yes,' she said. 'If you – meant it.'

'I meant it.'

'What – do you want me to do?'

'Announce our engagement.'

The sweat broke out on Gerry's forehead. She had a swift mental vision of Julian Barwise; his tall, massive figure; his satyr-like face with the drooping eyelids; the full, sensual lips. She grew cold as ice.

'Mr Barwise,' she said breathlessly, her mouth close to the telephone. 'Really ... oh, please ... you can't want–'

'I do want,' interrupted Barwise. 'And you know it. I'm madly in love with you, Gerald-ine. All day, all night, I say that name ... Geraldine!'

She shuddered.

'When our engagement is publicly ann-ounced, I'll sign the contract with Hulme,' added Barwise. 'Sorry if I'm forcing your hand, but you needn't do it if you don't want to, after all.'

'No,' she said, with an hysterical little

laugh. 'But if I say "no," the play goes back to Mr Hulme.'

'That, I regret to say, is so.'

'Beast,' she thought. *'Beast!'*

'Hello,' came from Barwise. 'Hello, Geraldine – are you there?'

'Yes, I'm here,' she said.

'Well, what am I to do? Shall I get hold of Hulme in the morning and get ahead with the production?'

One moment's hesitation. A gigantic mental struggle for Gerry. She was shaking so that she could scarcely hold the receiver to her ear. She thought of Nicky ... her well-beloved Nicky ... of dear, brave Macil who smiled so gallantly through a succession of disappointments. And she thought, too, of the night in this house when she had deliberately ruined Nicholas. The battle was won. She said the word that Barwise waited for so eagerly at the other end of the wire.

'Yes.'

'Hello – what? What did you say?'

'I said – *yes.*'

'Ah, my dear – then you'll marry me?'

'Yes, if I must. But it's not because I want to.'

'I'll make you care for me...'

'Never – you never will.'

'Oh, yes, I will, baby. You'll see.'

'No, I tell you!' she said distractedly. 'If I agree to marry you it's because I owe a special debt to Mr Hulme which I've got to pay and I'm paying it – this way.'

Barwise ignored that speech. It was inclined to make him ashamed of himself. That was the last thing he wanted.

'Well, anyhow, Geraldine, you will consider yourself engaged to me?'

'Yes,' she said.

'You'll tell your parents – and Hulme, of course.'

'Yes.'

'Good. Darling, you shall have everything in the world that money can buy. Good night. I'll see Hulme first thing in the morning and give him a contract. Then, if I may, I'll drive down to Hampshire and see you and the parents.'

'Very well,' said Gerry.

'Nine minutes. Will you have another three minutes,' droned a feminine voice.

'No, thanks,' said Barwise.

There was a click. Then silence. Gerry hung up the receiver. She wished she could stop shivering. She felt physically ill. She tried to picture Nicholas's joy and excitement in the morning when Barwise communicated with him. But somehow her brain refused to work on those lines. She could only picture his disillusionment in her; his contempt when he heard she was going to marry Barwise. He would, of course, think it a strange and incredible thing ... after all her vows; her feverish protestations of undying passion for him. He would come to the inevitable conclusion that Barwise's position; the gaiety of the theatrical circle; his knighthood; all appealed to her – had gone to her head. And then, *oh, God,* she thought, how he would despise her.

She walked into the drawing-room where her mother sat playing poker-patience with her father.

Mrs Wayde looked up when Gerry entered.

'That was a very long phone call, *mignonne.* Who was it?'

'Julian Barwise,' said Gerry.

'Really!' Mrs Wayde's fat face creased with smiles. 'My darling, he's very smitten with your charms, isn't he?'

'Oh, very,' said Gerry on the verge of hysteria. 'So much so that he proposed to me over the telephone just now.'

Austin Wayde looked up from the card-table and removed his horn-rims.

'What's that? Julian Barwise proposed to you?'

'Yes.'

'Well, I hope you turned him down,' growled Mr Wayde.

'Austin, *dear!*' protested Mrs Wayde. 'How many times do I have to tell you that he will be *Sir* Julian Barwise in the new year. He did a *great* deal of entertainment work for the Tommies during the War. And he is a gentleman and a most charming and entertaining fellow. My *dearest* Gerry' – she turned back to her daughter – 'just imagine … he has actually asked you to marry him! And so quickly. It must have been love at first sight. What did you say?'

Gerry looked blindly beyond her mother. 'I said – "yes".'

Mrs. Wayde blinked, and then rose with a great jangling of the beads around her fat neck. Her ample bosom heaved with excitement.

'Gerry – *grande chérie, c'est merveilleux!* You *accepted* him! You are going to marry Julian Barwise!'

'Yes,' said Gerry.

Mrs Wayde made a rush for her. Mr Wayde snorted.

'I can't say you look very pleased for a newly engaged young woman,' he said. 'Bless my soul … my child to marry one of those theatrical fools…'

'Be quiet, Austin!' screamed Mrs Wayde. 'Mr Barwise is a *delightful* man – and not a fool! My *darling!*' She gathered Gerry into her embrace. *'Que je suis contente!'*

But her contentment altered to concern. For Gerry closed her eyes and leaned heavily against her. Mrs Wayde called 'Austin' loudly.

Gerry had, for the first time in her mother's knowledge, fainted dead away.

This fainting fit caused extreme consternation in the Wayde household. Never had such a thing been known before. The family doctor was sent for. Mrs Wayde worked herself up into a state of hysteria. Mr Wayde retired to his study and confessed himself a little anxious but more perplexed than anything. He had thought Gerry was a strong, healthy, modern young woman not prone to Victorian 'vapours.' He had suffered for years from the sad knowledge that dear Désirée was neurotic, but he had hoped Gerry was different. And why a girl should faint dramatically into her mother's arms, immediately after the announcement of her engagement, was a problem Austin could not solve.

Gerry, when she recovered, was the calmest person in the house. She was annoyed that the doctor had been sent for. She allowed him to give her a sleeping tablet and then sent him away. She assured her mother that she was perfectly well, that she had a 'liver' which had given her a dizzy head and hence the faint.

'I'll talk to you – about Julian – tomorrow, duck,' she said, stumbling over that Christian name. 'I'm going to sleep now.'

And so the subject of Julian Barwise was not mentioned until the next day, although Mrs Wayde was bursting with curiosity and excitement.

Gerry spent that night in getting command of herself, and in a measure she succeeded. She did not give way to the desire to cry her eyes out. Hour after hour in her quiet, darkened bedroom, with a wet handkerchief steeped in eau-de-cologne across her aching head, she lay thinking over what she had done. And, having made up her mind to go through with it, told herself that she must bury the past behind her and begin again.

She must forget that she had ever loved Nicholas Hulme with a selfish passion. She must remember only that she wanted him to succeed, to gain his life's ambition, before anything else in the world. She must love him selflessly and, therefore, annihilate self.

She was angry with herself for fainting in the drawing-room. That had been a weak, stupid thing to do. But the telephone conversation with Julian Barwise had been such a strain and, foolishly, she had eaten nothing for the last day or two. But tomorrow, she told herself firmly, she would be sensible. She must either play the part she had chosen well, or not at all. And, of course, the best thing she could do would be to put Nicholas out of her mind altogether.

She pressed her fingers against her closed eyelids. They hurt her. Her whole body, as well as her whole heart, seemed to ache. Forget Nicky! How impossible. Equally hopeless to try and forget that little flat up in Golders Green in which she had known so many happy hours. Macil ... brave, kind Macil ... those jolly little boys.

Tomorrow they would all hate her. In the midst of the excitement of knowing that Nicky's play was to be produced, they would think of her with contempt.

Late that night, unable to sleep, Gerry got up, put on a dressing-gown, and stole along the passage to the oak room, which had not been slept in since Nicholas left. She switched on a light and entered. The big north room struck chilly. These September nights in the country were growing cold. The room looked desolate and ghostly with a white dust sheet spread over the four-poster bed.

Gerry, her face stony, regarded this room which was so full of memories for her. Memories chiefly of Nicky, sitting at that table writing his play ... running his nervous fingers through his thick, black hair.

She thought, with the most acute pain, of the wrong which she had done him months ago. Well, she was paying for it. She was making her reparation. She had wanted to do it. She mustn't squeal, now, when the chance presented itself.

She crept to one of the windows and looked out. How dark and cold it was outside. The sky was cloudy. There was neither moon nor stars. A white mist hung over the beautiful garden and curled round the distant beech woods. Somewhere from the grounds came the eerie, melancholy hoot of an owl.

Gerry shivered and turned back to the room. She switched off the light, closed the door quietly, and returned to her own bedroom.

She crept desolately into bed and turned her face to the pillow.

'Oh, Nicky,' she aid. 'Nicky, if you only knew...'

And now she was not so brave. The tears came, hot, bitter, pelting down her cheeks.

CHAPTER 21

A wire was delivered at the flat in Golders Green for Nicholas Hulme soon after breakfast.

Macil was making the children's beds when her brother, waving a slip of paper in his hand, rushed to her.

'Macil, my dear … wonderful! It's come! Barwise's sent for me.'

Macil lifted a flushed face from her bed-making.

'Oh, Nicky – really?'

'Really, old girl. Listen to this: *"Julian Barwise would like see Mr Hulme kindly call Julian Barwise Offices Propinquity Theatre W. half-past eleven this morning."* Well, what about it?'

Macil felt in her overall pocket for her beloved cherry-wood holder, and stuck a cigarette in it so that her brother should not see the tears in her eyes.

'Oh, my dear,' she said. 'I'm damn glad!'

'So am I. *Damn* glad,' said Nicholas. 'He wouldn't have sent for me if there hadn't been something doing.'

'Of course there is. I suppose Beatrice Philoman likes the part. Nicky, isn't Gerry a *sport?*'

'I shall never be able to thank her enough,' said Nicholas.

And he felt, as he had felt when he had first heard the news from Gerry, the intense longing to see her, to take her in his arms.

The excitement from that moment until a quarter-past eleven, when Nicholas put on his hat and left the flat, was intense.

'I shan't be able to go out. I must stay in and wait for you to come back and tell me what's happened,' Macil told him. 'Good-bye, my dear, and good luck!'

It was nearly one o'clock when Nicholas came back. Macil had not stayed in. Being a dutiful mother she had taken the boys out for their morning walk. But she rushed home, eager to hear the result of Nicky's interview with the great producer.

She found her brother sitting in the dining-room feverishly writing; sheets of foolscap all over the table and floor. When Macil entered, he sprang up and raised his pipe above his head:

'Macil, they're going to do it–'

'The play?'

'Yes. They're going to produce it at the Propinquity in December. Beatrice Philo-man will play Jean Strange. I'm to have the contract, early next week, with Barwise and the Chetwynd-Lacey crowd who always finance these shows.'

Macil took off her hat and shook back her

hair. Flushed, beaming, she stared at her brother. His eyes were brilliant.

'It's too marvellous to be true, Nicky.'

'Yes. I must tell you all about it...'

He launched into a detailed account of his interview with Julian Barwise. Julian was charming to him, he said. Not a bad fellow. A bit oily and his hair wanted cutting and he was the type Nicholas hadn't much use for, but a clever producer all right. Full of bright ideas. He liked the play immensely. They weren't sure of the title that blessed little angel, Gerry, had given it, but that was a detail that could be settled later on. Beatrice Philoman was crazy about the part of Jean Strange. Barwise wasn't sure who would play Ronald Grant, the hero, but he was going to approach Ivor Winter, who was just back from a huge success in New York.

Macil listened, thrilled and inarticulate. Nicholas walked up and down the room like a schoolboy; not a vestige of his depression, his bitterness, his gloomy outlook left.

'I'm working on that third act now,' he ended. 'Barwise wants me to strengthen it. I'm to get it done by Saturday. Macil, old girl, I'm damned if I don't take you out to Leoni's tonight and give you the meal of your life!'

She wiped her eyes. She had to. She tried to laugh.

'Darling, we mustn't be extravagant – yet.'

'We're going to celebrate this, tonight. Whatever happens to the play it will be publicity for me, and, with Beatrice Philoman in it, it's bound to have a chance. Macil, what about your favourite steak *Diane* tonight, what?'

'And your hot lobster, Nick!'

He rolled his eyes heavenwards.

'Perfect! There's only one thing missing.'

'Gerry,' said Macil at once.

'Yes, Gerry. It's all through her and I can't get hold of her … to thank her.'

'If only she'd come and celebrate with us.'

'It's the devil. I'm in such a delicate position with the Waydes…'

Nicholas stuck his pipe between his teeth and chafed at the thought of this. Never had he wanted Gerry so much. Hadn't she given him back all his enthusiasm, his self-confidence, his hopes for making money and a name? He wanted to be at her feet. He would be – for the rest of his life.

'I tell you what, Macil,' he said. 'I've just written to her, but I'll do something better. I'll go out after lunch to the post-office and get a trunk call to Ponders.'

'Yes, you can do that.'

'No one will recognise my voice. And if I'm asked my name, I'll say from Dalbeattie's.'

'Yes, do that,' said Macil eagerly. 'And try to get her to come up and celebrate with us tonight.'

Nicholas barely ate his lunch. He was as excited as a chid. Directly after the meal he rushed out to the local post-office. He got through to Graylingstone 26 – how well he remembered that number! – in a few minutes. His heart pounded when he asked to speak to Miss Wayde.

'What name shall I say, sir?' came a voice which Nicholas recognised as the butler's.

'Say – it's about her car – from Dalbeattie's, Piccadilly,' said Nicholas.

A few minutes. Nicholas whistled a tune as he stood there in the call-box. Then a voice... Gerry's...

'Hello – who is that?'

'Gerry – my dear,' he said eagerly. 'It's Nicholas – Nicky – speaking.'

Silence.

'Gerry – hello – are you there?' said Nicholas.

'Yes,' said a very faint voice.

'It's Nicky speaking.'

'Yes.'

'Gerry, I want to thank you. My dear, you don't know what a miracle you've performed. Barwise sent for me ... this morning ... he's going to produce my play. Gerry ... hello – are you there?'

'Yes.'

A little puzzled by her abruptness, he continued:

'Barwise is going to produce– Gerry, it's a

chance of a lifetime and I owe it all to you–
God bless you, my dear.'

A second silence. Then Gerry's voice –
very low.

'You're really glad?'

'Glad? I'm up in the air! Gerry, Macil and
I want you to come up if you can possibly
make some excuse to get away. We want you
to celebrate with us – at Leoni's for dinner
tonight.'

'I can't possibly.'

Some of Nicholas's fervour died.

'Gerry – hello! Hello ... are you there?'

'Yes.'

'What's wrong? You sound so funny.'

'Do I?'

'Yes. Anything wrong?'

'No.'

'But there is – my dear, what is it? Why
can't you come up?'

'I can't. We've got a big dinner-party on
here tonight. We're celebrating, too...' There
followed a somewhat hysterical laugh.

'Oh,' said Nicholas. He felt suddenly hurt
by her tone. 'I see. When shall I see you
again?'

'Oh, one day. Goodness knows when. You
see, I ... we're celebrating my engagement
at home tonight.'

'Your *what*?'

'My engagement.'

'Engagement to – whom?'

'Julian Barwise.'

Nicholas was struck dumb for a moment. His hand, holding the receiver, began to shake. His face grew hot. He wondered if he had heard aright. Then he said:

'Gerry – am I crazy or did you say you were celebrating your engagement – to Julian Barwise?'

'I said that – yes.'

'To *Barwise!*'

'Yes. I … I hope we'll always be friends – you and Macil and I. I'm awfully glad I helped get your play on. But you see I … fell in love with Julian … rather suddenly. *Are you there?* Rather suddenly, I said. We're to be married at Christmas. Won't you wish me luck?'

Another silence. Nicholas was white. He felt stunned; like one who had been given a crashing blow on the head. Gerry's voice came:

'Hello – are you there?'

'Yes,' he said in a flat voice. 'I must – congratulate you. Thanks for what you did for me. I don't know, now, why you troubled to do it. Good-bye.'

'Nicholas!' His name came over the wires with a sudden wild note of pain, but he did not hear it.

'By the way,' he added, 'you'll get a letter from me in the morning which I un-fortunately posted before I knew about your

– your engagement. Would you oblige me by burning it – unread.'

He hung up the receiver.

He walked blindly out of the call-box into the street. He walked back to the flat like an automaton. When Macil saw him she was horrified by his appearance. He had left the flat a gay, enthusiastic boy. He came back like an old, tired man.

'Nicky – what on earth's the matter?'

'Oh – nothing.'

'But there is. Nicky, did you get on to Gerry?'

'Yes.'

'Can't she come up?'

'No...' he gave a sudden laugh. 'She's celebrating down at Ponders. Her engagement.'

'Engagement!' repeated Macil, staring.

'Yes. To Julian Barwise.'

'Nicky, you're joking.'

'I wish to God I was. It's been the biggest shock of my life.'

'But it *must* be a joke.'

'No. She was serious enough. Very curt with me. Possibly a little ashamed of herself. I know she met Barwise at a party the other day. I suppose she's been seeing a bit of him. No doubt he's fallen in love with her ... and she with him...'

He paused. He had a sudden clear vision of Barwise's heavy face and drooping eyelids, his long hair and suave manner. Could Gerry be in love with that fellow? It wasn't possible. And only such a short time ago she had sat here in this very room on the sofa with his arms about her. She had clung to him; told him that she worshipped him, with reckless passion; told him that nothing mattered to her except his love. And after *that* – she could enter into an engagement with Julian Barwise!

He clenched his hands. His lips twisted with pain.

'No – she can't possibly be in love with him,' he said. 'It's his money – his position – the big Julian Barwise – the glamour of success. And his title. He'll be Sir Julian next year. She'll be Lady Barwise. That was too big a draw for her. Oh, my *God!*'

Macil stared at her brother. She was too shocked and surprised to speak for a moment. Then she said:

'I simply can't believe it. Why that child *adored* you, Nicky!'

'I thought so. Apparently it was an adoration that petered out when she was given the chance to marry a man like Barwise.'

'I can't believe it,' repeated Macil.

'Nor I...' he dropped his face in his hands. 'I suppose she doesn't understand what love is, Macil. She's an inconsequent child. All the rotten things I thought about her ... down at Ponders ... are true. You see for yourself. She has no moral stamina – no levels. She hates one moment – adores the next. She's totally untrustworthy. And she'll make anyone believe any mortal thing with that ardent manner of hers. Oh, my *God...*'

Macil drew in her lips.

'I simply can't believe it,' she said for the third time.

'It's true enough. Isn't it damnable? I was so damn glad about the play. I wanted to thank her ... to share my success with her. If she wanted success ... why couldn't she have waited? If my play had been any good I could have gone to Austin Wayde and held up my head and asked to marry his daughter. But Barwise got in first. Macil, I don't feel I care whether the play is produced or whether it isn't.'

'Oh, yes, you do, duckie.'

He looked up at her. His eyes were suffused.

'Yes, of course I do. I want to make a hit – for you and the kids. But she meant a lot, Macil. Such a hell of a lot.'

'I know she did.'

'Well – that's ended. We won't see her up here again.'

Macil lift a cigarette. Through the smoke her tired eyes regarded her brother's bowed shoulders and bent head. It seemed to her a tragedy that this hour of his success should be damped by such a hideous disappointment in the girl he loved.

But the more she thought of it the more impossible she found it to believe that Gerry did not love Nicholas any more. Why the child had not merely cared – she had *worshipped*. The last time Gerry had been here, when she had taken her into her room to bathe her eyes because she had been crying, Gerry had said:

'I do love him so terribly, Macil. I'd die for him.'

That couldn't have been all hysteria; acting; the emotion of the minute. Whatever it was, Macil decided that she was not going to let this thing happen to her idolised Nicky without making some sort of effort on his behalf.

'I'm going to see Miss Gerry,' she told herself. 'There's something very wrong, somewhere, and I'm going to get at the bottom of it.'

CHAPTER 22

The dinner-party celebrating Geraldine Wayde's engagement did not take place. It was fortunate for Gerry, who was in no state of mind to sit through festivities and smile when the whole of her world lay in ruins around her.

After the painful telephone conversation with Nicholas she had been perilously near to breaking down and giving the whole show away. She had felt weak and unsuited to play the part of a heroine. Only by the greatest effort she had managed to tell Nicholas those lies. Her one consolation lay in the knowledge that he was so full of enthusiasm about his play. She knew that. And she knew that she was giving him that chance which he needed for Macil and the boys. Hadn't he told her that was of primary importance in his life?

'Of course, he'll be terribly upset about me, now,' she thought drearily. 'But he'll soon come to the conclusion I wasn't worth a pin and then he'll forget me.'

She was gay – feverishly so – for the rest of that day. Her mother was delighted. Austin Wayde was sufficiently impressed that the girl had made a happy choice to give his approval. Julian Barwise was motoring down to Ponders that afternoon. Some of the 'family' – an aunt of Mr Wayde's – a sister of Mrs Wayde's – had been hastily wired for to come and take part in the engagement celebration.

Gerry went out riding for an hour before tea. It was a dull day with a coolish wind, but she wanted to feel that wind against her face and the stimulus of a gallop across the fields. She wanted to tire herself out, physically, so that she would be even too tired to think.

When she led her mare, Deirdre, back to the sweet-smelling box, she was more than tired. She was exhausted. Although her cheeks were pink from the ride, there were dark rings under her eyes. She put her cheeks against the velvet nose of the mare and shut those aching eyes for a moment.

'Oh, Deirdre,' she whispered. 'I'm so wretched! I'm not fit to be a heroine and make big sacrifices. I'm ready to crumple up at a touch. Oh, Deirdre, when that big, hateful, evil man comes down tonight, how shall I be able to bear it?'

She patted the mare's warm, satin neck and walked slowly from the stables up to the house. A slight drizzle was falling. She lifted her face to the grey skies and let the drops fall on her face. She felt that her heart was as grey, as leaden, as those skies.

While she was letting Taylor remove her riding-boots, the butler hurried to her.

'You're wanted on the phone please, Miss Geraldine.'

Gerry's heart jerked. Was it – could it – be Nicholas? Had he decided to ring her up again? Desperately she hoped not. In this condition of mind she would never be able to go on lying to him, to prevent herself from telling him the truth. But her heart-beats slowed up again when the butler informed her that it was Mr Barwise.

She walked into the morning-room and took up the telephone.

'Hello,' she said.

'Is that you, Geraldine?'

'Yes,' she said, grimacing.

'Darling!'

Silence. Gerry refused to answer that. She felt nothing but sullen resentment against this man.

'Darling, I'm more distressed and angry than I can say, but I'm afraid I can't get down to dinner tonight.'

Mr Barwise would not have been gratified could he have seen the relief on his newly-made fiancée's face.

'Can't you?' she said.

'No. And considering that it's our celebration, I'm heart-broken, little lady.'

'Why? What's happened?' she asked coldly.

'Just had a wire from Southampton. Pirbright, who does most of my work in New York, is arriving in London tonight and must see me on urgent business. If it had been anyone but Pirbright–'

'That's quite all right. I understand,' broke in Gerry.

'You'll explain to the parents?'

'Yes.'

'I must stay in town and see this fellow.'

'Yes.'

'But I'll come down to lunch tomorrow, if I may?'

Tomorrow! Yes, it was only postponed, she thought.

'You aren't being very nice to me, my little wife-to-be,' came Barwise's voice.

She gritted her teeth.

'I'm sorry. But you know the position…'

'Ah, my dear, I'll teach you to love me,' he broke in, laughing.

'Good night,' she said, almost rudely, and hung up the receiver.

She felt such bitter resentment against this man today that she thought she would willingly have killed him. With some satisfaction she went in search of her mother to tell her to postpone the celebration of her engagement.

And so she had another evening in peace. Yet there was no peace for her. The night, when she was alone with her thoughts, her memories of Nicholas, was one long agony.

She felt that once more she would suffer without ceasing, as she had suffered through her own fault when Nicholas had been asked to leave this house. Then, the pain had been born of remorse; of a futile longing to make amends. And now she was making amends and there had evolved a new pain ... equally unbearable.

'I'm a coward,' Gerry told herself. 'A miserable coward. I'm ashamed of myself.'

Once or twice she asked herself whether this sacrifice would be acceptable to Nicholas, and she knew that it would not. That made her a little uneasy. But he would never – must never – know. Sometimes she thought not of Nicholas but of Macil. She felt a very real grief because she would not see Macil again. She had grown fond of her. She was the finest woman friend Gerry had ever made. That friendship would be denied her now, as well as Nicholas's love. How hard it seemed.

But if Nicky's play was a success Macil would benefit. Gerry tried to concentrate on that thought. And if the play was not a success! Well, that would be too terrible. All her sacrifice in vain.

Morning came. Once again Mrs Wayde found endless amusement in making preparations for the 'engagement celebration.' More wires were sent to relatives. And Gerry, sunk in gloom, tried to pretend that she was excited, and to look as though she were a happily engaged girl, anxious to see her lover.

Then, about half-past ten, a wire came for Miss Geraldine Wayde. Gerry took it from Taylor, the maid, who brought it up to her room. She had been riding and was changing her clothes.

Gerry opened the wire in a bored fashion. But as soon as she read what was written on that oblong of pink paper, her whole attitude changed. The wire was from Macil.

'Come at once N. ill Robertson.'

Gerry's cheeks grew red and white in turns when she digested this. *N. ill.* That meant Nicky was ill. And Macil had sent for her. On top of what she had told Nicky over the telephone yesterday, Macil had sent for her. Nicky, therefore, must be seriously ill. Was it bronchitis, or pneumonia, again? Or had anything else happened to him?

Gerry became panic-stricken. That wire had a most electrifying effect on her. She knew that she must go up to town at once in answer to it. Macil had said *'Come at once.'* That was enough for Gerry. Whatever happened in the future she could not ignore such a summons. The very thought of Nicholas being ill – so ill that Macil found it necessary to wire to her – drove every thought from Gerry's mind but one. She loved him. She more than loved – she adored him. Her sacrifice, her engagement to Julian Barwise, everything must go by the board now.

She crushed the wire in her hand and rang the bell for Taylor.

'Taylor – my grey outfit – yes – and my pink hat and suède shoes. Quickly. I've got to go up to town at once.'

'Yes, miss,' said Taylor, surprised. She had thought Miss Geraldine was having a luncheon-party down here to celebrate her engagement.

'And my fur-lined tweed coat,' added Gerry, stripping off her riding habit with feverish haste.

The minutes later, dressed and ready, complete with driving gauntlets and bag, Gerry rushed down to the hall and told the butler to telephone through to the garage for the Triumph. She couldn't get a fast train now. She would drive. She would be up in town in an hour and a half.

She hurried into her father's study. Mr Wayde was out, so she could telephone quietly in there. She sent a telegram:

'Will be with you soon after twelve. Gerry.'

In the hall she collided with her mother who was coming in from the garden with a trug of freshly cut roses.

Mrs Wayde stared at her daughter. Why this attire ... the motoring coat ... the hat and gloves?

'Gerry, where on earth are you going?'

'Up to town, mother,' said Gerry and prepared for an outburst.

It came. Mrs Wayde put down the trug of roses and let out a torrent of questions.

'Up to town? Are you crazy, *chérie?* Your fiancé will be here in two hours' time. Why are you going up to town? Because a friend is ill? What friend? Someone I don't know? Gerry, this is impossible. I insist upon knowing! You won't tell me? But you can't go! You can't leave the house when your fiancé is coming to lunch – your aunts – the whole party arranged. *Mon Dieu,* what has come over you? What will Mr Barwise – Julian – say?'

Mrs Wayde, panting, paused for breath. Gerry looked at her with very bright eyes. There was a stubborn set to her lips.

'I know it's awful – my going – missing this party, but I tell you I've *got* to go, mother. It's a case of serious illness and I've been wired for.'

'But by whom? Is it Ivor – or Phyllis?'

'Heavens, no!...'

'Then who?'

'I can't tell you.'

Mrs Wayde's plump face crimsoned.

307

'Gerry, you're keeping something from me.'

'Yes, that's pretty obvious, mother.'

'Now, listen, Gerry – how dare you–'

'Look here, mother,' broke in Gerry. 'It's no use starting a row with me, now. We'll have it out when I get home again. I *am* keeping something from you. But it's no good asking me questions. I won't answer them. I'm twenty-one years of age and not a baby. I've got my own private affairs and I don't see why I shouldn't have them. I'm not going to be answerable to my family for every mortal thing I do!'

'*Gerry!*' gasped Mrs Wayde.

'Well, there it is. I'm going because it's a very serious matter and nobody shall stop me.'

'But I simply don't understand!' wailed her mother. 'Mr Barwise – your engagement–'

'You must explain that I've been called up to town to a sick friend and I'll be down again as soon after lunch as possible. You must entertain Julian Barwise for me.'

'*Mais, c'est affreux!*' said Mrs Wayde, beginning to cry. 'You're worrying me to death. If only your father were here–'

'Neither father nor anybody on earth would stop me from going up to town now,' said Gerry. 'I'm honestly sorry to upset things, but I'll be back as soon as I can.'

Gerry's green and silver coupé drove up to the front door. Mrs Wayde, like one paralysed, watched her daughter enter the car and vanish down the drive. Then she picked up the trug of roses and walked slowly into the dining-room. She was both bewildered and upset. The whole thing was beyond her comprehension. Gerry's behaviour was extraordinary, to say the least of it. Who was this mysterious sick friend? Man or woman? Mrs Wayde prayed it was not a man. And yet – Gerry was supposed to be engaged to Julian Barwise. Wasn't she in love with him? What *was* it all about? What *should* she say to Mr Barwise when he arrived? And to the other guests who had been invited to the party. It was enough to make anyone weep...

Gerry drove the Triumph up to town in just under an hour and a half. There was no doubt about it that she exceeded the speed limit that morning. It was raining when she reached London and the roads were greasy and dangerous – particularly along the Great West Road to Hammersmith. But Gerry – panicking to get to the flat and find out what was wrong with Nicholas – cut recklessly in and out of the traffic. Twice the Triumph skidded but righted itself. Once she narrowly escaped crashing into the wing of a lorry. The abuse of the lorry driver followed her down the road as she sped on. She didn't care. She kept thinking:

'Nicky is ill. I must get to him. I don't care what happens.'

It was so typical of her impulsive, ardent temperament that she should rush up to town in answer to Macil's wire in this fashion. Regardless of consequences. Forgetting that she had made up her mind never to see Nicholas again.

It was a pale, breathless Gerry who finally tore up the stone steps two at a time and rang the bell of Macil's flat.

Macil opened the door. A familiar sight to Gerry in one of her blue working overalls; the inevitable cigarette between her lips; the dark, thick hair, so like Nicholas's, pushed back from her forehead.

'Macil!' said Gerry in a gasping voice. 'I've come. Tell me quickly – what's happened – how ill is Nicky? What's happened to him – oh – is he all right?'

Macil did not answer for an instant. She looked intently at the younger girl. She saw the panic in Gerry's eyes – heard it in her voice. She was satisfied, before she asked a single question, that she had been right in what she had thought. Gerry had not broken the tie with Nicky and become engaged to this other man because she had stopped caring for Nicky. That stood out a mile. Macil removed the cigarette from her lips. She gave a peculiar little smile.

'Come in, Gerry,' she said.

Gerry followed her into the drawing-room. She could have broken down and wept for sheer joy at seeing the little room again; at being in this stuffy little top flat – Nick's home – and with Nicky's sister. And she had gone through hours of mental torture, trying to put this joy behind her and to wipe out the happy memories.

She said huskily:

'How is Nicky? Where is he?'

Macil shut the door and stood with her back to it. Her tired, grey eyes still searched Gerry's face.

'Nicky, so far as I know, Gerry, is perfectly well – physically. Mentally, of course, he is horribly cut up by what you said to him on the phone yesterday. And, so far as I know, he is on his way to the dentist with Robin who is having a tooth stopped.'

Gerry's heart beat very fast. She stared unbelievingly at Macil.

'But you – you wired for me,' she stammered. 'You said that N-Nicky was ill – that I must come at once.'

'I did, yes. And it seems to have succeeded admirably. You did come – at once, my dear.'

Gerry swallowed hard.

'Macil, I – you – really–'

She stopped and caught hold of the arm of the sofa beside which she was standing. Then Macil came up to her and pushed her gently on to that sofa.

'Sit down. You look white as a sheet, child.'

Gerry took off her hat and put both hands

up to her head. She felt suddenly weak and incapable of action.

'So – Nicky – isn't ill – at all!'

'No, thank the Lord.'

'And all the way I've been tormenting my-self – half off my head–' Gerry stopped and buried her face in her hands.

Macil sat down beside her and put an arm around the slim shoulders which were quivering.

'My dear, what the devil's all this about?' she said. 'Look here. I've got to know. I'm going to be quite frank. I tricked you up here. I was so astounded by what Nicky told me, I couldn't get it into my head that you'd chucked him and become suddenly engaged to Julian Barwise just because you preferred Barwise. You see, I am a woman, Gerry, and I know what women are. They may at times be unfaithful and changeable and all the rest of it, but they don't change quite as rapidly as all this. I mean – only a few days ago you were up here in this flat, crying your eyes out because you adored Nicky and couldn't be openly engaged to him. It wasn't possible for me to believe that you'd changed so completely within a few days.'

Gerry kept silence. Macil went on:

'So I made up my mind to send for you and to have it out with you. Lord, what a lot of lies I've told. I had to lie to Nicky, too. I made the dentist appointment all in a hurry so as to have an excuse to get Nicky out of the flat while you were here. I did it as soon as I got your wire saying you'd be up at twelve. Then I told Nicky I'd got an appalling attack of neuralgia and begged him to take Robin along. He was in the middle of writing and he didn't thank me, I tell you! But the poor old boy went off like a lamb. Now, Gerry, if you'd wired back to say you couldn't come I'd have left things alone. I'd have realised that you meant you didn't care a fig for Nicky any more. But you've rushed up here – looking like a ghost because you thought he was ill – and I know you love him still. Don't you? Tell me the truth, old thing. You can trust me.'

Still silence from Gerry. But her whole body shook and Macil knew she was crying. She stroked the bent, fair head.

'What's it all about, darling? Tell me. Nicky's my brother and I adore him, as you know. I'd half murder any woman who let him down. I've grown to like you such a lot, my dear, and to be so glad you and Nick were fond of each other. I couldn't bear it to end like this. It mustn't. And for the Lord's sake, child, if you love him enough to come tearing up to him like this, why have you become engaged to Mr Barwise?'

Gerry raised her face. It was flushed and wet with tears. She clung to one of Macil's hands.

'Oh, why did you trick me like this?' she said. 'You oughtn't to have.'

'Perhaps not. But I had to get clear on this business, Gerry, and I was thoroughly dazed. I *had* to see you. For Nicky's sake, too. He's as miserable as he can be. He didn't sleep all night. I swear that. I could see it in his face this morning. And last night he took me to Leoni's and we tried to celebrate the play being taken, and we couldn't either of us get up a spark of enthusiasm. You see' – she touched Gerry's hair tenderly – 'how fond we both are of you!'

That went straight to Gerry's heart.

'Oh, Macil,' she said. *'Darling* Macil!'

'Mutt,' said Macil. 'What's it all about? I keep asking you. Tell me.'

'Was – Nicky – so upset as all that?'

'Naturally. Wasn't he supposed to care for you?'

'Yes...' Gerry bowed her head. 'But I thought the success of the play would mean more.'

'It meant a lot. We were both off our heads with delight. But the one person we wanted up here with us was you. You'd done all the good work. Nicky was bursting to see you, dear. Then he came back from phoning you, like a broken reed. Poor old boy!'

The colour burnt Gerry's face. So Nicky cared as much as that? How wonderful to know it! How wonderful and thrilling to

314

hear it! But now that she had fallen into Macil's trap, what was she going to do? What could she say?

She stood up and wiped her eyes with a handkerchief.

'Macil, I can't let Nicky see me.'

'Why not?'

'You know. I … I'm engaged to Mr Barwise.'

'H'm,' said Macil. She twisted her lips. 'And are you in love with Mr Barwise.'

'No.'

'But you told Nicky you were. Why?'

Gerry turned to her, her hands clenched.

'Macil, you mustn't ask me.'

'I'm going to ask and I insist upon knowing. Look here, Gerry – Nicky's so dear to me that I can't bear to see all the stuffing knocked out of him, and that's what you've done. He believed in you. He was devoted to you. He simply can't understand why you've thrown him aside like this. It wasn't that he thought he had any claim on you–'

'But he had!' broke in Gerry passionately. 'Oh, he had.'

'No – he thought he hadn't – seeing what a position you're both in. But he did think you loved him, and it was a crashing blow to find you engaged to someone else – so suddenly.'

'Oh!' Gerry whispered to herself. 'What am I going to do?'

Macil rose and walked to her. She pulled a packet of Players from her overall pocket, lit one, and then handed one to Gerry.

'Smoke that, child, and tell me the truth.'

'I – can't–'

'Why?'

'I simply can't, that's all.'

'You've got something on your mind. Why not get it off?'

'Don't you see,' said Gerry in a tone of anguish, 'if I tell you, it'll spoil everything for *him.*'

'For Nicky?'

'Yes.'

'But how?'

'That's what I can't tell you.'

'You mean if you tell me why you're engaged to Mr Barwise it'll spoil things for Nicky?'

'Yes.'

Macil took the cigarette from her mouth and stared at the younger girl. Then her face grew suddenly hot.

'Good heavens, Gerry – you don't mean–'

'Macil – don't ask me – let me go away – don't try and drag the truth out of me,' broke in Gerry.

Macil looked at her hard. Then she said firmly:

'Gerry, I'm beginning to see daylight. I believe you've been a most incredible little mutt – a quixotic little idiot – and if what

I'm thinking is true – Nicky will be positively furious with you – *furious!*'

Panic seized Gerry. She wasn't going to be tricked, bullied into confessing what she had done. It would ruin everything – all her hopes for her lover. She tried to get past Macil to the door.

'I'm going now. I must go–'

But Macil caught her wrist.

'You're not going, Gerry. I've quite made up my mind. You're not going to leave this room until you've told me – *everything!*'

CHAPTER 23

Nicholas returned from the dentist with his small nephew. He was afraid he had made rather a poor show of chatting to the little kid during the walk home. But he had not felt like talking. He was thoroughly depressed. Before he had gone out he had tried to work on that last act of *Our Discovery* and failed to write a line. His head had ached. He had slept badly last night. And he was without any imagination. The trouble was Gerry. He couldn't stop thinking about her. He knew it was weak of him – he couldn't stop wanting her. Perhaps until he had lost her he had not been wholly conscious of the intensity of his love for her.

He found it bitter and difficult to believe that she was engaged to Barwise; that she cared so little for him, after all. He was alarmed, too, to discover how much she had mattered in his life; how empty any success he might achieve would be without her. Of course, it had all borne out his previous cynical theories, that women were, on the whole, untrustworthy. There wasn't one in a million like Macil. Yet somehow he had believed in Gerry's love. Once they had grown to understand each other and all that disastrous business down at Ponders had been wiped out and forgotten, he had been convinced that she genuinely loved him. He could not get over this shock, this blow, at all.

He felt, too, that it was so damnable that she should have become engaged to Barwise – of all men. She was at liberty to get engaged to whom she liked. He had never bound her. He had felt it his duty not to bind her because of his financial position. But it was pretty rotten to think that it was Barwise's name and position she coveted. He would never have believed it of Gerry. He had thought it so splendid of her to take all that trouble about his play. And now she was going to marry Barwise. It spoiled everything. He felt disinclined to see Barwise again – to go on with the play at all.

He hung his hat up in the hall and strolled moodily into the drawing-room.

He stopped on the threshold and stared incredulously at the figure of Gerry. Gerry, in a grey beautifully tailored ensemble that he had so often seen her wear. He remembered her telling him that it was called 'oyster' colour. He had said, 'You women do have some funny ideas about clothes and colours – I shouldn't have said it was oyster – I should have called it "dirty white"' – and she had laughed and said, 'How horrid you are, Nicky,' and kissed him.

319

Queer, how absurd incidents like that came back to one at the most crucial moments. Nicholas found himself recalling the incident of the 'oyster colour' now, when he faced Gerry after all that had happened.

She was standing by the window, smoking a cigarette. She looked a little pale and upset. She had been crying. Macil was standing with her, also smoking. Nicholas met Gerry's gaze. Then she flushed scarlet and hung her head. His nerves jumped; his whole body seemed to grow hot at the sight of her. But he said coldly:

'So *you're* here.'

'Yes,' said Macil, before Gerry could answer. 'She's here – the bad, ridiculous child.'

Nicholas glanced at his sister and frowned. Macil seemed very ordinary and she was actually smiling. Why? And why the devil had Gerry come here? Just to see how damned unhappy she'd made him?

Then Macil said:

'Come in and shut the door, Nicky. There's a lot to tell you. Where's my Robin?'

'He's gone into the nursery to Tony.'

'I'll go to them.' She turned to the girl. 'Tell him everything, my dear, or I shall.'

Nicholas stared. He was bewildered. He saw Gerry's face grow scarlet.

'Oh, Macil, you oughtn't to have dragged it all out of me,' she protested.

'I'm jolly glad I did, my dear. If I hadn't

and you'd gone on with this *infamous* affair and Nicky had found out, he'd never have forgiven you.'

'I suppose not,' said Gerry in a whisper.

'What's all this about?' asked Nicholas.

'I'll leave Gerry to tell you,' said Macil.

'But I can't!' broke out Gerry, in a panic. 'I simply can't!'

Macil stopped at the door.

'Very well,' she said. She looked grimmer than Nicholas had ever seen Macil look. She threw her cigarette-end into the grate.

'He's going to know, my child, and that's a certainty. Nicky. Do you know why Julian Barwise has taken your play?'

'Why?' He asked the question quietly, but he felt suddenly afraid.

'Because,' said Macil, 'Gerry agreed to marry him.'

Nicholas looked at Gerry. She did not meet his gaze. Her face was crimson and unhappy.

'I don't think I quite understand,' said Nicholas.

'It's only too simple,' said Macil. 'This absurd child went to Barwise with your play and asked him to read it. He read it. He said he liked it and he agreed to give you a contract – on the sole condition that Gerry became engaged to him.'

'Good God!' said Nicholas.

'I should think it is "Good God!"' said Macil. 'I'm completely shattered. I've never heard such a disgraceful thing. The man ought to be poisoned. And Gerry – well – I'm not going to call the poor child any more names. I've already jumped down her throat and told her she's a quixotic little idiot and various other things besides.' She turned to Gerry and smiled. There was a wealth of tenderness in that smile. She added, huskily: 'It was absolutely heroic of her, really, Nicky. She wanted to help you. She said she owed it to you. But I told her you'd rather die a pauper than have such a thing happen.'

Nicholas did not speak. He could not find words. He could only look at Gerry, who still refused to meet his gaze. Macil opened the door.

'I can't think what made me send for her today, Nicky,' she added as she passed him. 'But I seemed to feel in my bones that there was something peculiar about that engagement. Now, give her a lecture, old boy. I must see about food.'

The door shut behind her. Gerry and Nicholas were alone. Gerry lifted her head and looked at Nicholas almost timidly. She struggled for speech.

'I – I – oh, I feel so ashamed of myself,' she stammered.

'Ashamed – yes – so you ought to be,' he said. 'For *daring* to presume I'd find such a sacrifice agreeable.'

'No – not for that,' she said. 'I'm ashamed

because I've been so weak. I ought to have gone through with it and never let you know. But Macil b-bullied me.'

'Bullied you! I'd like to do more than that,' said Nicholas. 'I'd like to shake you, Gerry!'

She gave a hysterical little laugh.

'Go on, then,' she said.

He suddenly moved to her side and put his arms around her. Roughly he drew her against him; pressed her so close that she could scarcely breathe.

'Oh, you little damn fool, Gerry,' he said furiously. 'You little *damn* fool! How dared you do it? How dared you? It was unforgivable. To strike a bargain like that – to – to sell yourself – for me. Good God, do you think I'd like to see a play of mine put on the boards and wake up and find myself a second Rattigan – knowing that you were marrying Julian Barwise as a bribe? How dared you do it?'

She trembled and caught her lower lip between her teeth. His angry voice and the hard, painful grip of his hands did not trouble her. It was ecstasy to be in his arms again. But she was still ashamed that she had been so little a heroine; that her sacrifice had lasted so short a while.

'Answer me,' said Nicholas. 'Do you suppose such a thing would have been acceptable to me?'

'N-no,' she whispered.

'Do you think success and money counted so much to me that they recompense me for losing you?'

'I – I don't know.'

'You do know, Gerry. Answer me!'

'I *don't* know,' she protested, her cheeks on fire. 'You've said all the way along that you couldn't marry me because you had no money, and that your first duty was to Macil and–'

'To Macil!' he broke inn. 'Good heavens, and do you suppose Macil would like to benefit by such a sacrifice? Not she. I bet she's as damned angry with you as I am!'

'Oh, Nicky!' said Gerry, and crumpled up; clung to him very tightly indeed; stood on top-toe and pressed her hot cheek against his. 'Oh, Nicky – *Nicky!*'

'My dear,' he said. 'My darling–'

His voice lost all its anger. He hugged her until she winced with pain. He covered the fair, bright head with kisses.

'My darling,' he repeated. 'If you knew what hell I went through when I thought you'd turned me down for that poisonous fellow.'

'I went through hell, too, Nicky. I nearly died of misery. I can't bear him!'

'What in heaven's name possessed you to make such a bargain?'

'It was for you, Nicky. He – he was attracted by me at the party. Then, when we

324

lunched together at the Savoy, he said he had fallen in love with me and wanted to marry me. He said he'd take your play and put it on – if I married him, and if not – he'd send it back!'

Nicholas squared his shoulders.

'I'll kill that swine!'

'He is a swine,' said Gerry. 'But there it is – he made the offer and I accepted it, so it's my fault as much as his. I could have said "no" and let him send back the play.'

'I wish to God you had. It would have saved me the trouble of going round to his office and knocking him down.'

'Nicky – you mustn't do that. No – don't – please – to please me. There'll only be a fuss – a scandal. You can't do it, Nicky. He'd turn nasty and have you up for assault, and you couldn't make the facts public. It would be too awful.'

'That's true,' said Nicholas. 'Damn it. I'd like to have laid the dirty scoundrel out.'

'It doesn't matter now.'

'No. I suppose not. I shall just tell Mr Julian Barwise to return my play and go to hell.'

'Oh, Nicky – your play – all your hopes!' said Gerry miserably.

'I don't care a pin about the play,' he said. 'Don't you understand yet that I love you, Gerry? If I made a success and lost you – the play would mean nothing. Oh, I know I want cash for Macil and the kids – and I daresay it'll mean an uphill fight to get it. But Macil was right when she said I'd rather die a pauper than you should tie yourself up to a fellow you don't like.'

'I loathe him,' she whispered.

'If you'd cared for him – well and good. He's got a position and can offer you something – and I'd have wished you luck.'

Gerry's arms tightened about his neck.

'Luck? Oh, Nicky ... and it would have been like death – to marry any man – except you.'

'Gerry – I can't get over it. You'd have married that swine – for my sake.'

'I meant to. But I've made a pretty poor show of things. Macil got the truth out of me in ten minutes. I'm not much good at – at heroics–'

He took one of her hands and raised it to his lips.

'Little fool,' he said huskily. 'You had no earthly right to attempt heroics of that kind. I don't want you to sacrifice yourself for me. I don't want you to be a heroine. I loathe the novel prig of a heroine who makes sacrifices. She's a frightful creature. I want you to be just – yourself.'

'But, darling,' she said, and the tears stung her eyes. 'Don't you understand – I – I behaved so rottenly to you once – I wanted to make up for it.'

'My dear,' he said, 'it was sweet of you –

sweet and wonderful. But that business in the past is all over and forgotten, and there's no need for you to remember it, or consider you need make up for it. You have made up for it – in a thousand ways. I love you, my dear. Go on loving me. And we'll let the future take care of itself. Something'll turn up – you'll see.'

'Kiss me, Nicky,' she whispered, closing here eyes. 'Last night I lay a wake telling myself you'd never kiss me again, and I couldn't bear it.'

'Last night I lay awake telling myself that women weren't to be trusted, and vowing to die a bachelor,' he said. 'But I dare say if I can make any money in the future it's a vow I'll break, sweetheart.'

'Oh, Nicky darling – *do!*' she said.

He laughed and kissed her. It was very quiet in Macil's little drawing-room for a long time after that.

It was some while afterwards that Gerry lifted a radiant face to Nicholas and said:

'Do you realise that it's lunch-time, and I'm suppose to be home soon afterwards. I shall never get there. I must go out and phone.'

'To your mother?'

'Yes – and to Julian Barwise. Nicky – he's there, down at Ponders, lunching with the parents – celebrating our engagement.'

'Oh, is he,' said Nicholas. 'Well, it will be the briefest engagement *he's* ever celebrated.

I'll see him when he gets back to town.'

'Nicky, I don't want you to, please—' She caught his arm and looked at him with beseeching eyes. 'It's best left alone. I shall explain to him on the phone that the deal is off, and you can write and ask for your play back, but *don't* see him.'

'Why?'

'I've explained why. It'll be most unpleasant and you might lose your temper and there'd be a row.'

'I should be certain to lose my temper. The whole show was infamous.'

'But it's over now. Let sleeping dogs lie. Please. I ask it as a favour, Nicky. Things will be unpleasant enough as they are. I've got the family to deal with. Mother will have hysterics of disappointment and father will say I'm off my head.'

Nicholas found his pipe and began to pack it. His eyes stared moodily out of the window. The rain was pelting down from a melancholy sky. There was a sudden depressing feeling of autumn in the air. Nicholas was depressed. To know that Gerry still cared for him – and so much that she had been prepared to make a big personal sacrifice for him – was a great and comforting thing – a tremendous thing in his life. The thrill of her in his arms; of her warm, sweet kisses; still lingered with him. But being a man and practical, he came down to earth more quickly than Gerry, and he saw nothing but trouble ahead. He thought of the dinner with Macil at Leoni's last night. That celebration had been a bit previous. The play would never be produced now. His heart sank a little.

Gerry saw the gloom in his eyes and her own heart sank.

'Nicky,' she said. 'I suppose even now you won't let me tell father about you.'

'No, dear,' he said. 'It's impossible. I *must* get on my feet first.'

'Well, Julian Barwise isn't the only producer in London.'

'No–'

'And there's your other play which I've always had such faith in.'

'Which other?'

'*At Boiling Point.* I've still got it at home. Nicky, that's your best effort, and you're going to have it, and finish it, and send it to Johnson Fairwright. Didn't you write it for him?'

'Yes, I did.'

'Then finish it and send it to him. Let's show Julian Barwise what we can do.'

Her eyes were bright and eager again. She imparted her enthusiasm to Nicholas. He took her hand and lifted it to his lips.

'All right, sweetheart,' he said. 'Send it to me. You're right. We've got to show that swine what we can do – without his help. And we will!'

CHAPTER 24

Gerry drove home late that same afternoon, and she reached Ponders in time for dinner. It was still raining. She had had a nasty drive, and Nicholas had been as loath to let her go as she had been to leave. But they had a few amazingly happy hours together, and Macil had seemed as happy as the lovers. If that very gallant person shed a few tears in private – from sheer disappointment because all hopes of Nicky's play were dead – nobody knew it. Macil had had so many disappointments and she knew how to face them. When she had stood in the doorway beside her brother, saying good-bye to Gerry, she had said:

'Well, *au revoir,* darling, and I'm sure we shall all sleep soundly tonight now all this nonsense is cleared up.'

Gerry had said:

'But it's such a rotten thing for you – about the play, I mean.'

'Rotten it may be,' Macil had replied. 'But Nicky and I prefer that you don't walk gracefully out of our lives. Our heads are bloody but "unbowed" – aren't they, Nicky?'

Nicholas, with his arm about her shoulders, had answered, 'They are!'

It was impossible for Gerry to go home feeling unhappy. Yet her most passionate desire was to help these two beloved people, and she seemed unable to achieve her end.

It had given her a lot of satisfaction, however, to have a three minutes' call over the wires to Julian Barwise, from the Golders Green post office. She imagined the fury on the face of the gentleman in question, when she told him that he need not consider himself her future husband.

'But what the devil–' he had begun, and she had cut him short.

'Mr Hulme has decided to withdraw his play. He will not be wanting a contract from you, Mr Barwise, so I find no need to accept your offer of marriage.'

'So you've told him, have you?'

'Yes.'

'Wasn't that a little foolish?'

'From your point of view. Not from mine. Please explain to my people that our engagement, such as it was, is off.'

'You're quite sure–'

'I'm certain.'

'Very well,' Barwise had said in a furious voice. 'But you may regret it.'

'I don't think so.'

'The play wasn't so great that your friend will find it easy to get it produced on his own efforts.'

'That remains to be seen. Good-bye,' Gerry had said, and walked out of the call-box, her cheeks crimson, her eyes blazing.

'Spiteful brute,' she thought.

She found, later, that Julian Barwise carried his spite further. Both she and Nicholas had overlooked the fact that he might tell her parents about the play *and* its author. When she reached home she was unprepared for the scene that awaited her.

She took off her coat and hat, which were wet with rain-drops, walked into the library and found a grim-looking father. Her mother, she was told, had been made quite ill by the shock she had received. After a delightful luncheon with Mr Barwise and some of the family, Mr Barwise had been called to the phone, and told them, afterwards, that his engagement with Geraldine was at an end. That had been bad enough. But nothing compared to the bombshell he had burst at their feet when he told them that they might like to know that their beautiful daughter was interested in a certain Mr Nicholas Hulme, and it was doubtless because of this Mr Hulme that she had broken the engagement.

Later he had driven back to London, assuring them that he was indebted to them for their charming hospitality and murmuring the hope that the 'beautiful Geraldine' would not commit the indiscretion of marrying an impecunious playwright.

The family aunts departed, not a little horrified by what they thought a lamentable instance of the hysterical conduct of the moderns. Mrs Wayde had palpitations and retired to bed. Austin Wayde, thoroughly disgusted by the whole affair, raged alone until his daughter returned from town.

He had cordially disliked Barwise. He had deplored the idea of accepting him as a son-in-law. The man was too old and too much of a *roué* for Gerry, he had thought, and he could not stand the suaveness, the artificiality of these men who had anything to do with theatricals. But, for hours, Désirée had nagged at him; pointed out that Barwise was to be knighted, enlarged on the features of his money, his big position, the amusing life Gerry would lead as his wife. And finally he had made up his mind to accept him and hope for the best.

He had felt definitely relieved when he had heard that the marriage would not take place. But the whole thing had seemed to him unseemly and undignified. It had meant a loss of dignity to him, and that was one thing Austin Wayde could not stand. On top of it all, to learn that his daughter had been secretly seeing his late secretary, put him thoroughly out of countenance. He was in a formidable humour when Gerry came home. She saw it the moment she entered the library. He was standing with his back to the fireplace. A log fire was burning to take the raw edge off this wet autumnal night. Mr Wayde held a half-finished glass of sherry in one hand and an evening paper in the other.

When Gerry came into the room he put the sherry down and glared at her.

'Well,' he said. He tapped his knee with the newspaper. 'What have you got to say for yourself?'

'Nothing very much,' she said.

'Oh, indeed,' said Mr Wayde. 'Nothing very much, eh? Well, let me tell you, Gerry–'

'Wait, father,' she broke in. 'Why this rage?'

'Why this rage?' he repeated, reddening. 'After your scandalous behaviour!'

'Do you mean you're so annoyed because I'm not going to marry Mr Barwise?'

'Look here, my child, perhaps it doesn't strike you that the whole affair has been an outrage – an insult to your mother and myself.'

'Insult – why?'

'You informed us last night that you had promised to marry Julian Barwise. You arranged for him to lunch here today and your mother sends for Aunt Susan and Aunt Jessica. He comes along. We have a party and you – you take it upon yourself to be absent – to career up to town to a sick friend. Sick friend indeed!' Mr Wayde coughed and cleared his throat resonantly. 'In the middle of this luncheon-party you telephone from London to say that your engagement is off. Mr Barwise leaves the house and we are given to understand that you've been up in town with Mr Hulme. *Mr Hulme* – whom I dismissed from my service because of his scandalous behaviour with you! And then you have the impudence to say, "Why this rage?"'

Gerry stared at the floor. Her heart jerked uneasily. So Julian Barwise had told them about Nicholas? Of course, she might have known he would, out of sheer malice. What a disaster. Well, there was nothing to be done now but to tell the whole truth.

Mr Wayde picked up his glass of sherry and finished it. He wiped his moustache in an irritable fashion. He looked at his daughter again.

'Gerry,' he said. 'I demand an explanation. Your mother is in bed. She's worked herself up into a state of nerves over this thing and damme, I'm not surprised. First of all – is it true that you were in town with Hulme today?'

'Yes.'

'Good God! And have you been seeing him ever since he left Ponders?'

'Not ever since. Not for a long time afterwards.'

'But you have been seeing him?'

'Recently – yes.'

'Then you *were* carrying on an intrigue here, when he was living under my roof?'

'No.'

'I'm sorry, Gerry,' said Austin Wayde coldly. 'But I fail to understand the position.'

She walked across the room and stood beside him, before the fire. She put one cold hand out to the flame. She said in a low voice:

'Look here, father, you and I have always been good friends, haven't we?'

'Up till now, yes, Gerry. You're my only child and – well – it's a bitter disappointment to me that you should have behaved like this.'

Gerry put a hand through his arm.

'Father, dear,' she said. 'I don't doubt it must all seem very extraordinary, but look here – if I do explain and tell you the absolute truth – will you believe me?'

He bridled a little. He glanced at her and coughed.

'I don't know...'

'Father, you must believe me, if I'm going to tell you everything. Look at me. I haven't ever lied to you. As a kid I never lied. You know that, don't you?'

He looked down into the dark eyes raised to him. Wide, deep, honest eyes, certainly. They were inherited from his side, those beautiful eyes with their long lashes. Austin

Wayde's favourite sister had had eyes like that. She, too, had been called Geraldine. They had named Gerry after her. She had died during the War; one of the tragic war victims; sunk in a hospital ship in the Channel. It was queer, but tonight, when he was most annoyed with this daughter of his, Austin Wayde was struck by the resemblance to the sister who lived in his thoughts as a beloved martyr. And he knew that Gerry was right. As a child she had always spoken the truth. She was a very decent child, too. There came upon him, suddenly, a feeling of guilt. After all, he had been a busy man; so tied up with politics; he had left Gerry's upbringing entirely to her mother. Désirée was a good sort – but she was a stupid, neurotic woman – heaven forgive him for thinking so. Was Gerry to blame, after all, if she herself behaved stupidly?

'Well, my dear,' he said, after a pause, 'I know you don't, as a rule, lie. I'll believe what you tell me. But your conduct about Mr Hulme hasn't been very open, has it?'

'I wanted it to be, father. But it wasn't possible. Nicholas felt the difference in our positions so keenly – he wouldn't consent to an engagement of any kind between us.'

Mr Wayde stared at her.

'You wanted to be engaged, you two?'

'Yes.'

'You'd better tell me about it.'

So Gerry told him. Told him everything. Even about her attempted sacrifice for Nicholas Hulme.

'So you see, father,' she finished. 'I may have behaved badly, but I've got a little excuse. I love Nicholas more than anybody, anything, on earth. It's been my one desire to make amends to him for that time here at home, when I really did behave badly.'

'I see,' said Mr Wayde.

And he looked at his daughter with new eyes. He saw her not as a badly behaved young baggage; not as the stupid child of a stupid mother. But as a rather fine and gallant young woman with a strength of character he would never have given her credit for. All his anger about his late secretary evaporated. He put an arm about Gerry's shoulders.

'My dear child,' he said. 'It seems to me that you've gone through an unnecessary amount of unhappiness – both of you. Knowing that you really love young Hulme as much as this and that he's behaved so well – I'd have done something for you. You know that. I'd have made things easy.'

'But Nicholas would not let you make things easy. He wouldn't – he won't now – accept any help of any kind from my father. He says he's got to get on his own feet before he can come to you about – marrying me.'

'That's very praiseworthy,' said Mr Wayde,

'but all the same–'

'No, father,' said Gerry. She smiled and shook her head. 'I'm glad you know all about it, but it's no use your being a dear and offering to help Nicholas. He won't be helped. We've just got to wait and see what he can do on his own.'

'Well, well – if you say so.'

'I do. But now tell me – before I go up and see mother and make my explanations to her – wouldn't you prefer to see me married to Nicholas Hulme than to Julian Barwise?'

Austin Wayde poured himself out another glass of sherry.

'Good God, yes!' he exclaimed. 'I always liked young Hulme. I regretted his unfortunate departure. When he's shown what he can do, I shall be delighted to see him again. He has intelligence and he's a Conservative. Why, good God, your friend, Barwise, doesn't know the first thing about politics. He has never voted in his life. The man's one of these damned theatre fellows. I hate 'em. I told your mother I hate 'em. For heaven's sake marry a man who knows a bit about the government of this country!'

'In that case,' said Gerry smiling, 'I couldn't marry anybody better than your late secretary – could I?'

She felt as though there was an enormous load off her mind now that she had told her father about Nicholas, and cleared his name. In the happiest frame of mind she went upstairs to tackle her mother. And that good lady – after a few faint protests, an outpouring of her most succulent French idioms, and a few tears – accepted the position as it was.

'It's most unsatisfactory for you to have no proper engagement, and you might have to wait for years before Mr Hulme makes his way in the world!' was Mrs Wayde's final wail.

'I'm only twenty-one, Désirée duck,' said Gerry, sitting on the end of her mother's bed and patting her hand. 'And I can quite well wait a few years, though I hope Nicky will make his way shortly with one of his plays. Now say you're glad, do!'

'Of course your father did dislike Mr Barwise. He said his hair was much too long and that he couldn't understand the first thing about politics,' said Mrs Wayde, sighing. *'Mais, ma chérie,* I would have liked you to have made a brilliant marriage.'

'If I have the good luck to marry Nicholas Hulme – it'll be brilliant enough for me,' said Gerry.

CHAPTER 25

It was Austin Wayde who made the big gesture by writing, himself, to Nicholas Hulme and asking him to come down to Ponders and see him.

'Gerry has explained a great deal, and perhaps I owe you an apology, Hulme,' he said. *'My wife and I understand that you and Gerry care for one another. Very well, come and talk it over. I know that you feel the difference in your positions, which is most commendable, but let us talk things over. I am pretty certain the present government will be out of power in a very short while and I shall want your help in the election...'*

Gerry was enchanted by this letter, which her father gave her to read before he sent it. But she knew what Nicky would reply before his answer came. It was typical of him.

'I am grateful for your kindness, but you must forgive me if I don't come down until I have achieved something on my own. I love Gerry and I want, more than anything in the world, to make her my wife. But I cannot tie her down to me until I am on my feet...'

Then Austin Wayde wrote again:

'Very well, if you're so obstinate, young man, come along as our guest and let's leave the other matter alone for the time being. It is Gerry's wish that we should see more of you and meet your sister. Come down next week-end and bring Mrs Robertson. My wife will write to you…'

Mrs Wayde did write. She wrote as Gerry directed and told Macil that Robin and Tony were included in the invitation. It was an invitation that Nicholas saw no occasion to refuse. And, indeed, he was touched by the Waydes' sympathetic acceptance of the position.

Thus it was, one week-end in September, when the days were still warm and sunny enough to make life in the country beautiful, Nicholas found himself back at Ponders. And it was at Ponders, in his old bedroom, the famous and historical oak room, that he finished his play. In the atmosphere where *At Boiling Point* had been conceived it was completed, and the word *'Finis'* was written.

It was an extremely agreeable week-end. Mrs Wayde having made up her mind that her daughter was going to marry Nicholas Hulme, grew used to the idea and even began to like it. After all, Nicholas was a very charming and good-looking young man, and he might one day write a successful play. Which thought consoled Mrs Wayde for the end of her hopes that Gerry would marry a title or an American millionaire. She set herself out to be nice to both Nicholas and his sister, and nobody could be nicer than Désirée Wayde when she chose.

She was delighted with Macil because that ever-understanding person lent a sympathetic ear to her, and Mrs Wayde spent most of the week-end pouring out her troubles to which Macil listened seriously. Few people ever did.

As Macil said to Nicholas at the end of the week-end:

'The old lady isn't a bad soul, Nicky. But what a pity she won't forget she was brought up in France. I'm positively dazed. I've come away from Ponders not knowing whether to say "*mon Dieu*" or "my God!"'

The boys had the time of their lives. The big gardens and the woods, which they were able to explore without restriction, fascinated them beyond words. After a life in Golders Green, Graylingstone was a paradise.

Macil found it rather delicious not to have to worry about food and housework, and she abandoned herself to the luxuries of life at Ponders and was unashamed of the frank pleasure she got out of them. After all, it was good to laze about in the sunshine and be waited on, hand and foot. One could get used to hardships, to strict economy, to an uncongenial atmosphere. One did. But it was good, all the same, to come down to a place like Ponders for a bit, and specially pleasant to see the children having such a heavenly time.

For Gerry, it was, without doubt, the happiest three days of her whole life. It gave her the most unalloyed delight to see Nicholas back in this house. To see him sitting at his old place opposite her at the table, that first night he came down. To see that he was back on the right terms with her father – on much better terms. To know, in fact, that he was reinstated and that the wrong she had done him had been righted again.

That same night, by mutual consent, whilst Macil was talking to her host and hostess, Gerry and Nicholas slipped out into the garden and wandered down to the woods.

The beech trees were no longer young and green as they had been in the spring before Nicholas left Graylingstone. They had blossomed to full maturity and turned to the rich red and gold of autumn. To Gerry, everything seemed to have matured. Woods, flowers, even the full moon, which on this September night looked down on a misty world with a grave and golden face.

Gerry walked along the beaten track beside Nicholas, thinking of the other walk they had taken there. Perhaps, he, too, was thinking of it, because he paused, took her gently in his arms, and held her close for a moment without speaking. Then he said:

'You remember?'

'Yes,' she whispered. 'And you tried to run away from me … which was what I deserved. But you won't try to run away again, will you?'

'Never, if I can achieve something for you, my dear.'

'Oh, even if you don't – you must go on loving me, Nicky. I couldn't bear you not to.'

'I will do that, dear, all my life. You can be sure.'

She lifted a hand and smoothed the hair back from his forehead. She looked at him with passionate tenderness.

'I do love you so, my darling. Do you know, weeks and weeks after you went away in the summer I used to come here and lie down under the trees and think of you – want you. I suffered – absolute hell. You'll never quite know how much.'

'I think I do know. But don't talk about it.'

'I want to – in a way. It makes me realise how happy I am now.'

He looked down at her. She wore a brown silk dress and had put her fur coat over her shoulders. There were golden roses pinned to her dress. Some of the third and last crop of the Ponders roses. They smelt very sweet. Her hair smelt sweet to him, too. He put his lips against it.

'It's rather wonderful,' he said, 'that we should be so happy now. What a good thing it is that one is made to suffer, Gerry. When you've been through hell, heaven seems better to you, doesn't it?'

'Forgive me for any hell I've caused you, darling Nick.'

'Forgive me,' he said.

They stood in the dim, moon-pierced woods in each other's arms. She felt closer to him, spiritually, than she had ever been since he had become her lover. She marvelled at her own happiness.

Perhaps she was never conscious of her closer spiritual union even in the later days when there came physical possession and her intense and passionate contentment as his wife. She remembered, always, the serenity and sweetness of their embrace, that September night in the beech woods, when the old wrongs and griefs were blotted out finally.

But, of course, there were fine and rapturous hours to come. The day, for instance, when Nicholas achieved his life-long ambition and saw a play of his produced in London. A play produced without influence, without prejudice, and on its own merits.

That play was the one which he had begun and finished in Gerry's home. The one which she had saved from destruction and pieced together and made him complete. And it was Johnson Fairwright, the actor-manager, for whom Nicholas had originally intended the leading role, who produced *At Boiling Point* and played in it one night in the January of the following year.

It was a thrilling night for everybody concerned. Of course, the Waydes were there. Mrs Wayde in her element, in a gorgeous new gown, glittering with diamonds and talking to everybody with fluent outbursts of French. To the friends and acquaintances who happened to be there, she proudly pointed out the fact that the very pretty, fair-haired girl in the author's box, wearing a white dress and holding an old-fashioned Victorian posy, was her daughter, Geraldine.

'It isn't official yet. Keep this a *dead* secret,' whispered Désirée Wayde to all and sundry at the end of a most successful second act. 'But Gerry is more or less engaged to Mr Hulme. Such a *brilliant* young man!'

There were many who agreed with Mrs Wayde at the end of the third act that Nicholas Hulme was a brilliant young man. The last curtain came down on a storm of applause. There was that thrilling call of 'author' – a general atmosphere of excitement, of enthusiasm, which was a sure sign that *At Boiling Point* had been well received. Nicholas, overwhelmed and much too shy to appear before the footlights, refused to make a speech and left Johnson Fairwright to say one or two graceful things. In the author's box Gerry and Macil sat clutching each other's hands. Their hearts were bursting with pride and satisfaction.

'He's done it, Gerry,' Macil whispered. 'It's got across, my dear. They like it, and the whole cast acted magnificently. Gerry, isn't it splendid?'

But Gerry could not answer. She was inarticulate with emotion. Her thoughts were winging back to a night, months ago, when she had first seen Nicky bending over his table in his room, working feverishly on this play. And also to the bitter day when she had picked up the torn and scattered pieces of the manuscript and put them together again. She was thinking:

'Thank God ... thank God ... Nicky, I have done something for you after all.'

Later there was a wonderful supper on the stage and wonderful bits of news leaking from all quarters. The Press was full of enthusiasm. They called the play a certain success. Nicholas Hulme was made ... his name was made ... his future as a dramatist was assured. The libraries had taken half the house for the next two months. That was always a good sign. Shanon Maltry, the dramatic critic on the *Mercury*, prophesied a six months' run for this play, at least, and possibly – with Johnson Fairwright in it – it would run a year.

It was all beyond Nicholas's wildest dreams. But perhaps the most wonderful moment of all was when he managed to get Gerry away from the crowd and drive her in a taxi, back to her hotel where her mother and father awaited her.

'My dear,' he said, holding her close in his arms. 'My dear, do you realise what it means?'

'I do, indeed, darling Nicky. It means money, success, everything that you deserve. Everything for Macil and the boys.'

'Yes,' he said, 'and more than that. It means that I can ask you to marry me, Gerry. You dear, darling thing. It was because you kissed me and said "Good luck, sweetheart" before the show began that it has been a success!'

She leaned back in his arms, rubbed her cheek against his shoulder and drew a long sigh.

'Oh, Nicky darling! I expect we'll get married now, don't you?'

'Would you like to?'

'Just a little bit. Anyhow, I must oblige Macil by taking you on and keeping house for you. She wants a change.'

He laughed down into the sparkling eyes that were raised to his.

'What do you mean by that, you horrid little thing?'

'How blind men are,' said Gerry contemptuously. 'They never see anything. Haven't you noticed that Macil wants to get rid of you?'

'No. Why?'

'Dr Agnew, of course, mutt.'

Nicholas whistled.

'Peter Agnew! I see. So she wants to get married, too, does she?'

'Well, she whispered to me tonight that she thought she might. She'll never care for anybody again as she did for her husband, but she's awfully fond of Dr Agnew and he adores her.'

'So he ought to. Macil's a wonderful woman.'

'And I agree.'

'And I know another wonderful woman!'

'Who?'

'The future wife of the celebrated dramatist...' Nicholas thumped his chest.

'I know somebody who hates himself,' she jeered at him.

Then his arms went round her again. She could not longer jest. She laced her fingers behind his head; her eyelids closed. The taxi-driver had to open the door and tell them, crossly, that they had reached the hotel. Gerry and Nicholas did not know it.

The publishers hope that this book has given you enjoyable reading. Large Print Books are especially designed to be as easy to see and hold as possible. If you wish a complete list of our books please ask at your local library or write directly to:

Dales Large Print Books
Magna House, Long Preston,
Skipton, North Yorkshire.
BD23 4ND